Title Page

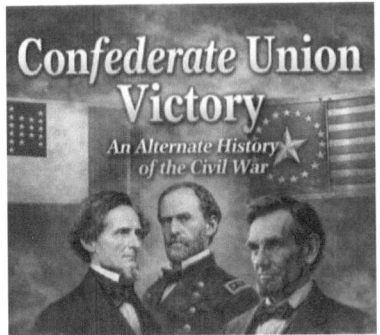

Copyright by Alan Sewell

Rev. 03/17/2026

https://www.amazon.com/Alan-Sewell/e/B00557PQDY

Feedback: alsnewideas@gmail.com

Contents

This is the concluding Volume IV in the **Confederate Union** series based on an alternate Civil War between a secessionist Free State North and a Unionist slavery-expansionist South. The series does not seek to glorify the Confederacy or the belief of many of its people that slavery should be maintained and expanded. The Confederates are acting within the context of their times. This alternate history speculates on how each side would react if their roles were reversed.

Alternate history serves a useful purpose when it encourages us to consider real history in greater depth. Real history has a sense of inevitability that obscures other alternatives. How would we feel if the roles in the Civil War were reversed such that Southerners fought to maintain a slavery-expansionist Union, while the Northern Free States decided they must leave it?

Why **would** Southerners in the Slave States want to preserve the Union? *"We've been trying to get out from under the Damn Yankees* *for years. Now they've gone and done us the favor of leaving our house, and Damnfool Davis wants to catch them and bring them back!"*

As we will see, the Slave State South might contest the secession of a rebellious Free State North, especially when Southerners control the government. In the 1850's none other than Senator Jefferson Davis, who in real life implored his fellow Americans to preserve the Union:

"It needs the united power, harmonious action and concentrated will of the people of all these States to roll the wheel of progress to the end which our fathers contemplated, and which their sons, if they are wise and true, may behold. This great country will remain united."

Abraham Lincoln, on the other hand, concludes that the secession of the North is necessary to prevent the Free States from being submerged in slavery. As a real-life congressman in 1848 he said:

"Any people anywhere, being so inclined and having the power, have the right to rise up, and shake off the existing government, and form a new one that suits them better-- This is a most valuable -- a most sacred right -- a right, which we hope and believe, is to liberate the world."

Confederate Union, the first book in the series, makes its departure into alternate history the year before the Civil War began. In April 1860 the national Democratic Party met in Charleston, South Carolina to choose its party platform and presidential nominee. In actual history, the delegates failed to agree on a platform or a candidate, so the party fragmented into three competing factions --- Northern Democrats, Southern Democrats, and Border State Democrats. The Republicans united behind Abraham Lincoln, electing him President with less than 40% of the popular vote.

Confederate Union presumes an election in which the Democrats did not divide their party at Charleston, but instead united it under the ticket of Stephen Douglas and Jefferson Davis, a combination suggested by many in real-life. The united Democrats campaign more vigorously than their rival factions did as separate entities. They add California, Oregon, Illinois, and Indiana to their column in 1860, defeating Mr. Lincoln's Republicans by an electoral vote of 156 to 147.

After the election, hostility between the Free States and Slave States intensifies. Slave catchers resume their incursions into the North to capture runaway slaves. Fighting breaks out when slave raids are resisted by Abolitionist militias. President Stephen Douglas orders Regular Army units to restore order. The fighting spreads throughout the North. Northern Republicans declare the Free States to be an independent Republic known as The United States of Free America.

Regarding characterization, bear in mind that living personalities are more complex than their historical stereotypes. In this alternate history Civil War, Democratic Party Unionists including Stephen Douglas, Jefferson Davis, George McClellan, Edwin Stanton, and Robert E. Lee are fighting on the same side to restore the Union, while Abraham Lincoln's Northern Republicans are fighting for Free State independence. Thus, the participants may show different aspects of their characters than those stereotyped in conventional Civil War histories.

For example, the stereotype of the petulant, pettifogging Jefferson Davis does not appear in this story. He is surrounded by a larger talent pool than he in the actual Civil War when he had to appoint generals who detested him and sought to undermine his authority. He is ebullient in leading a war with his National Democratic Party comrades to preserve a pro-Southern "Confederate Union." This more complex picture of President Davis is shown in this book --- not to vindicate Mr. Davis, but to show how he might have reacted in different circumstances.

Likewise, George McClellan, a real-life protégé of Jefferson Davis, is more aggressive in fighting alongside his Democratic Party colleagues than he was in fighting for President Lincoln, whose "radical" (i.e. anti-slavery) politics he rejected. The pompous, paranoid side of McClellan's character is not developed in this story because he has no reason to disrespect and mistrust his friend President Jefferson Davis.

Robert E. Lee also shows a more nationalist outlook. Most Southern military men of his generation were stationed at posts from New England to Florida to California to Oregon. In the 1830's Lee was assigned by the Army to improve the navigation of the Mississippi River between Illinois and Iowa. So, when Robert E. Lee speaks of his familiarity with Illinois and regards it to be part of his country it is because he has **been** there. He is not the man who cares only for Virginia, as he is often stereotyped.

Because the Democratic Party does not rupture, other career Democrats like Edwin Stanton and Benjamin Butler never become closely acquainted with Abraham Lincoln and therefore remain loyal to the Confederate Union.

The secession of the North also causes Abraham Lincoln to react differently. In real-life, the North's superiority in men, equipment, and financial resources provided Lincoln a cushion that enabled him to tolerate bungled chains of command and other inefficiencies that degraded the Union's war effort during its first two years. As President of the United States of Free America, which has parity rather than superiority with the Confederates, he will have to organize a more effective management of the war than he was able to accomplish in the real Civil War.

Please note that I have written the dialog as it was spoken in the 1860s, so there may be some differences with modern grammar.

There are four books in this series, in Kindle and Paperback:

www.amazon.com/dp/B00AKG0LZI/

www.amazon.com/dp/B00GLHV8IY/

https://www.amazon.com/dp/B00RC08EBS/

https://www.amazon.com/dp/B07J3NGCFD/

Also, thanks to Richard Moncure for editing.

Now, the final volume of the Confederate Union Series, *Confederate Union Victory! (will there be one?)*

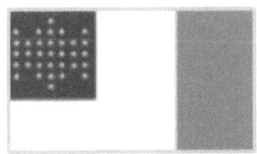

Confederate Union of America. Capital: Washington City.

Field Commanders: Jefferson Davis (taking the field), Robert E. Lee, Thomas J. "Stoneballs" (alternate history appellation) Jackson, John Logan, George B. McClellan

Strategic objectives 1862: Capture Chicago and southern Ohio; confine the Free State Rebellion to the territory east of Lake Michigan and north of Latitude 40. Plan to close out the Rebellion in 1863.

United States of Free America. Capital: Cleveland.

Field Commanders: William T. Sherman, Ormsby Mitchel, Ambrose Burnside, John C. Fremont, U.S. Grant.

Strategic objectives 1862: Defend Providence, inland New England, Philadelphia, Chicago, units surrounded in Central Illinois, northern wards of Cincinnati. Build reserve army in Southwest Michigan for counterattack at Chicago; build inventory of Spencer Repeating Rifles. Obtain possession of the Pacific Northwest. Plan to clear Confederates from all free states and territories in 1863 and secure independence of United States of Free America.

1. "A Confederate Union for a Confederate Century"

New York City, September 9, 1862

"Welcome back, Mr. President," said New York Tribune Editor Horace Greeley. "I suppose you've come to tell me that you've won the war."

"I've come to show you how the country will be reconstructed when the Yankee Rebels **and** the Southern Fire Eaters abandon their foolishness," Davis replied evenly. He took the rolled-up map he called **The Reconstructed Confederate Union** out of his satchel and handed it to Greeley.

Greeley showed a skeptical face. His tone was far less friendly than a year ago, when he presented Davis with a proposed peace settlement the Free State Rebels had agreed to. He couldn't understand why Davis had rejected what seemed a fair division of the old United States between the Confederate Union and the United States of Free America.

Southern "Fire Eaters" couldn't understand it either.

"We've been trying to get out from under the Damn Yankees for years," said Davis's Southern critics. *"Now they've gone and done us the favor of leaving our house, and Damnfool Davis wants to catch them and bring them back!"*

Davis deplored these extreme Southern Rights men who sought to undermine his government from the safety of their homes. He thought less of them than the Free State Rebels who had proven they would fight, and die, to defend their self-proclaimed country and their principle that all men should be free. The time had come to show rebels from both sides of the Ohio River that their defiance must cease, or it would be conquered.

Greeley unrolled Davis's **Reconstructed Confederate Union** map across his desk, holding down the edges with lithograph plates. A fresh breeze blowing in from the sea fluttered the curtains. Metropolitan New York was a low-lying, steamy archipelago in summer. Sea breezes made the city tolerable. Davis looked out the open door of Greeley's office and through the window across the hall, where he saw the twin city of Brooklyn, the nation's third largest city, across the East River. The window in Greeley's office nearest him showed the suburban towns spreading westward across the Hudson into New Jersey.

Davis observed two flags flying over the cityscape. The new "Confederate Union" flag, with its broad white and orange-red vertical bars, flew over the residences and businesses of ardent supporters of the Confederate Union.

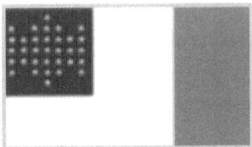

It was designed by P.G.T. Beauregard, Superintendent of West Point, when the Free State Rebellion began, to distinguish his forces from the Free State Rebels flying variants of the old United States flag. West Point had since been evacuated by Beauregard, but his improvised battle flag was now the de facto flag of the Confederate Union.

Over the horizon, beyond the Confederate fortifications ringing the metropolis, flew the "Gold Star" Flag of the United States of Free America.

It had eighteen small stars arranged in a circle in its canton, representing only the Free States that claimed to have established a new country. Its large gold star in the center symbolized a Federal Republic with a dominant central government, not a confederation of sovereign states.

New York City and Brooklyn had mostly stayed loyal to the Confederate Union. Their businessmen bought Southern cotton and resold it to Northern and European mills. Their banks loaned money to

Southern planters. Their workers, especially the immigrant Irish, wanted Negroes to remain slaves, so they could not come here to compete for jobs, thereby undercutting wages. New York City's Mayor Fernando Wood was as much a Southern Rights man as any homegrown Southern Fire Eater. Wealthy New Yorkers were buying Confederate Union War Bonds whose 7% coupons were paid in gold. Loyalty followed its paymaster.

However, about 200,000 ardent Republican voters had removed themselves to Free State territory. They were offset by a similar number of Confederate Union Democrats from Pennsylvania, New England, and New Jersey, who sought refuge in the city. The population exchange all along the military frontier was hardening the divide between the two nations.

According to some, three nations now occupied the territory of the former United States, New Jersey having proclaimed itself a "Transcendentalist Republic" separate from either of its warring neighbors. The Jerseymen sought to prevent any further warfare on their soil. The majority voted Democratic and were therefore attached to the Confederate Union by political sentiment. But as a Free State, New Jersey had no attachment to slavery. Its legislature had declared the state to be "a free and independent republic that will decide its destiny independently of the federations of warring states."

The Confederate Union and the United States of Free America paid scant attention to New Jersey's claims of sovereignty. They tolerated it as a convenient neutral territory allowing people and businesses on both sides to make the necessary exchanges of goods and currencies that were officially prohibited by the belligerent governments. "Going to New Jersey" had entered the vernacular of both nations as a way of saying that somebody was up to something slightly disreputable.

"Sit down, please," said Greeley, after he had flattened out the map and arranged chairs for Davis and himself beside it. Before perusing the map, he pressed the button on his desk, which Davis surmised was an electromechanical device like a miniature telegraph. Greeley's butler, a Negro, appeared at the door.

"Minted tea, salt crackers, and chopped fruit, please," said Greeley, whose healthy diet also suited Davis.

"Yes, sir," the butler responded.

"Would you please serve my adjutant waiting downstairs," requested Davis. He was referring to Robert E. Lee's son Custis who accompanied Davis on his trips.

"Right away, sir," replied the butler. If he had any animosity toward Davis, his face didn't show it. Most Negroes in New York City had left for the Free State lines as soon as the war started. The Fugitive Slave Law allowed any white person from a Slave State to claim any Negro in the North as a runaway slave. The secession of the Free State North had been touched off by Southern slavecatchers attempting to kidnap Negroes who had run away decades before. No free Negroes had yet been kidnapped from New York, but the threat loomed. Greeley's butler was courageous to remain here.

"You see how unnecessary slavery is," Greeley said as the butler left. "Would any slave in the South have responded more efficiently? Of course, I must pay his wages, but I don't have to buy his food, clothes, and shelter. He buys those for himself. His purchases prosper our merchants. They in turn advertise in my paper and prosper me. So, you see, I get every penny I pay my free Negro employees back, and then some."

"Uh, huh," muttered Davis. He didn't like being hectored by anti-slavery men. Then he decided it would be best to answer courteously. Greeley had so far reported on the war as fairly as he could reasonably expect. He wanted to maintain his good will.

"I'm telling you this in strictest confidence: we recognize that slavery must be modified. I can't speak of it in public because anything I say will be misconstrued. The Yankee Rebels will say, 'Davis admits that slavery is wrong; we were right to rebel against it.' The Fire Eaters will say, 'Davis has betrayed us; we must secede from the Confederate Union and create a true Southern Confederacy.' I can tell you this: it will be easier to improve upon the institution of slavery if the Confederate Union is made whole. If we are defeated, the Fire Eaters may take over the government and expand slavery, while reopening the slave trade."

Greeley nodded reluctantly. He didn't want slavery "improved upon." He wanted it eliminated. But he was pragmatic enough to understand that if the slaves were to be liberated, emancipation would have to come from inside the Confederate Union.

Davis drew Greeley's attention to the map.

"The Reconstructed Confederate Union will consist of twenty-two Slave States and eighteen Free States. Of the Free States, seven will be permitted to settle free Negroes. The other eleven Free States, including the new State of Jefferson, will be reserved for Whites. The yellow line shows the division between slave states and free states. The red line shows the territory reserved exclusively for white settlement."

Greeley frowned. He could see that Davis wanted to consolidate New England into a single state to reduce its Republican / Abolitionist vote in the Senate from 12 to 2. The consolidation of Indiana and Illinois would eliminate two more Republican senate seats. Davis subdivided

Texas into three states to increase its Democratic Senate vote from 2 to 6. He divided California into two states, the portion south of the restored Missouri Compromise Line becoming the slave state of California, while the portion north of the line would become the free state of Nevada.

In the middle of the country, in what was starting to be called "The Near Northwest," Illinois and Indiana were divided laterally to confine the Republican / Abolitionist vote to a single state around Lake Michigan. The southern portions were to be combined into the new state of "Jefferson." The old state of Indiana was to become defunct, but its name would live on as "New Indiana" when the Indian Territory north of Texas was admitted as a new slave state. The South was to be allocated ten more Senators --- four new ones from Texas, two from the new Whites-only State of Jefferson, two from New Indiana, and two from the redrawn state of California.

"You know that when the Free State men see this map, they will fight even more ferociously for their independence," predicted Greeley.

"Please assure them it isn't a vindictive Reconstruction," implored Davis. "It's only meant to ensure permanent reconciliation. The Slave States must have supremacy of states in the Senate, while the Free States have supremacy of population in the House of Representatives. Both sides will thenceforth rest assured that they will not be dominated by the other. We are calling it 'A Confederate Union for a Confederate Century.' All the states, free and slave, will fulfill their destinies within it, as our fathers intended."

"No more 'Confederate Union, United Expansion?'" asked Greeley, recalling the campaign slogan that had elected the Confederate Union ticket of Douglas and Davis in 1860.

"We will emphasize developing the land we've already acquired," confirmed Davis. "The Free States need not fear being dominated by more slave states acquired from Mexico. Nor will the British need to fear any designs by us to take the Canadas from them."

"I believe you are sincere in renouncing the acquisition of more slave states," said Greeley. "But who can say who'll follow you as president? It could be Yancey, Rhett, or another Northern man with Southern sentiments like Stephen Douglas. Your Reconstructed Confederate Union would disfranchise the Free States from the Senate."

"They'll still have the House," countered Davis. "That will be enough for them." He fixed his gaze on Greeley.

"I'm hoping you will persuade your errant abolitionist friends to accept reconciliation on these terms *before* it becomes a vindictive Reconstruction. If they give up the rebellion before November's election, they may resume their rightful places as citizens of the reconstructed Confederate Union. If the Rebellion persists past the election, it will take on a formal character of treason. The Rebels may be disfranchised, their leaders brought to trial, and their reconstructed states governed as territories under Confederate National Authority. Those who have removed themselves to the Yankee Rebel lines may have their properties confiscated and sold to loyal people. Please let your people know that I want them to return to the government of their fathers of their own volition. I do not desire to conquer a peace against my fellow Americans."

"I will convey your sentiments," promised Greeley, "but I doubt it will induce them to surrender. They feel that you betrayed them before, in revoking the Missouri Compromise. They will not believe that you, or whoever may follow you, can be trusted to keep your new promises. Nor do I believe you can conquer a peace. Even if you could conquer the Free

States, you would not have peace." He recalled the ancient lament of one of the peoples the Romans had conquered: *They have made a desert, and now they call it peace!*

"You cannot hold them down by bayonets, not unless you intend to turn this country into a military dictatorship," Greeley insisted. "Allow the Free States to go their own way, and they will vex you no more. All you can gain by continuing this war is to send thousands more of your best young men to moldy graves and encumber the Confederate Union with debt that will not be repaid for generations. Is that what your people elected you to do?"

Greeley's butler returned with minted tea and a plate of chopped fruits, crackers, and cheeses. Davis smiled. "Thank you so much," he said to the butler. "This is a most welcome refreshment after a wearying journey."

"I'm glad you enjoyed it," replied the butler cordially, perhaps forgetting for the moment that Davis owned people of his race as slaves.

Greeley could tell from Davis's courtesy to the butler that he saw humanity in the black race. Many white people in New York, especially the newly arrived Irish, cringed whenever they saw a black person, as if they were looking at a gorilla. Might it one day be possible to talk Davis and other progress-minded Southerners into liberating their slaves?

When the butler had finished laying out the food, Davis took a drink of minted tea and begin reminiscing in a relaxed way.

"You know, when I entered the Senate in '57, my first act was to convince Congress to appropriate funds to expand our Capitol to accommodate the hundreds of new Congressmen who will represent our great Republic when it is populated from sea to sea. I will not allow the country to be torn asunder by an inflamed minority while I am President.

Douglas and I were elected by a majority of 63%. We won the electoral votes of every slave state, plus the free states of Illinois, Indiana, New Jersey, California, and Oregon. We won 48% of the vote in the State of New York and 49% in Connecticut. Am I supposed to abandon my voters to the tender mercies of Abolitionists --- those very same Abolitionists who paid John Brown to come into the South and incite our slaves to rise against us? No, Mr. Greeley, there will not be peace if we let them go off into their own country, where they would construct a sword of aggression around their nest of treason."

"You're nowhere near being able to force them back into a Union with the Slave States," argued Greeley, while chewing a quarter-slice of an orange. "They will fight you to the bitter end, rather than be part of a country that embraces slavery."

"We've taken St. Louis, Cincinnati, Boston, and Portland," Davis reminded him. "We'll be in Chicago soon, and perhaps in Providence before Chicago. We are near Philadelphia. When any one of those cities falls, the Rebellion will crumble like a house of cards in a hurricane."

"You've taken the *ruins* of St. Louis and Cincinnati and Boston and Portland," countered Greeley. "The flesh and blood and brains of those cities have removed themselves to the Free State lines. Now they're fighting you from prepared positions. You've run out of tricks to surprise them. Their trade is open to the world through the Canadian ports. The British are loaning them money to buy the food and equipment they require to continue the war indefinitely".

Greeley pointed his finger at Davis. "You'll have to fight your way into their cities, building by building. It will wear down your armies. The British have warned that if you destroy another Free State city by artillery bombardment, they'll stop the war by interposing their forces between you and the Free States, thereby guaranteeing their independence…"

"British rules of war!" scoffed Davis. "Oh, yes, what great humanitarians the British are! They don't mind slaughtering their Darkies in India whenever they are inconvenienced by the least hint of defiance, but they presume to tell us not to disturb the nests of our Free State Rebels! What obnoxious prattle! If we let the Rebel States go, they'll be in league with the British. They'll combine forces against us and try to confine us south of the Potomac and the Ohio. They'll try to cut us off from California and the West. They'll drive us out of New York City, and you would help them, wouldn't you? We'll have the Yankees and the British lording it over us, and perpetually inciting our Negroes to insurrection!"

Greeley picked up another orange, then looked at Davis.

"I rather think it is the war that is causing all this distress. End it, and there will be no more risk of British interference. Even without the Free States, the Confederate Union will be a mighty country. Surely you will be able to defend yourself against any and all other powers. With the coming of peace, the British will have no reason to remain hostile. They'll still need your cotton. They'll still want to sell you manufactured goods. They'll still want to invest in profitable opportunities to build your railroads and canals. The men of the Free States will want those things from you as well. They need you. You need them. The peace will be enduring, based upon necessity."

Greeley furrowed his brow.

"Please think about something, Mr. President. Imagine that you and Senator Douglas had never made the Confederate Union Compact. Imagine if Mr. Lincoln had prevailed in 1860, and your Southern Fire

Eaters had carried out *their* threat to secede from the Union and establish themselves in a new Southern Republic. *You* would have gone out with them, would you not? *You* would have become President of the Confederate States of America, and *you* would have made war against the Union of the Free States until they recognized your independence. *You* would have led the Rebellion from the other side, would you not?"

Davis had never considered that possibility. He struggled for an answer but couldn't come up with an honest one.

2. The New Country

Blue Island, Illinois, September 11, 1862

Thomas J. "Stoneballs" Jackson was uncharacteristically idle and therefore uncharacteristically melancholy. From the heights of Blue Island Ridge he saw the smoky sky over Chicago sixteen miles away, and the line of clouds that formed in the afternoons where the warm air from the land met the cooler lakefront breezes.

He drew his spyglass and looked across the flat terrain. The Yankee Rebel lines in front of the city were just visible at that distance. He knew that with Free State General Ormsby Mitchel in command, they were being strengthened every day.

My men, who were primed to enter the city in victorious celebration, are becoming homesick and demoralized. They see the sun hanging lower in the sky each day and meeting the horizon at a steeper angle. Those bright nights of June have become the black nights of August. Soon they will become the cool nights of autumn, and then winter nights of ice and snow. If my plan had been followed, we would be billeted comfortably in the city, and I would be planning the attack toward Cleveland next spring to drive the final stake into the heart of the Rebellion.

I must not allow these disappointments to cloud my mind. I must pray for Providence to guide me in subduing this wicked Rebellion.

He had viewed this scene every day since arriving in the second week of June, a few hours too late to take the city on the march. Free State commanders George Custer and Ormsby Mitchel had arrived just ahead of him. Custer had sacrificed his command at the "Last Stand" Battle of Blue Island, buying time for Mitchel's men to occupy the rail junctions leading into the city from the south. Now lines of entrenchments, manned by Free State veterans, barred the way into the city.

Instead of destroying the Yankee Rebels in their western nest, Stoneballs now had to dedicate himself to the uninspiring work of consolidating his gains. He was slowly extending his lines to the north and east to constrict the Rebels' freedom of movement in and around the city, while strengthening his organization of the railroads and telegraphs that linked his new front with its bases down in Central Illinois.

A publicity-seeking general might have used the lull as an opportunity to write boastful letters to superiors, and to invite reporters from newspapers and magazines into his headquarters for interviews. Stoneballs didn't want any more publicity. His star had risen since the dawn of the war when he rescued General Lee's men trapped at Gettysburg. There he had earned his moniker "Stoneballs" by breaking off the ornamental stone balls on the walls of the homes and farms around Gettysburg and firing them out of his cannons to blast a line of retreat after he exhausted his stock ammunition. He fought his way out of another encirclement during last year's Battle of the Salient.

He had studied those setbacks and gleaned the necessary conclusions. For this current offensive across the broad prairies of Illinois, he had honed the Confederate Army of the Northwest into smaller, more mobile, all-arms divisions moving rapidly and fighting independently, thereby surprising the Rebels at places they didn't expect.

His partner, flamboyant Illinois Congressman John Logan, had devised the line of attack up the "forgotten" Illinois River. A well-orchestrated feint by General Lee had drawn U.S. Grant's attention and the bulk of his army eighty miles west to the Mississippi. The Confederates had moved up the undefended Illinois River, Stoneballs' army heading on toward Chicago, while two other Confederate forces disrupted the Free State lines to the east and west.

Therein lay the source of Stoneballs' frustration. The Free State army was split into thirds, according to plan, but so were the Confederate armies attacking them!

Grant's portion of the fragmented Free State Army had been roughly handled by Lee's pursuing Confederates during its precipitant retreat across the Mississippi and up into Iowa. But, like George Washington's army at Valley Forge, it was still sufficiently intact to defend the interior of the country west of the Mississippi and north of its juncture with the Des Moines River. Lee, commanding all Confederate forces in the Northwest, had been drawn far away from the center of the battle around Chicago.

Down in Central Illinois, the Confederates had wrapped a cordon around the bypassed Free State divisions still holding out between Springfield and Decatur. This, too, was a less favorable exchange than it appeared on the maps. It tied down seven Confederate divisions in an indefinite siege defended by Free State militiamen and volunteer army divisions in strong entrenchments.

Stoneballs' mobile divisions were strung out trying to maintain a continuous front between all those points. John Buford's cavalry was patrolling the Des Plaines River west of Chicago to prevent the Rebels from breaking out and threatening Lee's rear. Logan's corps was screening the Indiana / Illinois state line to prevent the Rebels from cutting in behind Stoneballs in force and linking up with the Free State forces bypassed in Central Illinois. Despite Logan's vigilance, the thin Confederate enveloping lines were stretched so taut down there that Free State wagon trains from Indiana slipped through from time to time to revictual their encircled comrades.

He folded his spyglass and slapped it into his palm a bit harder than usual.

We tried to do too many things all at once. If we had concentrated all sixteen divisions into a rapier thrust against Chicago, as I advised, we would have taken the city and won the decisive victory that would have broken the back of the Rebellion. General Lee's insistence on destroying the Rebel armies in the field before moving on Chicago resulted in neither their destruction nor the capture of the campaign's objective.

He turned his gaze to the southwest where he saw his men camped around the town of Blue Island. Nearest were the Indian brigades of General Albert Pike, whose great warrior chiefs Stand Watie and Opothle Yahola had defeated Custer's command at the Battle of Blue

Island. The Indians, ferocious in battle, were asking when they might return to their homes in the Indian Territory now known as New Indiana. So were the Arkansas men in Pike's other two brigades, who pined for their homes in the Ozark Highlands.

Roberdeau Wheat's rambunctious Louisiana Tigers, told that Chicago was a fleshpot that shamed even New Orleans, were getting restless. If Chicago was not taken soon, they were liable to take off on their own and ransack Joliet and other outlying towns. The Negroes were getting harder to control too. They had picked up their masters' ideas of celebrating a victorious campaign by running amok in conquered Chicago. Their disappointment in not reaching the city was manifesting itself in their lackadaisical work.

If we do not get to Chicago soon, the men will cease to think of themselves as instruments of a victorious army. They will become a rabble that withers away by illness and desertion. But what can I do, other than strengthen my defenses and wait for events beyond my control to develop?

He decided to do what he always did when he felt frustration welling up, which was to go to the nearest church and pray for patience until Providence revealed its will. He walked down the footpath from the top of Blue Island Ridge, past the fields of blue flowers adding their hue to the misty air over the ridge. He reached the town at the base of the ridge and checked into his headquarters at the Blue Island House to inform his staff officers that he would be praying at the Methodist Church, the only fully constructed church in the recently settled town.

He walked past the minister's little house, one of many homes that took in the wounded from the Battle of Blue Island. The house no longer had its doors open to admit scurrying doctors and orderlies. The wounded had either recovered sufficiently to be released on parole to the

Free State lines if they were Rebels, returned to duty or furloughed home if they were Confederates, or had finally succumbed to their wounds and been taken to the soldiers' cemetery on the other side of the ridge.

The Free State Rebels had taken to calling Blue Island "Our Alamo" and telling an exaggerated tale about how Custer's men had fought to the last against "Confederate Indian savages." Custer had indeed lost more than one third of his men killed outright. The rest were said to have been incapacitated by wounds, although a complete accounting of the battle revealed many lightly wounded, and more than a few unwounded who had thrown down their weapons and surrendered when the painted Indians came screaming at them. The Rebels nevertheless insisted that every man had fought to the death at Custer's side. The story became ever more embellished each time they shouted, "Remember Blue Island!"

The usual congestion of wagons crowded the streets around the church. Most belonged to civilian refugees. When Stoneballs had first arrived in June, Democrat-voting Confederate loyalists in Chicago, expelled from the Free State lines, were seeking new homes south of town. Now Free-Soil people of Rebel sentiment were removing themselves from Confederate-occupied territory. Stoneballs never liked being reminded that so many people preferred to give up their homes in the Confederate Union to go to live among the Rebels. As he entered the church, he encountered a woman who looked to be about his age draped in a black shawl, her head covered in a black veil. Her three children, aged from about six to thirteen, were with her.

"Peace be with you, ma'am. My condolences for your sorrow."

"My husband died last year," said the woman. "He was fighting with John Pope's division."

"He has gone to live in the Lord's House," Stoneballs consoled, in his accustomed way of comforting grieving families --- some whose loved ones were killed by the war, but many more by the eternal diseases that struck down one in four children, and one in ten women, including Stoneballs' first wife, in childbirth. "Death is the Lord's way of breaking our bonds with our loved ones on Earth, and thereby preparing us to leave this earthly life when our time comes."

"Our 'earthly bonds' are being broken now," replied the woman, starting to cry. "Our neighbors ran us out of Alton. They said it was a Confederate town now, and Free Soil Rebels weren't welcome. They told us we must swear allegiance to the Confederate Union or leave. They said Confederate refugees had lost their homes when the Free State men took over in Northern Illinois, so it served us Rebels right to lose ours, now that the tide has turned."

"I don't approve of running people out of their homes," said Stoneballs, "no matter what their sentiments. Those who want to stay out of the war should be allowed to proclaim their neutrality and not be bothered by either side. Alas, in times of conflict, Man becomes a wicked creature who turns against his neighbors and even his own flesh and blood. I want to end this war before our American family estranges itself and reconciliation becomes impossible."

The woman dried her tears. "You're the general they call 'Stoneballs' aren't you? Our newspapers say you're a righteous man, though fighting for the most unholy cause!"

"Yes, madam, I am General Thomas Jackson. Ever since the battle at Gettysburg, they've taken to calling me 'Stoneballs.'" He shrugged. "I can think of better monikers, but I've given up on trying to discourage the appellation."

She smiled, upon realizing that even an esteemed general cannot command the name he is known by.

"General Stoneballs, I know you are doing your duty to end this war as your conscience commands. And I am following my conscience in hoping that the Free States remain beyond your grasp."

"The Lord is perfect in His wisdom, but reveals only portions of it to us mortals," Stoneballs consoled her. "Seeing only a part of what He sees, we find ourselves in perpetual conflict with each other, I suppose since the time Cain murdered Abel."

The woman looked at the crucifix on the wall. "Only One obeyed the perfect will of the Father and suffered for all us wayward people."

Stoneballs bowed his head and nodded. "Where are you going?"

"To Michigan. My sister is in Grand Haven. She sent her husband through the lines to fetch me and bring me back. She says the town is booming with refugees from the parts of Illinois, Indiana, and Ohio the Confederates have taken. I think we will be happy living among our own people. It is a new country the Confederates will never take from us."

"We will meet again in better days of peace," Stoneballs assured her. "May the Lord protect you and yours." He opened the door and watched her and the children climb into their wagon. It was driven by a man Stoneballs presumed to be her brother-in-law. He watched them drive off and turn on to the road leading to the rail junctions south of Chicago. They would pass around the south side of Lake Michigan and on up through Indiana to Michigan.

She is going off to live in what she calls her new country. Illinois is a new country too, no longer descended from the Virginians who conquered it from the British during the War of the Revolution. It has gained nearly a million people in just the last ten years, more than Old Virginia has gained in the seventy years since the first census. Virginia is a land of farms and county seat towns, growing slowly, if at all. A third of our people are slaves. Illinois is a land of cities, railroads, and factories. It can grow for generations yet to come, and not a slave among them.

I am three hundred miles inside the state, but still nearly a hundred miles from its northern border. There is also Indiana, Ohio, Michigan, Wisconsin, Iowa, and Minnesota, all being populated by New England Yankees, British and Canadians, and Germans, who are Free Soil people.

General Lee says that if these people become a nation, they will grow too strong for us to resist. They have proven, with John Brown's Raid, that they cannot be trusted to leave us alone. They will hector us to free our slaves and incite them to rise against us if we do not bring them back into our Union. Our purpose is to conquer their rebellion and force them to live under our authority. Which party is right? Why is the Lord so reticent to give us guidance as to which side should prevail?

His favorite Bible verse came to mind: *"And we know that all things work together for good to them that love God, to them who are called according to his purpose."*

He stood up, feeling that the outcome of the war had not been pre-ordained by Providence. **Whichever side fought with the most effective combination of bravery, intelligence, will, and resources would prevail. It would be a difficult and ugly war.** Many more families were destined to lose husbands, brothers, and sons; and to be run out of their homes by hostile neighbors.

In his mind, he kept hearing the woman's phrase, "It is a new country the Confederates will never take from us."

3. *The Fireman*

William Tecumseh 'Cump' Sherman --- newly appointed General of the Armies of the United States of Free America --- contemplated the view from the West Michigan dunes rolling north toward the Grand River two miles away.

The dark blue waters of Lake Michigan met the azure sky at the horizon. Waves lapped against the white sands of the dunes along the shore, crowned with green hardwood forests. Sun-tinted mist rose from the warm waters of the lake. A cool breeze from the north rustled the green leaves in the trees above Sherman's head. Here and there the smaller and weaker trees were showing their first hints of autumn's yellows.

"If there's a heaven, I'll wager a month's pay it looks something like this," said Sherman.

Sherman's subordinate, Major General Ormsby Mitchel, winced. As a man of religious spirit, he was willing to wager far more than a month's pay that there was a happier world beyond this one. "The Good Lord has provided us with a blessed land," he counseled. "Unfortunately, we too often insist on defacing His glorious creations."

Mitchel was looking beyond nature's beauty and toward the sprawling shack town around the mouth of the Grand River housing thousands of Free State refugees. Malodorous smells of cesspools, livestock, barnyard fowl, animal manure, mud, and rancid water in the dirt streets blew in on the north wind, wrinkling his nose.

His eyes were offended by the shacks of roughhewn warping green pine with gaping holes plugged with tree branches, rags, newspapers, and mud. The newly arrived were sleeping in wagons, if they had them, after selling their horses and mules to be butchered. Beyond the shacks, people sheltered under "tipis" of piled up branches and pine straw. Lean, hungry people, and their raggedy children meandered about, still in shock from being suddenly uprooted from their prosperous homes and farms in Confederate-occupied Illinois.

He reminded himself that these refugees were not to blame for the squalor. Thousands of women and children, elderly and infirm had been forcibly removed from their residences by the Defense Council of Chicago, that he commanded. Food rations had to be allocated to people manning the fortifications around the city or performing essential work within it.

Other refugees had come in from the farms and towns of Illinois occupied by the Confederates during their summer offensive. They could have stayed behind and prospered by trading with the Confederates, but they had chosen to follow the retreating Free State armies. Some had recently fled the oppression and poverty of the European empires, arriving in America only to become refugees once again in their new country.

"It's taking much longer than I thought to get those people sorted out," said Mitchel. "I'd hoped we'd be able to duplicate your success in New England in cut time."

"Circumstances are entirely different here," Sherman remarked. "The Connecticut Valley was settled two hundred years before we brought in the refugees. Michigan is a frontier state. You're starting over from scratch here. It's bound to take longer."

"I should have thought of that," confessed Mitchel. "It would have been better to relocate them to Indiana. It's a longer-settled state that could have better accommodated them. But it looked like we were going to lose the rail junctions south of Chicago in June, so I sent them here. Then I became absorbed in the defense of the city and didn't pay attention to organizing these refugees. They're in bad shape. If we don't get them better shelter, they'll freeze when the snow starts flying --- if cholera doesn't kill them first, or they don't become insane wandering around in that filth."

"Don't worry," Sherman consoled. "These people may look like meek little bunny rabbits, but we'll get them knocked into shape. The Connecticut Valley looked even worse at the beginning of last year when we took in the refugees from Boston and the coast. Now they're producing surpluses of food, clothing, and weapons. The men are trained to use the new Burnside rifles we're producing --- the ones that stopped the Confederates from getting into Providence. The 'Sherman Line' as they call it, is impregnable. The territory behind it is self-sufficient in all necessary productions. This land will be too."

Mitchel looked again toward the squalid chaos down there along the Grand River. "Tell the truth, I don't know where to start. It's too late to put in a crop. I don't have any inventories of material to get these people working on permanent constructions, and...."

"I'll get you some help," Sherman interjected. "You can't be expected to defend Chicago and take care of these people. I'll ask Burnside to send some of his best men out here to organize them, so you can dedicate your efforts to defending Chicago."

"Thank you, sir!" exclaimed Mitchel. He sounded relieved, but not enthusiastic. Sherman didn't blame him. Mitchel hadn't seen what Sherman's New Englanders had accomplished after evacuating their homes in Boston and other coastal towns.

Sherman's gaze followed Mitchel's to the shack town. "They'll pick up the cudgel once they're organized. Our people have stuck with us, at least the ones this far north."

"If there's anybody further north than this, they'll be at the North Pole!" replied Mitchel. The Grand River was the frontier line of settlement. In the 3,300 miles of emptiness between here and the northern pole, there were only scattered Indian settlements. "Like I said, if I'd thought it through, I would have spread them out in Indiana, instead of way up here."

"You put them in the right place," Sherman assured him. "The rail line from Grand Haven runs directly to Montreal. Secretary of State Seward has obtained another $50,000,000 loan from the British to enable us to buy what we need from the Canadas. I'll put in an order for lumber, bricks, mortar --- and rations --- from Montreal to expedite construction of real buildings here. That will keep the people fed, housed, and gainfully employed until they can put in a crop next spring."

Mitchel nodded.

Sherman's eyes followed the railroad running inland. "I can use the Canadian railroad to move my New England men out here without making it obvious to the Confederates that I'm building up a reserve army to surprise them when the time comes. This place is also good from a human aspect. The people will apply all their energies to improving a wilderness they will one day own. It will expedite the development of Michigan. We'll build a new city here, with houses, merchants, schools, and everything else they had in Chicago. We'll establish factories, farms, and shipyards all over Western Michigan. We'll make this our base for the reconquest of the Great Northwest!"

Mitchel's face showed relief. "I suppose I didn't do too bad then, even if I didn't plan any of this."

"Sometimes things work out for the best without your planning them. That's known as 'serendipity.'"

"Serendipity? That's a good word to describe what brought you here. I don't imagine we would've held out for long if you'd taken the Confederates up on their offer to put you in command of their army."

Sherman's mouth bent a wry smile. "No, I don't expect you would have ⋯ not with Davis, McClellan, Lee, Stanton, Jackson, and all the rest of the Old Guard lined up against you. I came here to even the odds and make it a fair fight!"

Sherman wasn't exaggerating. When the war broke out, he'd been the Superintendent of Louisiana's Military Academy. He was an esteemed friend of Louisiana's governor and its leading politicians, businessmen, and military officers. President Stephen Douglass had sent Robert E. Lee out to offer him command of the Confederate Union's Army of the Northwest.

He'd declined the offer, then stayed neutral until his brother --- Speaker of the House John Sherman --- and Free State President Lincoln had persuaded him that the Free State's cause was just. Had it not been obvious that the United States of Free America was unlikely to survive without his services, he might have remained neutral and returned to San Francisco to sit out the war.

He brushed back his blowing hair, which he rarely greased into place.

"I came at the right time. By the time I declared my loyalty to the Free States, Fremont was settled in at Philly; Grant and McDowell were holding the line here in the Northwest; and nobody had thought to safeguard New England. I was the only man they had left to travel between the fronts. With your help and Grant's, we defeated the Confederates at the Wabash last year. Then I moved on to stop the Confederates in New England and caught them with their pants down at Camden. I happened to be at all the right places at all the right times."

Mitchel was moved by Sherman's humility, which few officers manifested.

"You're modest in not boasting about your strategic genius that made those victories possible. We couldn't have won without your clear thinking that rallied us when defeat seemed imminent. Horace Greeley has taken to calling you 'The Fireman' because Lincoln sends you to put out the fires, wherever they are burning. Now you've come to put out another one in Chicago!"

Sherman looked out over the lake in the direction of Chicago a hundred miles southwest.

"I don't know about Chicago. I'm not so certain they'll try to bull their way into it. Davis has got them in high feather with his

Reconstructed Confederate Union talk. He wants them to believe the war is all but over and will be achieved soon and without much loss. They'd spill oceans of blood fighting their way into Chicago --- maybe ten times as much as they lost taking St. Louis. The British won't let them blast Chicago off the map the way they destroyed Cincy. Davis may ask them to attack someplace else where he thinks a decisive victory can be won without excessive bloodshed and destruction."

"Oh?" replied Mitchel. "Where would you attack if you were them."

"I'd try for a wide envelopment around Indianapolis. Or, better yet, I'd attack eastward along the Wabash to Fort Wayne, then follow the Maumee to Toledo, to take another bite out of us."

"What about Springfield?"

"I'd leave it alone. It would take another veteran army corps to reduce the place. Yates' militiamen survived the worst of the Partisan War. They'll fight to the death. Better to starve them out than kill them all and create another 'Alamo' legend, while wrecking an army corps you can't afford to lose. By the way, Lincoln asked if it was feasible to organize a relief expedition. He wanted to travel with the expedition and speak to the people of Springfield, to show the Confederates that they might temporarily occupy our land but will never conquer our people. I had to recommend against it. Springfield's too far from our main line to justify the risk."

"Mr. Lincoln thinks big, doesn't he?"

"Another reason we'll win the war, so long as everybody does their part. We must be patient now and wait for the Confederates to fully develop their attack. We must not act precipitately and let them whipsaw us again by pointing their armies at one place, then blindsiding us in another. We must let them think they've won a victory and can let down their guard. Then we must hit them with all our reserves like we did last year on the Wabash."

Sherman crossed his arms and turned to face the east. "Since the New England front will likely stay quiet, I will be transferring up to sixty thousand men to this theater. We're hoping to arm some with Spencer repeating rifles. I've tested them. They're three times more effective than Burnside's rifles; ten times more effective than muzzle loaders. If we can hit the Confederates in the flank, while they're out of their trenches and moving about in the open, we'll slaughter them like pigeons."

Mitchel rubbed his chin and thought for a minute. "These newfangled weapons rarely live up to their billing, but you seem convinced that this one will. Can we obtain enough to make a difference?"

"We're getting satisfactory production of mechanical subassemblies from the components factories we've established along the Connecticut River," answered Sherman. "Final assembly is taking place at the Remington factory at Ilion, New York. That's taking longer than we thought, but Remington is expanding their facilities and hiring on more workers. Our engineers are field-testing the mass production models. If they pass muster, several hundred a day will be produced, beginning in early September. We hope to arm at least ten thousand of our men before committing them. Be careful not to say a word about this. We must assume that some of those people down there are Confederate spies."

"It would be good for morale if we could at least let our people know, in a general way, that improved weapons are coming."

Sherman shook his head. "If they knew they'd be getting better weapons, they'd hold back from risking their lives in battle until they got them. They've got to fight as hard as they can now, with whatever arms are available."

"I understand," acknowledged Mitchel.

"We **can** tell them they're not fighting alone. The British and Canadians are invested in our freedom. If our cause fails, they'll never see their loans repaid. Tell your people that British and Canadian families are on short rations so our people can eat. Tell them the British have warned the Confederates not to destroy any more of our cities. If they want any more of our cities, they'll have to take them house by house, and pave the streets with their blood and guts like we made them do in St. Louis. Let's see how much more of that they can stand!"

"It's important that the people know we are not fighting alone," agreed Mitchel. "When might I expect your men from New England to arrive? Their arrival will let our people know the rest of the country has not forgotten them."

"I'll telegraph Burnside to expedite them on their way before I leave tomorrow. I'm going across the lake to Milwaukee and then on across Wisconsin to meet with General Grant in Iowa. It's imperative that I meet with Grant and inform him of our strategy, and his place in it. He's got to hold on to Iowa and Minnesota even if our communications across Wisconsin are disrupted."

"Wisconsin?" asked Mitchel. "I'd forgotten about it. The Confederates haven't shown any interest in moving north past Chicago on that side of the lake."

"They're stretched thin, like we are. They can't do everything all at once any more than we can. I'll stop by Madison to talk to Governor Salomon and make sure he understands we haven't forgotten about him.

He's defending the state with militia. If he needs any Regular Army men to stiffen them, I'll see what I can spare from New England."

"Will you be returning through Chicago?"

"Yes. I'll see you there in about four days. Then I'm going down to Indianapolis and from there to Cincinnati. I want to see what I can do about getting the Confederates out of the Ohio River counties east of the city. If I get busy down there, you'll be on your own up here. So, I'll tell you the same thing I'm going to tell Grant:

"The Confederates have one last ace up their sleeve, and they're going to play it soon. They may succeed in breaking up our front for a time. If the front becomes discontinuous and you lose contact with me, your orders are to defend Chicago and as much of adjoining Indiana and Michigan as you can, in the way Barrie and Yates are defending Springfield. Establish contingency plans to fight for every defensible position, such as along the St. Joseph River.

"If the worst happens, we'll fight on as fortified city-states --- relying on the Canadas as our backdoor railroad and the Great Lakes to keep us in communication by water. If we can hold out through spring, I'm confident we'll have enough Spencers to beat the Confederates back across the Ohio. Their next offensive will be their last ace. Once it's played, it'll be our turn to deal the deck. Stay confident, and the people will be confident --- and ready to give their all when the time comes."

"Yes, Fireman Sherman!" Mitchel replied, this time with full confidence.

Fireman Sherman. Sherman liked that appellation. He had a premonition that history would remember him by it.

4. The Ghost of Stephen Douglas

Egg Harbor City, New Jersey, September 13. 1862

Major General George B. McClellan embraced Jefferson Davis and his aide-de-camp Major Custis Lee in the foyer of the Germania Gasthaus.

"What a pleasant surprise, Sir!" exclaimed McClellan. "I'm so happy you were able to visit my humble encampment." He turned to Custis. "Next time you write your father, please convey my admiration for his victory over Grant in Illinois."

Davis gave an approving glance at the well-furnished room. "Your encampment isn't so humble. This is a tidy little town, prosperous by the looks of it. It's entirely settled by Germans, I understand."

Davis had noticed the town's prosperity as soon as he detrained. The streets were clean, the houses freshly painted, the gardens tended. Merchants of well-inventoried stores were gossiping with farmers returning from their fields outside of town to take a midday rest from the heat. The brisk strides and spotless uniforms of the troops who occupied the town were evidence that McClellan was in command. The townspeople were as clean as McClellan's men, proving they didn't need anyone giving them orders to look their best. Even the farmers wore overalls without patches.

"They've platted it out to rival New York," McClellan explained, "Seven miles long and a mile wide. The founders say it will become the German metropolis of America. 'The Freedom of America, and the abiding happiness of Germany' --- that's their pitch."

Davis smiled. "They'll need to come up with a more appealing appellation than 'Egg Harbor City', if they want to attract people who'll fulfill those grand expectations!"

"It doesn't even have a harbor," added McClellan, "and probably never will, given the shallow river. Nevertheless, it's a strategic location on the railroad between Philly and Atlantic City. My engineers are building a real harbor at Atlantic City, to expedite our resupply. It will facilitate the growth of this area after the war."

"I despise war and seek to avoid it until it becomes unavoidable," remarked Davis. "But it does prune the rotten branches from society and allow new ones to emerge. Places like this will develop more rapidly after the military has improved their communications. Men who never would have traveled more than twenty-five miles from their homes in civilian life travel far and wide with the army and learn to take a larger view of life, and a larger view of their country. Our progress will be more rapid after this war than it would have been without it."

Davis drew his handkerchief and wiped sweat from his face and neck. This far inland there was no hint of the ocean breeze that usually kept New York City tolerable.

McClellan waved his hand invitingly toward the stairwell. "Please accompany me downstairs to the Rathskeller --- that's the German word for basement. It holds the night's cool air. My engineers installed a barrel of ice down there, and the proprietor keeps a keg of cold beer he brews fresh every day."

"Twist my arm!" shouted Davis.

McClellan called for his orderly to take their bags up to the guest quarters, then took Davis and Custis Lee downstairs.

The cool dry air in the Rathskeller felt as refreshing as the air from a limestone cave. Sure enough, there was a barrel of ice sitting over an iron tub. A handpump connected to a vulcanized rubber hose ran into a drain in the floor to remove the meltwater.

"Aaahhh!" said Davis, loosening his collar to allow the cool air to sink into his shirt. "When I get back to Washington City, I'll have the engineers build a couple of these devices in the White House. There's no place worse than Washington in summer. Not just the heat, but the diseases that ride the fetid air. Stephen Douglas, God rest his crafty soul, weakened his constitution with strong drink, but typhoid fever put him in his grave. Keep it under your hat --- that when this war is over, I'll ask Congress to create a new capital district in the highlands, where we can breathe healthy air and drink pure spring-fed water."

McClellan nodded, while wondering what people with homes and businesses in Washington City would say. Davis appeared not to have considered the storm of opposition bound to arise from people who had invested their lives there. Davis, like everybody else, was wise in some things, but naïve in others.

They pressed up to the bar. McClellan introduced them to two of his staff officers, then to the proprietor and his wife.

"Mein Gott, the President of the United States in my establishment!" exclaimed the proprietor. "Vot an honor is dis!"

Davis noted that he, like most everybody he'd met in New York City and New Jersey, still referenced the country the old way. What would the country be called when the war ended, hopefully with the reunion of all states?

McClellan put a gold dollar on the bar, while asking for beer and privacy. The proprietor held the coin high. "Look here, Hedvig," he said to his wife, "vot luck dis var is for some people!" He poured their beer and then motioned for his wife to leave. "Come, ve go to de stores while dese gentlemen talks. Dey may help demselves to all de beer dey vants." The two officers sitting at the bar quickly drained their glasses and left with them.

"What do these Germans think about our war?" Davis asked when they were out of earshot.

"They say they came to America to escape the wars between the German states. They want nothing more to do with our war between American states. Neither do most other Jersey men. They say they're citizens of a Border State that isn't attached to the cause of the North or South. Governor Olden and the legislature have declared New Jersey to be an independent republic, so people will have a moral and legal basis to avoid taking sides. Here's what they're saying:" McClellan got up and pulled a brochure down from the bulletin board and handed it to Davis. It was titled *The Transcendentalist Republic of New Jersey*.

46

Davis looked at the cover. It showed a triangle inside a circle with the words, "Knowledge, Reason, Morality" placed at the points where the circle and the triangle touched. Inside the circle was a lithograph of farmer in his field, with a manufactory lurking in the background. He opened it up and frowned.

"Says it's written by Henry Thoreau, Ralph Waldo Emerson, and Walt Whitman --- crazy New Englanders, of the stripe that provoked this war." He flipped the page. "Oh, the introduction's written by Horace Greeley. Let's see what he says:

'We are proposing that New Jersey should establish itself as an independent Republic whose society is organized around the principle of 'Economy of Associations.' Capitalists must remain free to accumulate wealth and invest it in business opportunities. They must continue to profit from their investments. Their employees must become part-owners of the businesses employing them, and thereby receive a fair share of the profits. We must become a society of shared ownership and shared responsibility, including responsibility for making certain that all our people have employment, adequate food, and sanitary housing.'"

"Not as crazy as you thought, is it?" asked McClellan.

"No," Davis admitted. "It isn't. Secretary of War Stanton advises me to get the people looking beyond the war by talking about these economic issues of capital and labor. People are leaving the farms to work for wages in town. Steady work with steady pay is what they care about. Slavery will always be with us, but it is bound to become less important as the wealth from city work increases. Stanton says that if we ever hope to persuade the Free States to give up their rebellion, we need to be talking along these lines. Let the Yankee Rebels know we can look out after their interests as well as our own."

"I see it happening that way too," concurred McClellan. "In another fifty years, we'll be as populous as Europe. Probably more so, because we're better governed than they are --- at least we were until the war started. I met many intelligent and ambitious Germans and Russians when you sent me to Europe to study the Crimean War. Millions will immigrate here, like the Germans in this town, to live under our enlightened government. We'll need those people on our side, living in one country with one flag. If we fragment ourselves into multiple nations constantly at war with each other, how are we any better than Europe?"

The foam on their beers settled. "Cheers," said McClellan, raising his glass. "A toast to the Confederate Union for a Confederate Century."

Davis drank a long swig from his beer, a rare indulgence for him.

"Delicious!" he exclaimed. "I haven't enjoyed a cold one so much since those days at West Point when we'd sneak over to Benny Havens after those hot days on the parade ground. What a delight!"

"Oh, Benny Havens! We'll sing reminiscences of Benny Havens," intoned McClellan offkey, as he had sung it as a cadet a decade and a half ago.

"You know, old Benny is still alive and kicking," added Custis, who'd graduated West Point in 1854. "His place is still causing a bit of trouble. I was almost expelled when my roommate smuggled a flask of spiced rum into our room."

"I had a controversy over that, too," said Davis. "I successfully argued my case that West Point forbids cadets from consuming spirits, but not ale!"

Davis took another drink, then sang a verse from long ago:

"To our comrades who have fallen, one cup before we go,

They poured their life-blood freely out *pro bono publico!*"

A trace of tear welled up in Davis's eye.

"A soldier's life is lonely and often short. I lost classmates in the Seminole Wars and in Mexico. Now we're killing our classmates on the other side; what a tragedy *that* is. Even the survivors will carry scars of war with us until our dying day." Davis winced because the ache in his foot, shattered at the Battle of Buena Vista, came into his mind.

Davis drained his beer. McClellan picked up the mugs and took them to the keg to pour another round.

"We must win this war and stop the bloodshed before it consumes your generation," Davis said to Custis Lee. "Our generation is responsible for this war. Bad faith by stubborn old men who should have known better. We are insulting the kind Providence that gave us this blessed land."

McClellan came back with the beers and sat down. "What's going on Out West?"

Davis sighed. "Not as much as I'd like. Our men are stuck around Chicago, Springfield, and Indianapolis. Springfield's been surrounded and cut off from reinforcement and resupply, but they have about 40,000 --- and by some reports as many as 60,000 --- armed Yankee Rebels defending the town and a couple others nearby. They're mostly militia units commanded by the governor, stiffened with a couple of volunteer army divisions that stayed behind when the Free State Army broke up. We'll eventually starve them out, but maybe not before the end of this year.

"Lee's in a stand-off with Grant on the Mississippi. Buell still hasn't taken the north end of Cincinnati. And here we are, in stand-offs in the East. Your plan to capture Philadelphia was well-conceived. What do you think blunted it? Did the Rebels get wind of it in advance?"

"Not likely," answered McClellan. "Our spies inside the Free State lines say we fooled Sherman into thinking we were going to attack up the Connecticut River, using the same tactics we did in Illinois. He positioned his men to let us ascend the river, obstruct it behind us, then swarm us when we started to debark. He didn't know Philly was our objective until our cavalry reached Camden. He got to Philly fast because he wasn't a prisoner of his planning, like most generals are. He cut across Fremont's front on his own authority and hit us hard in the flank."

"Fortunes of war," said Davis, raising his glass.

"At any event, our attack was partially successful," contended McClellan. "It panicked Mr. Lincoln into ordering Fremont to pull his men out of northeastern Maryland, thereby allowing us to restore direct communications between Baltimore and Wilmington. We're tying down their men around Philly and keeping them away from the other fronts. It's their major procurement city. They can't carry on the war without it."

"We're gnawing at them," opined Davis, "but we've got to grab them by the scruffs of their mangy necks and shake them. Otherwise, time will start to work against us. Being stuck in stagnant camps is hard on the men. Desertions and infractions are rising, especially in Illinois. As much as Braxton Bragg would like to shoot every man who deserts or cusses an officer, I cannot allow it. We are a volunteer army of citizens who must depend upon morale, rather than the firing squad and the stockade, to maintain discipline. We need a decisive victory to maintain the morale of our men and their families at home. Otherwise, the Fire Eaters will fill the Congress and force us to call off the war. They don't want the Yankee Rebels back."

The beer was having its effect on Davis. "Tell the truth, I don't want some of our **Confederates** back. Joe Johnston will be released in our first prisoner exchange. He's already written me a letter. Says he's entitled by seniority to be promoted to General of the Armies. What a pain in the posterior!"

McClellan slapped his hand over his mouth to keep from laughing out his beer. "Old Joe's coming back! You should've offered to let some more Rebels go if they'd agree to **keep** him!"

Davis grimaced. "Stanton didn't want the prisoner exchange. He said the Yankee Rebels are fighting a defensive war, and that every man fighting on the defense is worth three on the offense. According to him, we're effectively giving the Yankee Rebels three men back for each one of ours. Even if that's true, I had to agree to the exchange. Those prison camps are killing more of our men with disease than we're losing in combat. I couldn't stand to see our boys go through another winter up there."

"How many men are we getting back?" asked McClellan.

"Approximately twenty-four thousand. That'll be a more-or-less even swap for Kirby Smith's men the Yankee Rebels captured on the Wabash last year, for Grant's men we captured in Illinois this year."

McClellan raised his glass, took a drink, and set it down. "I understand Stanton's position, but you were right to agree to the exchange. It's the necessary thing to do to save the men's lives, and we can put them to good use. Since they're mostly from Kirby Smith's corps, we can reconstitute them as a unit immediately and get them back in the field."

"A lot of them will be in bad shape with wounds and disease; they'll have to be furloughed or discharged from service," advised Davis.

"Yes, unfortunately. But let's optimistically assume we can return two-thirds to service right way. Where will they be exchanged?"

"Franklin, Indiana, between Louisville and Indianapolis."

"That's the best place to receive them," said McClellan. "We can arm every man who's strong enough to carry a gun and get them into action right away. They're going to be rip-roaring to fight after being cooped up in those prison camps for over a year. We can reinforce the released prisoners with the cavalry brigades of Jubal Early and Jeb Stuart, and Dick Ewell's men. They're not doing anything commensurate with their capabilities here. We'll break the Rebel line at Indianapolis, then roll it up all the way to Chicago. If we play our cards right, we might even recapture those Rebel prisoners we'll be turning loose!"

Davis smiled wryly, then squinted his eyes. "Have you by chance been communicating with the ghost of Stephen Douglas? This is the sort of design he'd cook up!"

"Stephen Douglas," replied McClellan wistfully. "I'd hadn't thought much about him since he passed away. He seems a part of the old country before the war, the part that's gone away, never to return."

McClellan recalled how Douglas had persuaded Davis to join him in creating the Confederate Union Compact, based on the dubious scheme of invading Mexico with Southern state militias, then annexing the country as new Slave States without the consent of the Northern-dominated Congress. Douglas had counted on mollifying anti-slavery

Northerners by bullying Britain to cede the Canadas to the Union as Free States.

Before that, in 1854, Douglas had schemed with his cronies in Congress to overturn the hallowed Missouri Compromise. He intended to double-cross the Abolitionists in the North and the Fire Eaters in the South, thus enabling the moderate men of both sections to govern. Instead, it had encouraged the Abolitionists and Fire Eaters to wreck the Union by making armed incursions into each other's territory, thereby pulling the ground out from under the moderates and making compromise impossible.

McClellan contemplated Douglas' selection of Davis to be his Vice President. "At least he had sense enough to put you on the Confederate Union ticket. I don't know if he could have saved the Union without you. As much as I liked him personally, I never put much stock in anything he promised. You are a man of integrity who thinks carefully about his principles and honors them once they are made."

Davis put his glass down hard. "Douglas didn't like that about me. He thought I was too stubborn in sticking to principle. He believed in sticking his finger in the air to see which way the wind was blowing, then hoisting the mainsail to catch it. His one and only principle was preserving this Union, no matter how much chicanery he thought he had to employ. He thought he could keep double-crossing people on both sides of the Ohio, then charming them into giving him another chance. That worked until people on both sides of the Ohio took their cue from him and started double-crossing each other."

"You know, the Europeans say that about Napoleon," concurred McClellan. " 'He was as great as a man can be who has no virtues.' He liberated the peoples of Europe from the monarchies confining them to the class they were born into. He set them free to rise to the level their merit warranted. But he never implemented the democratic institutions of congresses and courts required to make his empire larger than himself. When his generalship failed, his empire crumbled. He died a broken man. I am sad to say it, but Stephen Douglas will be remembered the same way."

Davis nodded. "At least he kept our party together in 1860. Without him, I know we would have fragmented into several parties. We wouldn't have prevailed in Illinois or Indiana, and perhaps not in California and Oregon. Mr. Lincoln would have been elected president with those electoral votes. Our Southern Fire Eaters would never have tolerated Lincoln's government. They would have busted the Union, and the opprobrium of secession would have fallen upon the South."

McClellan winced. "A possibility too dreadful to contemplate. As much as I despise 'the original gorilla' Lincoln, I think I would have been forced to fight for the preservation of the Union under his government. Douglas and Stanton would have sided with the Union too. It would have been excruciating for our Northern Democrat to fight for the government of a man we despise in order to save the Union we love."

Davis shuddered at the horror of a civil war instigated by Southern secession. How could he have fought against McClellan, whom he cherished as a son? And if McClellan would have fought for Lincoln's government to preserve the Union, how many millions of other Northern Democrats, who had heretofore been friends, would he have had to fight against?

I am not sure we could have prevailed in a war of Southern Secession, with the entire North, Northwest, and Far West against us. Even if we had managed to establish a separate national independence, after years of bloodshed and expense, we would have been a diminished republic, entirely wedded to the interests of slavery.

If we prevail in this war against Northern Secession, we will preserve our destiny to become unique in the world in our power, wealth, and influence. It falls upon my shoulders to restore the Union on sound principles, so that it will never be torn asunder by the ephemeral politics of fanatics in the North and South, or by the chicanery of wily politicians like Stephen Douglas.

"When this war is over," said Davis, "it will be up to young men like you to govern the restored Union in good faith and fairness to men on both sides of the Ohio and Potomac. If the union has been restored by 1864, then I think I will not be inclined to run for a second term. I will endorse you as our party's nominee, if you desire. Then it will be up to you, as a Union-loyal Northern man of military acclaim, to reconcile the Northern people to reunion, and to govern the Southern Fire Eaters with a firm hand, so they will understand there can be no profit in disunion mischief from their side.

"We must henceforth run our restored Union according to principle. We must no longer tolerate politicians who encourage either side, or in the case of Douglas encourage both sides, to double cross each other. Let us remember Stephen Douglas as a patriot, but let's never disinter his ghost."

5. *"If the Damn Yankees don't beat us, Damnfool Davis will!"*

Atlanta, Georgia September 16, 1862

William L. Yancey, "The King of Southern Fire Eaters," had never liked Atlanta, and liked it even less as a center of wartime commerce on the boom. The city was everything he had dedicated his life to preventing the Slave State South from becoming --- a noisy cacophony of self-important merchants, speculators, and factory owners shoving wads of paper money in everybody's faces by day, while the hired hands spent their paychecks drinking in cheap saloons and fornicating with prostitutes in the alleys behind them at night.

He had seen enough of that while growing up in the industrial towns along the Erie Canal, after his Yankee Abolitionist stepfather married his widowed slave-owning South Carolina mother and moved the family to Troy, New York. He grew up viewing North / South relations through the microcosm of his parents' turbulent marriage punctuated by domestic violence. He came back to the South as an adult, dedicating himself to separating the Southern States from the "degenerated Yankees."

Now, as he detrained at Atlanta's Union Station, he saw once again the "Yankee degeneration" transported into the very heart of his beloved South! With the coming of war, Atlanta had found its destiny as a railroad hub and military procurement center. The Confederate Union government, after a bumbling start with snarled railroad traffic that blunted its first offensives, had finally got its railroads sorted out and running at full chisel. Their operations were now coordinated by Richard Taylor, who had fought at Robert E. Lee's side during the first year and a half of the war, thereby learning by experience that armies cannot advance faster than their supplies.

Taylor had decreed that every rickety wooden-railed road in the South be replaced with forged steel rails and sturdy bridges capable of bearing heavy loads of war material. Every under-powered locomotive with leaky boilers must be replaced with a durable machine capable of hauling its heavy loads up the hills north of Atlanta and over the Appalachian hump in Tennessee and Virginia. Atlanta's rolling mills and locomotive works were working triple shifts turning out iron rails and refurbished locomotives. Its lumber yards were milling replacement ties for worn out tracks, and for new ones to double-track from Atlanta up to the acres of supply bases building up around Louisville.

Trains cleared through the city, loaded with cornmeal, molasses, salted pork and beef, fruit, citrus, hardtack, and new army enlistments from Georgia, South Carolina, Alabama, and Florida. They stopped in Atlanta just long enough to pick up uniforms, saddles, tents, knives, pistols, ammunition, and cannons fabricated from the industrial establishments growing up in and around the city. Then they chugged on up through Chattanooga, Nashville, and Louisville, and on to the

Northwestern Front stretching from Cincinnati to the outskirts of Chicago. Yancey grimaced when he saw this abundance, hewn from the soil and the labor of the South, shipping north.

Can't the commissary officers resupply our armies in Ohio, Indiana, and Illinois where they're fighting? Is there no pork and corn north of the Ohio River? Why take the food from our people in Georgia, Alabama, and South Carolina, who never even wanted this war?

His annoyance increased when he saw Atlantans boisterously exuberant. Their purses were stuffed with Confederate Union notes, issued by the government to purchase every production needed to sustain the war. And yet a discerning person, as Yancey surely was, could see fissures in the superficial prosperity. For one thing, the promiscuously issued paper notes were not holding their value at par with gold. It was illegal for sellers to post different price schedules for Confederate Union paper notes than for gold specie, but insofar as the Confederate Union hadn't enforced that law, people were ignoring it. The black-market exchange rate had fallen to a hundred Confederate Union paper dollars exchanged for 84 gold dollars. Those with financial acumen could calculate that if the rate of depreciation went on for another year, the currency would be devalued to around seventy cents on the gold dollar.

The yokels think they're becoming wealthy because the government is stuffing their pockets with paper notes that can't hold their value. In a couple years they will be using them to plug the holes in their outhouses.

A discerning person would also realize that those who did not earn their keep by producing goods and services of value to the Confederate Union's war effort were losing ground every day. The requisitioning of the lion's share of farm produce by Confederate

58

commissary agents decreased the supply available for civilian consumption. Flour, cornmeal, salt, sugar, meat, and imported coffee were becoming scarcer in Atlanta's city markets. Prices seemed to rise every day, with a growing gap between prices posted in paper notes and gold. Woe be to those who did not have a steady income of Confederate Union notes!

The only people who seemed to be truly prospering were the New York speculators who came to town with their purses bulging with the gold specie the Confederate Union government had contracted to pay on its war bonds. Their gold gave them first call on buying what was left on the farms after Confederate commissary agents made their requisitions. They brought it into town and sold it at inflated markups to the city people who paid with paper dollars. They demanded the Confederate Government to accept *their* paper dollars at par for gold when they purchased the next issue of war bonds. The Confederate Union Treasury took in the paper notes and reissued them to the public, thereby --- in the eloquent words of Yancey's newspaper partner Robert Rhett --- "redeeming without redemption and paying without acquittance, all for the profit of Yankees who are making war on us while picking our pockets clean!"

What an outrageous scandal when Yankee charlatans get paid in gold, while the honest people of the South get government notes that depreciate the paper they're printed on! Yankee speculators haven't lost a drop of blood fighting this war to force their Abolitionist friends back into the Union. They do the buying; we do the dying!

New Yorkers were buying up store fronts and stocking them with Yankee-made gewgaws that caught the eye of Atlanta's uncultured yokels. Around the edges of the growing city they were constructing those crude Yankee-style balloon frame houses built fast and cheap. They offended Yancey's taste for the ornate Greek Revival mansions on Southern plantations and county seat towns. Atlanta's dirt-red streets trampled by throngs of scruffy laborers offended his senses accustomed to well-groomed white masters directing docile slaves working the cotton fields in the rich black dirt around Yancey's plantation outside Montgomery, Alabama.

White laborers who came pouring in from the farms and crossroads towns were becoming as cocky as the Yankees. Their pockets bulged with Confederate Union notes. They didn't care if the banknotes depreciated tomorrow, so long as they bought whiskey and wenches today. Atlanta's laborers had never been particularly deferential to slave-owning landed men like Yancey, and now they were even less so. They no longer felt like they had to bow and scrape to the aristocracy.

The young men transiting the city in military trains also worried Yancey. They wore the blue Confederate Union uniforms instead of the state militia "multiforms" their fathers and older brothers had worn while fighting Mexicans and Indians in previous wars. The men were amalgamated into numbered regiments. Gone were the storied militia names like The Montgomery Blues, The Wetumpka Warriors, The Macon Southern Guards, and The Tifton Tigers. This was a national army, organized like a machine by George McClellan at the dawn of the war, and now woven tight by Secretary of War Stanton. These Deep South regiments would be brigaded with men from the Upper South; with Confederate Union loyalists from southern Illinois, Indiana, and Ohio; and with Irish volunteers from the Northeastern cities who had mostly remained loyal to the Confederate Union.

Our men from the Cotton States are being split up and put in with men who will indoctrinate them with Northern ways of thinking. Their loyalty to their states will be subverted. They will be schooled in loyalty to the Davis Government. If Davis should decide to become a dictator who erases the sovereignty of the states, they will side with him rather than us.

Worst of all were the Negroes. "Confederate Negroes" they called themselves because they worked for contractors supplying the Confederate Union government. The contractors hired the Negroes from their owners for the going rate of a dollar a day and paid the Negroes fifty cents to feed, shelter, clothe, and entertain themselves when they finished their 12-hour shifts. So long as they stayed in their teeming "Niggertown," they could eat where the pleased, sleep where they pleased, entertain themselves as they pleased, and worship in the African churches if they wanted.

Free Negroes from New York City, St. Louis, Baltimore, and Louisville were arriving to set up shops. Taverns, eating establishments, gambling dens, boarding houses, and all manner of other businesses owned by free Negroes sprung up. They were shoddy affairs of worm-holed pine logs covered with tent cloth, but they fulfilled the ancient need of men to buy goods and services with the money the sweat of their brow had earned them.

After buying food, tobacco, and liquor for themselves, the Negroes bought bolts of cloth, threads, and needles to send to their women back on the plantations, and little knickknacks for their children. They were providers for themselves and their families. They began to think and act as free men. They saw the free Negro shopkeepers prospering and wondered why all Negroes should not be free.

Even the Confederate Union government had begun hiring Negroes to work in its arsenal here in Atlanta, and in the new gun powder works at Augusta, thereby stamping its imprimatur on the principle that Negroes should be paid for their labor. Yancey no longer dared bring his servants to Atlanta, fearing they would become incited by freedom and difficult to control.

He hired a carriage for the ride to the Delaney House he and Robert Rhett had purchased as a headquarters and rooming house for themselves and the floating crew of the new Confederate States Party. He kept his city clothes there. He carried with him only a bottle of Laudanum opium tincture and a flask brandy to deaden the chronic pain in his kidneys and hemorrhoids. Barely forty-eight, he felt the anguish of a man whose life and dreams were slipping away. He had to persuade his colleagues to act quickly to save the South --- not from the Yankees, but from their own Confederate Union government!

The corrupt Yankee-loving government of Jefferson Davis and the rest of that rat pack of Southern traitors is determined to destroy us. Our slaves will become indentured servants. Then share-croppers and wage-sharers. Davis will bring the Yankees back into the Union to agitate our Negroes incessantly until they strut about in equality with Whites. He is giving our gold to the Yankees, so they can buy us and make us their slaves, while our Negroes are to be liberated!

*I wanted to make Davis the President of the Confederate **States** of America. Together we would have expanded our Slave States into the tropics, from the Ohio River to the Isthmus of Panama and beyond! But, no, he had to do the bidding of Stephen Douglas, whom nobody on either side of the Ohio trusted!*

Then I gave him a second chance to get rid of the Yankees by instigating the slave raid that caused the Free States to declare their independence. And low and behold if Damnfool Davis doesn't go and start a war to bring them back! Damnfool Davis and the Damnyankees deserve each other. We loyal Sons of the South don't want to be bothered by either.

Yancey knocked on the door and entered when the elderly house slave opened the door.

At least there's one Nigger left in Atlanta who knows his place. That won't last long at the rate things are going. The young Negroes will learn to count their wages earned by city work, to read and to write, and to understand the topics of their masters' conversations. We will have to watch them night and day lest conspiracies of rebelling against us should rise in their heads.

His mood brightened when the door opened to reveal his cronies gathered in the sitting room. He waved to newspaper publishers Robert Rhett --- his partner who had relocated his *Charleston Mercury* to Atlanta after the Great Charleston Fire of December 1861 --- and John M. Daniel who owned the *Richmond Examiner*.

Congress having recessed until December, he greeted Senators John Slidell of Louisiana and Louis T. Wigfall of Texas; and Congressmen L.Q.C Lamar of Mississippi, and Laurence Keitt and William Porcher Miles of South Carolina.

Southern Rights publisher Edmund Ruffin came bounding down the stairs, the third man in the "Fire Eater" triumvirate of secession, after Yancey and Rhett. Ruffin looked the part of the aging fanatic, with long mane flowing behind him. He had the energy of a young man with a razor-sharp mind. He was smiling as he warmly embraced Yancey.

"I knew that was your voice, you old scalawag!" he shouted. "How the hell are you?"

"The usual maladies afflict me," replied Yancey. "Riding in from Montgomery on the night train didn't help. Awful jarring on those loose wooden rails. I'll be glad when they're replaced by steel. We need to get a Pullman Car on that line too, so people can lay down and stretch out. I'm stiff as a board, but much improved in the company of friends!"

"Atta boy!" exclaimed Ruffin.

The others got up and clasped Yancey's hands. Rhett motioned for him to sit down in the favorite chair next to the ice cabinet.

"Halleluiah!" exclaimed Yancey, stretching out his legs out and arching his back in the soft chair. "It's wonderful having a home of our own. I was getting sick to death of the hotels."

"It's safer here," added Congressman Porcher Miles. "Stanton no doubt has loaded those hotels with spies. We must be careful that our confidential conversations don't leave this house."

"Stanton is a sneaky bastard," confirmed Rhett. "I wouldn't be surprised if one of his men started the fire that burned us out of Charleston."

John Daniel laughed. "Stanton is a tough customer, but not **that** tough. Most likely it was a Negro lighting up an outdoor fire. I understand there was a howling wind on a tinder dry night that spread it."

"If the Negroes had been tending their masters' business on the plantations instead of wandering around the city lighting fires on a windy night, Charleston wouldn't have burned," claimed Rhett. "They were hired to work in the shipyards, but nobody keeps an eye on them at night. It didn't help that most of our firefighters are off fighting the

Damn Yankee Rebels. I blame the fire on Davis and Stanton, whether they ordered it or not."

The house slave brought Yancey a coffee with iced peaches and cream. Yancey opened his brandy flask and laced his coffee. "Anybody like an 'eye-opener?" He passed the flask around.

"Ah, that puts a little pink in the day," said John Daniel.

"To your health," said Laurence Keitt, raising his cup.

"And to our new nation, the Confederate States of America!" added Porcher Miles.

"Hear! Hear!" they cheered.

"Spiffy flag," remarked Yancey to Porcher Miles, who had designed the Confederate States of America flag nailed to the wall. It was based on P.G.T. Beauregard's design, but with a striking 21-starred saltire canton replacing the old field of stars:

"You have improved markedly upon Beauregard's original." Yancey glanced at the campaign banner next to the flag, carrying the slogan originated by Laurence Keitt:

The Yankees contend that Slavery is wrong, and the government is a consolidated national democracy. We of the South contend that slavery is right, and that this is a Confederate Republic of Sovereign States.

He smiled in admiration. "An excellent encapsulation of the founding principles of the Confederate States. "Even the simple-minded will understand why we must secede from the Confederate Union and establish a true Southern Confederacy!"

"Attorney General Alexander Stephens is coming here next week to talk up Davis's Reconstructed Confederate Union," Keitt informed him. "We'll need to be ready to talk about reconstructing the Union *our* way --- without the scurrilous Abolitionist States."

"Davis and Stephens," muttered Senator Louis Wigfall. "Crawling around like two baby snakes, hatched from their same mother's egg."

"I love that phrase," exclaimed Daniel. "I'll use it in my next editorial!"

"I don't know what got into Stephens," commented Congressman Lamar. "He used to be rock solid on slavery. Now he's apologizing for it. Says we've got to educate our Negroes so they'll be competent to be hired out for city work. He wants us to let them marry legally and keep their families together. I don't like that. There's no halfway house between freedom and slavery."

"Damn right," agreed Yancey. "We don't need to be apologizing for slavery. We need to be making the case for expanding it into the tropics, where we can work our Niggers all year. We want to reopen the slave trade. We want Niggers cheap, so even the poorest peckerwoods can own a few. We want more Niggers and more land to work them on --- enough land and Niggers to supply the cotton demand of the whole world. That's what Alex Stephens used to say until the Northern men sunk their hooks into him. Davis is talking crazy too. Tarnation seize me if Damnfool Davis doesn't want to free our Niggers and then combine them with the Yankees to lord it over us!"

"We need to make it our business to educate the people to the danger," concurred Ruffin. He raised his finger. "Douglas and Davis won the election by the skin of their teeth. Even if we reconstruct the Confederate Union the way Davis wants, the Northern States will continue to outpace us in population. They're bringing in millions of low-born hirelings from all the degraded nations of Europe. They'll train them to vote Republican. Then they'll elect an Abolitionist President. They'll pack the courts and public offices with Abolitionists. When they're strong enough they'll reverse Reconstruction. They'll divide New England back into six states. They'll subdivide the other Northern States to give them a three-fourths majority in the Senate..."

"They can thank Damnfool Davis for teaching them that trick," interjected Yancey.

Ruffin resumed: "...and when they have complete control of government, they'll liberate our Negroes either by passing a constitutional amendment or by expanding on John Brown's Raid a hundred-fold. They'll kidnap our Negroes in the Border States and squirrel them away in the North. They'll send their immigrant hirelings into the Border States. Slavery will become insecure in Delaware,

Maryland, Kentucky, Missouri, and the District of Columbia. What good does it do us to gain New Mexico, Arizona, and California, when the Border States are abolitionized and turned against us?"

"We must warn the people of these dangers," implored John Daniel. "We must prepare them to cast off the Davis Government. The Negroes running loose in our cities are becoming insufferable. One of them is bound to kill a white man or rape a white woman. Or maybe careless Negroes playing with fire burn up a couple more of our towns. Then all hell is going to break loose, especially if it turns out the miscreant Negroes are working for Yankee paymasters."

"The people will tire of this infernal war to coerce the Abolitionists back into our house," added Ruffin. "Let's make our pitch then. Pull the Cotton States out of the Confederate Union. Just South Carolina, Georgia, Alabama, and Florida, if they're the only one who'll follow us for now. They will form a core around which the other Southern States can rally when they see the folly of this war. The Yankees have got a new general-in-chief. It's Sherman --- the one who beat us at the Salient last year, halted McClellan in New England, and beat him at Camden. He might just teach Davis another hard lesson. If he does, we'll call upon the states to dissolve the Davis Government and leave the damn fool sinking in the quicksand of his failing war."

Yancey poured more brandy in his cup, drank it, and slapped the table. "I never thought I'd pray for the Yankee Rebels to beat us. But if the Damn Yankees don't beat us, Damnfool Davis will!"

6. Eddie's Epiphany

Sangamon County, east of Springfield, Illinois, September 21, 1862

Eddie Bates shoveled another load of manure from the abandoned pigsty into the wheelbarrow. His back ached, and his mind revolted at the boredom of days of mindless work. He was no stranger to hard work. He'd done plenty of it as a soldier in the Free State Army, but nothing as mind-numbing as this. He hated every minute of it and longed to throw down the shovel and walk away.

"When I said I'd do any job to help the Free States win this war, I never thought it would be this!"

"What can we do?" answered Gabriel Bellamy, the middle-aged black fellow working beside him. "You've got to learn to put your mind on pleasant things while you work. Then the day goes by fast."

"Sorry, for making a bad job worse," said Eddie when he choked down the vomit and regained his voice. "I haven't smelled shit like that since I was locked in a coffin four days by slave raiders. I'm Eddie Bates, one of the Michigan Negroes saved by the Free State men at the Battle of Delphi in May of '61."

Gabriel put his shovel down. "I knew I'd seen you somewhere before. I remember you spoke about that at the rally with Governor Yates right after the Confeds surrounded us. What are you doing here?"

Eddied leaned on his shovel and watched a drop of sweat fall from his head to the ground.

"Figured I needed to make myself useful. The only thing I did before I enlisted in the army was to get kidnapped by the slave raiders last year. I lay chained in a coffin, wallowing in my own shit like a pig. It was my wife Emma Brown who busted loose and went and got our Sheriff Parker and put him and his men on the trail of the slave raiders. Some of my neighbors got killed fighting to save me, so I figured I ought to do some fighting for myself. That, plus I didn't want white folks to say, 'Listen to that fancy Nigger talk. That's all they're good for.' I wanted to fight so people would respect me."

"Why aren't you fighting now?"

"Because I was captured at Bloomington when the Confeds broke through! My regiment was left behind to guard the base when Grant's men moved west to fight on the Mississippi. The Confeds were on us before we knew it. Our colonel surrendered without firing a shot, other than for one sentry who got excited and blowed his own foot off. The Confeds paroled me, which means I can work, but I can't bear arms until I'm exchanged."

"This work ain't so bad then," surmised Gabriel, "not when your only other alternative is gettin' shot at or poked with a bayonet."

70

Eddie shuddered. "I had a terrible bad nightmare about being run through with a bayonet. A Confederate was charging me with his bayonet. I was so scared I froze until the bayonet went inside me. I woke up screaming. At Bloomington our regiment surrendered before I had any time to be scared. I may never know if I have the courage to stand and fight."

"Oh, I expect you'll be fine when the time comes, like the rest of our men. The Confeds been pushing them around, but they ain't whipped them. We're doin' our part to help, so don't worry about not doing nothing.'"

Eddie laughed. "Well, I *hope* we're helping them! I'd hate to think we're shoveling this shit for nothing!"

"Yeah, I wondered about that. Sometimes white folks put us to work doin' nothing just 'cause they think we'll steal something if we're idle."

"Ain't that the truth!" exclaimed Eddie. He glanced over at the crew of white militiamen who were tearing down the barn on this abandoned farm to salvage the lumber for construction of military works going up on the line around Springfield. That was hard work too, but they had a dozen men to spread it around. Some were resting while others removed the boards and carried them to a wagon. They were taking their own sweet time. If they saw Eddie and Gabriel slacking, they'd be over here in a heartbeat screaming: "You goldbrickin' Niggers better get to work or we'll tan your worthless hides." Eddie and Gabriel kept moving their shovels while they talked out the sides of their mouths.

"Governor Yates said he wants this shit to make saltpeter, which is what goes into making gunpowder," Eddie explained. "They're going to put it in a big pile and then piss on it to make the saltpeter."

Gabriel snorted. "That's another job they gonna assign us to do --- piss on shit! But tell me, now, how did you come to know Governor Yates? Was it because you two spoke together?"

"That's part of it. But most of it is that after I was captured and paroled at Bloomington, I was talking to the Confederates' Negro teamsters. They said they had orders to get ready to move toward Chicago. I heard a Confederate officer confirm the order. I decided to come down here and let Governor Yates know about it. The army men were trying to get him to take his militia with them to Indiana, but he was saying that Springfield, being the capital of the state, had to be held.

"After I told the governor and the army men what I heard, they decided that since the Confederates were going on to Chicago, the governor might be able to hold the line between Springfield and Decatur with his militia. A couple army divisions of Illinois men stayed here too, after the rest packed off to Indiana. When the Confederates found out we were going to stay, they had to hold some of their men back to keep an eye on us. They's probably madder than a wet hen about being stuck down here watching us instead of going on to Chicago with the rest."

"You done a lot for one man, haven't you? Someday they may be writing about you in the history books."

Eddie laughed. "Won't be much to write about: 'The Nigger who got hisself captured twice!'"

"That's the way white folks will tell it," agreed Gabriel, "But we know better. One day Negroes will be writing books. We'll tell your story the way it happened --- that you come down here at considerable risk to your life to help Governor Yates save Springfield from the Confederates! Who knows but if the Confeds had cotched you, they'd have sold you back into slavery?"

"They have legal title to me. My Pa took us and run away from our master in Maryland in 1833. Beat my hoppytoad if that Yancey scoundrel didn't go and dig up the title after all these years and come after me and the other runaways who were settled in Cass County, Michigan. What about you. Were you a free man before the war?"

"I was 'til I met my old woman!"

Eddie howled with laughter. The white workers at the barn turned their heads. Eddie and Gabriel moved their shovels faster. Eddie said, "We'd better keep our voices down."

When the white men returned to their work Gabriel told his story. "I was freed in 1828 when *Maître* Bellamy passed away. He was a Frenchman. When Illinois become a state, they said the French could keep their slaves as long as their masters lived, but they couldn't sell them to nobody. That's why we was freed when *Maître* passed."

"You're lucky he didn't take you out of the state and sell you to somebody down south before he passed."

"The French didn't see us as property to sell to the highest bidder the way slaveowners do today. Long as we did what they say, we was like family. I don't remember my Pa ever having a grievance against *Maître* and *Maîtresse*. We loved them and cried when he passed. After he died *Maîtresse* sold the place, and we went to live in Nigger Springs, with the rest of the free Negroes in Gallatin County."

"Same with us," said Eddie. "We made it across the line to Pennsylvania. The Quakers sent us out to the Free Negro settlement at Cass County Michigan. White folks in Michigan protected us. They done told the Southern slave owners that they'd kill them if they tried to capture us, and they were as good as their word."

73

"The white folks around us used to be decent like that too," agreed Gabriel. "They didn't like us working in their towns or getting too friendly with their women. But they were right neighborly in everything else. We traded with them for a while and even got invited to their church socials. It started to get worse after the *Dred Scott* Decision."

"How so?"

"Kentucky masters started buying farms up here and bringing their slaves in to work during the summers. *Dred Scott Decision* said that slaveowners could take their Niggers anywhere they wanted, even into the Free States. Do you know that the State of Illinois doesn't allow free Negroes from outside the state to settle here anymore? Be careful you keep your nose clean. They arrest a Negro from another state, and they will sell him into indentured servitude to the highest bidder for the rest of his life."

"I didn't know about that," said Eddie. "That doesn't happen in Michigan."

"Don't think it won't, if the Confeds win. They'll turn the people in every state against us."

A booming sound arrived on the wind. Was it thunder? More booms came at five-second intervals.

"The Confeds are letting us know they're here," said Eddie.

"Keeping the Confeds busy here keeps them away from Chicago," observed Gabriel. "That's what we got to do for as long as we can."

Eddie thought about that. *The Confeds are here because we're still fighting them here, and we're still fighting them here because I came down here from Bloomington to tell Governor Yates that the Confeds were packing up to go to Chicago. Maybe I kept the Confeds out of Chicago long enough for the Free State men to get there and hold the city. If that's what happened, then I've more than done my fair share of duty. Everything else I do from here on out is extra.*

Eddie's mind was at ease, and his shovel seemed lighter. He threw the next shovelful of manure into the wheelbarrow with energy.

"If we don't win this war, we might be sent back into slavery," predicted Gabriel. "I heard a preacher say that we Negroes are like seeds buried deep in rocky soil. All these years, since they brought us here, we been pushing our way up toward the sun. When the day of jubilation comes, we will break through the soil to see the blue sky, and feel the sun on our faces, and enjoy the sweet fresh air of freedom. When we got our freedom papers in '28 I felt that day was coming soon for all Negroes Now, I feel that no matter how hard we push up toward the sky, the Confeds will just keep heaping more dirt on top of us. We got to win this war Eddie, so we can stay free, and our children and their children can stay free, and one day all the Negroes in America can be free."

A couple drops of rain fell on a gust of cool air from the cloudy sky. The mist near the horizon showed heavier rain to the north, meaning it would soon be raining heavier here. One of the white men walked over. "It don't look like we're gonna get another lick of work outa you lazy asses, so put this load in the wagon, and call it a day."

Gabriel dipped his shovel in the manure one more time. "Every little shit helps."

Eddie was raised not to laugh at vulgarity, and the joke wasn't all that funny, but he laughed anyway. *What a strange and wonderful life this is. This war started when I was kidnapped by the slave raiders. By coming here, I may have kept the Confederates out of Chicago, which may be enough to win us this war, and keep us Negroes in the North from*

75

being sold back into slavery. I won't be getting no credit for it. In a couple minutes I'll be riding in the back of a wagon full of pig shit in a soaking rain! 'What can we do?'

He laughed again. It was the happy, light-hearted laugh of a man who suddenly knew he was fulfilling his life's destiny.

7. The New Heart of the Confederate Union

Floyd's Knob, Indiana. September 24, 1862

"How do you like the view?" asked Richard Taylor.

"Magnificent," replied Jefferson Davis. "I wouldn't have guessed this place existed. I remember the land north of the Ohio being as flat as a table top all the way up to Chicago."

"Most of it is, except for this corner of Indiana," explained Taylor. "We call these highlands 'knobs.' You don't see them from the city on hazy summer days, so you may not have noticed them before. I explored them as a boy. I still come up here whenever I need to clear my head with fresh air and a wide horizon. Custis said you were heartily sick of the lowland heat of Washington City, so I thought you'd enjoy it up here."

Louisville lay below in the valley across the Ohio River. A steamy mist hung over the river, the city, and the acres of army camps and supply bases around it. Military trains transiting the city added their palls of black smoke soot to the clammy air. More smoke rose from the furnaces bending metal down by the river where ironclads were being built to control the Ohio River.

Summer's heat and humidity sometimes lingered on until the end of September in the Ohio Valley. That made Louisville even more uncomfortable, as people waited expectantly for autumns' relief, which always came later than anticipated. It was hot up here on the top of the ridge but not sweat-soaking hot. A hint of the coming autumn's freshness filtered in on the north breeze every now and then. Custis Lee and Dick Taylor's men were roasting a pig over by the wagons just out of earshot of Davis and Taylor, who enjoyed ties of friendship and family as well as military command.

Tears welled in Davis's eyes. He pointed to a church steeple along the Ohio River just beyond the city. "Knoxie and I were married there." Davis had married Taylor's older sister Sarah Knox Taylor in Louisville in 1835. She died of malaria soon after near Davis's plantation in Mississippi. Zachary Taylor, Mexican War general later elected president, was the father of Knoxie and Richard.

"She is never far from my thoughts," reminisced Davis, his voice choking. Taylor surmised that Davis and his sister had shared a true love whose memory still burned bright in Davis's heart.

"Our ages were too different for me to have known her well," said Taylor. "All I really remember about her is the grieving of our family after her passing. I regret that Zachary's grief cast its misguided anger on you for taking her away from Kentucky. It wasn't reasonable for him to imagine her living here the rest of her life. I'm so glad that Providence reconciled you and Zachary and decreed that you both should become presidents."

"Thank you, Dick. Losing Knoxie took the life out of me, too. Providence, in its graceful mercy, has provided me with a new family, so that I may finish this earthly life. We'll never understand some things in this life. Perhaps we will gain a fuller understanding in the next world."

"In the earthly life we are but shadows of the perfected creatures we will become," pronounced Taylor. "We can no more understand the designs of Providence than a shadow can understand the mind of the creature who cast it."

Davis looked off to the horizon. "When this war is concluded, I will ask Congress to authorize the removal of our capital to a place like this, high in the mountains, with healthful fresh airs and water. I lost Knoxie to the foul airs of the lowland South. My first son Sam died in Washington in 1854. Stephen Douglas died there. Last night I received a telegram from Varina that Little Joe and Jeff Jr. have taken sick." He tried not to let his worry show on his face, but it showed in his unsteady voice. "I don't…. I don't want to lose them or see anybody else lose their children to Washington's fevers."

"Little Joe and Jeff Jr. will be in my prayers," promised Taylor. "Perhaps you should return to Washington to look after them?"

Davis shook his head. "If I could help them by my presence, I would. However, it is doctors who know medicine. The war requires my presence here. Until we regain control of the Baltimore & Ohio, the trip back to Washington would take six days each way. I am needed here. The front hasn't advanced in weeks. It we don't get it moving soon, we will lose the initiative, and the war."

"I understand," said Taylor, a self-educated military historian. "The value of the initiative in war cannot be overstated. It surpasses in power mere accession of numbers."

Davis put his hand on his friend's shoulder. "You have profound insight into the nature of war. I need your counsel. Let me begin by asking what is happening with the men coming through Louisville? I'm informed that none are arriving at Jackson's front around Chicago where we need them."

This question was yet another sign that the authority of the "Davis Government" was strengthening its grip on the Confederate Union. Davis had appointed Taylor Director of Military Railroads, making him one of the most powerful men in the Confederate Union. Taylor's grip on the railroads was as firm as the steel in their rails. He approved the manifests of every rail car in the Confederate Union. He was taking in men and materiel from all parts of the Confederate Union, sorting them out into well-equipped formations at Louisville, and pushing them up toward the thousand-mile Northwestern Front from Ohio to Kansas.

There were complaints. *"Davis is usurping plenary powers not exercised by any chief magistrate of the English-speaking race since the Magna Carta,"* as Fire Eater newspaper editor John M. Daniel put it.

"Since General Lee commands the Northwest," answered Taylor, "most of the men are being sent to his front. It extends from the Mississippi River falls around Keokuk on out across the top of Missouri to Kansas. Besides keeping Grant from moving east, Lee is trying to stop the murderous bushwhacking between Missouri partisans and the Abolitionist Jayhawkers.

"Other than that, I'm sending men to plug the gaps in the line between Indianapolis and Chicago. The Yankee Rebels are riding through the gaps to supply their friends in Springfield and Decatur with percussion caps and other necessities to keep them fighting. We're adequately covering the lines near the railroads but are stretched thin in between."

Davis pursed his lips. "Should Lee be receiving the lion's share of reinforcements? Shouldn't he be keeping Grant confined to the Trans-Mississippi with an economy of forces? Our maximum concentration of effort should be between Chicago and Cincinnati. We need a commanding general who can see the war as you see it from your perspective, of the Northwest being a unified command, instead of a disconnected series of independent efforts."

"Have you thought of bringing Lee over to Jackson's headquarters outside Chicago to exercise command from there?"

"I've queried him, and he recommended against it. His blood is boiling to fight Grant. He says Grant is the most dangerous Rebel general, and his army must be destroyed in the field before we move on Chicago. However, I fear he is losing perspective on the more important objectives of our campaign, which I see as taking Chicago, Indianapolis, and Cincinnati before breaking up Grant's army in Iowa."

"What about McClellan?"

"Mac's busy in his New Jersey bailiwick. He's fortifying the Jersey shore of Delaware Bay, trying to bull his way into Philly in combination with the navy. He thinks that losing Philly will knock the Rebels out of the war, because it's their largest procurement city. He also wants to be close to New England in case the Rebels start stirring that kettle. But we do need somebody to assist Lee in commanding this department. If you were a West Point man, it would be you."

"What about you?" Taylor asked. "Is there any reason you shouldn't assume command? You don't have to go back to Washington. Congress is recessed until December. Stanton can run the War

Department on his own authority. Why don't you direct the Northwestern Department from Louisville? You can send for your family to join you here when the boys are well enough to travel."

Davis's face brightened. The years went flying back in his mind to those vivid days of command during the Black Hawk Indian War, and the Mexican War.

"I would be pleased to take command of this department if General Lee concurs that it will be advantageous for him to concentrate his full attention on defeating Grant."

"I served alongside Lee for a year, and you may be certain he will give you his full approbation," Taylor assured him. "He knows we've pushed our Army of the Northwest so far forward that it can no longer fight together as a single field command. He has not a thought for himself, but only what is best for the army and the nation. He will be pleased for you to assume strategic command of the department, while he wages his tactical battle against Grant."

"Thank you," answered Davis. "That puts my mind at ease. I want to be careful to avoid those vile political and personal controversies that vexed your father during the Mexican War. Those animosities prolonged the fighting a year longer than it should have lasted. It disturbed me deeply that men in the ranks should lose their lives because their leaders would not forsake their political and personal squabbles. That must not happen in this war."

At least it won't happen unless Joe Johnston is returned to duty, thought Davis.

At least it won't happen unless Davis appoints Braxton Bragg to high command, thought Taylor.

"Stephen Douglas promised me command of our militias he planned on sending to Mexico to preempt the French from seizing it," recalled Davis. "I will be pleased to command armies, though I would infinitely prefer to be fighting Frenchmen in Mexico than Americans in Illinois."

"I remember Douglas calling up the southern militias," replied Taylor. "Then Yancey's raid into Michigan sparked the Free State Rebellion, and we forgot all about Mexico. If Yancey had left well enough alone, Douglas would have sent our men into Mexico under your command, and we would have acquired Mexico as Slave States, as Yancey said he wanted."

"Yancey's always been a troublemaker," agreed Davis. "But I can't say as I blame him for being skeptical of Douglas. Douglas often made promises while intoxicated that he never intended to keep."

"Do you intend to fulfill his promise to annex Mexico when the Free State Rebellion is suppressed?"

Davis shook his head. "No. I can see now that the solution to our sectional antagonisms can't be found in Mexico. The land isn't suited for plantation agriculture. Even if it was, the Mexicans will never accept the return of slavery to their soil. We'd have to fight them, the Catholic Church, and maybe the governments of France and Spain, and England. Douglas thought he was going to keep us united by acquiring Mexico for more Slave States, then hornswoggling the British out of the Canadas for more Free States. The most likely outcome would have been a war between us and an alliance of Free States, Mexicans, British, Canadians, French, and Spanish. We'd be stretched a lot thinner than we are now."

"Douglas seemed like he had a good heart for the nation's best interests, but he didn't think a lot of his ideas through," replied Taylor.

"Our troubles became unamenable when he repealed the Missouri Compromise. He didn't understand why principled people in the North would object to it."

"He was every inch a patriot," confirmed Davis. "I'll give him that. But in my book patriotism alone can't make up for lack of principle. If there is no principle behind a country's governance, people will try to get out from under it and make a new country with a new government, to the extent they are able. Look where we are now: The Abolitionists are trying to take the Free States out of the Union. Yancey's Fire Eaters are looking for an opportunity to discredit our government and set the Cotton States up as an independent republic. We have become spoiled children squandering a rich inheritance."

Davis pointed to the south. "The Gulf of Mexico is about 650 miles." He pointed to the east. "The Atlantic Coast is about 650 miles." He pointed to the north. "The northern limit of our country, along the shore of Lake Superior, is about 650 miles." He turned west. "The Pacific is about 1,800 miles.

"Providence has bequeathed us special dispensation --- one-twentieth of the land area of the Earth, all of it in the temperate latitudes. Mankind has never before been blessed with such a magnificent country. All we have to do to claim our inheritance is to quit fighting among ourselves. Until now men of bad faith on both sides of the Ohio have been cutting the ground out from under patriotic Americans.

"Tomorrow I will announce the creation of the new State of Jefferson. I intend it to be the new heart of the Confederate Union. There will be nothing to fight about in Jefferson --- no slaves; no free Negroes; and no Fire Eaters and Abolitionists to roil the waters! It will be a lesson to Americans in all the states to put aside our differences as residents of Slave States and Free States and go back to being **Americans**."

"You may want to consider extending Jefferson eastward through Ohio's southern counties," suggested Taylor. "We're making progress there. The towns are settled by Yankees, but the countryside is owned by Southern people who crossed the river from Kentucky. The Yankee Rebel government in Ohio has been hard on these people, so they've been coming into our lines. We're arming them and sending them back to fight for their homes."

"Yes, it would be beneficial to have Jefferson protecting Kentucky along its entire northern border," agreed Davis. "Slaves wouldn't be looking across the Ohio River for Abolitionists to row over and spirit them away."

Davis took a deep breath and stretched his arms. "Thank you so much for inviting me here. I've done more productive work with you in one afternoon than I've done in Washington in weeks."

"Then I'll look forward to you joining me in the Galt House until Congress returns in December," said Taylor. "We can bring in Lee, Jackson, Harney, and Buell, as need be, to help us plan and execute our recovery of the Northwest."

"I'll join you there, but I hope only for a couple days. The Galt House is too public. I'll be watched like a gorilla in a zoo --- by our people, by the newspapers, and by Free State spies. I'll be badgered by every pestilential favor-seeker who wants me to appoint his nephew postmaster of Weedsville. This place would be much better, in terms of comfort and privacy. Could you set up a camp here for us to work out of?"

"I'll have it ready day after tomorrow."

"Excellent! Then I'll spend a couple of days renewing political connections in Louisville and Frankfort, while announcing the creation of the State of Jefferson."

The smell of roasting pork wafted in on the breeze. "Let's see what the boys have cooked up for us," said Taylor. Davis glanced in that direction in time to see a couple of Taylor's men tapping a keg of beer brought up from Louisville on a wagon. The German brewers in Cincinnati and St. Louis, along with many other businesses, had relocated to Louisville, as it appeared the destroyed cities would be a long time in getting back on their feet. Louisville seemed destined to become a much larger city than it would have become without the war.

Davis glanced once more over the Ohio Valley, where lay the State of Kentucky, the original core of settlement of the Inland States. He and Abraham Lincoln were born almost in sight of each other from here. Davis's father, a man of modest wealth, had moved his family to the heart of Slave State Mississippi. Mr. Lincoln's father, a poor man, had moved north into the heart of Free State Illinois. Tens of thousands of other Kentucky-born families had divided between the North and South. And thus divided, Americans had grown apart.

He turned northward to the proposed State of Jefferson he would create as the **new heart of the Confederate Union**. He thought of **his** destiny --- as president, and as father of the State of Jefferson, and now as commander of the Armies of the Northwest. He smiled, as a man whose sees his life's destiny revealed.

8. *Return to the Far Country*

Cleveland, October 10, 1862

Saturdays were becoming easier for Abraham Lincoln. With the devolution of military command to Sherman, he no longer had to argue with Congress about the minutiae of military strategy. His suppression of Salmon Chase's attempted coup last June allowed him to manage the government with confidence that he would not be removed on the whim of the Provisional Congress, as the Free States' first provisional president John Fremont was removed before him. At least he was unlikely to be removed so long as there were no more stunning Confederate advances.

For the moment, the military situation appeared satisfactory. Sherman assured him the Confederates couldn't break the "Sherman Line" in the Connecticut Valley or capture Philadelphia or Providence. In the Northwest, Sherman was confident that if the Confederates hurled their armies at any point between Chicago and Cincinnati, they would be roughly handled by his reserve armies building behind the front

--- the tried-and-true method he'd used to defeat the Confederates at the battles along the Wabash and at Camden.

Down in Central Illinois, general Barrie and Governor Yates were maintaining their bypassed positions along the Springfield to Decatur line. Phil Sheridan's cavalry corps had broken the Confederates' spotty encirclement long enough to bring in a thousand fresh men and wagons loaded with cartridges and rations.

If there was any disappointment, it was with the progress of the manufacture of the Spencer repeaters, more specifically their ammunition. The copper cartridges were being manufactured in quantities suitable for single-shot muzzle loaders, but not for rapid-fire repeaters.

Sherman had advised that rather than equipping an entire army with repeaters whose ammunition would be expended in the first hour of battle, it would be better to arm a single division with 1,000 rounds per man. He said it would only be necessary to break the Confederate line at one point with concentrated fire. Conventionally armed men could then pour through and attack the Confederates from their rear, when they were panicked and easier to capture.

Sherman forecast ammunition enough to assault the Confederates around Chicago at the end of February, when they would be fatigued in their snowy trenches. By March, another division would be armed and ready to fight in New England or New Jersey. More divisions would be equipped with Spencers each month until the Confederates were driven out of the Free States.

Besides feeling more confident about the military future, Mr. Lincoln was relieved that he had not been forced by the Provisional Congress "to employ the harsh measures of hanging and confiscation" against Free State Democrats who favored the Confederate Union. Many dissident Democrats had removed themselves to Confederate Union lines. They were replaced by Free State Loyalists evacuating Confederate-occupied territory, thereby concentrating the Free State men in a more compact, and more easily defended territory.

He grasped the idea that "victory will go to the side that produces the strongest sinews of war." That meant having a strong economy with sound money people and businesses would accept in exchange for their productions. The Free States' paper notes, backed by $100,000,000 of British loans, traded at a premium to Confederate Union notes, thereby enabling the Free States government to buy war supplies from domestic farms and factories, as well as from the British and Canadians. Mr. Lincoln had grown up during the early days of the United States when silver and gold coins, including Spanish pieces of eight, were the money. The notion that paper notes could be as good as gold and silver coins intrigued him.

The real wealth of a country is not how much gold and silver lies under its territory, but rather the value of the productions of its farms, mines, and factories. Our government must henceforth become accustomed to printing paper dollars, and declaring them legal tender, thereby allowing them to summon up the value of all this productive wealth created by the minds and hands of our industrious people.

For now, we must pledge that our paper dollars may be redeemed in gold when the war is over. But there will come a time when the good faith and credit of our government alone will give them value. We will no longer be held captive to the tyranny of how much gold and silver we can mine and mint into coins. We will be limited only by the ingenuity and creative energies of our people, who are the true engines of wealth.

He was more than satisfied with the assistance the British were providing, which stopped just short of entering the war as a belligerent. The Free States' railroads across the St. Clair and Niagara rivers were now fully integrated with the British North American railroads running to the port of Montreal. Montreal's cold-water port, icebound four months of the year, could not fully replace the New England ports lost to the Confederates. But it did maintain the people's confidence that the Confederates could not blockade them into submission.

Relieved of those worries, he made Saturdays an informal day. His Saturday mornings were devoted to rest and leisurely reading, and the afternoons to socializing with political friends. It was not a lazy man's day. He continued to rise at dawn, come downstairs, have coffee, walk on the lawn to take fresh air, and then come inside to doze lightly in his most comfortable chair. Mornings were becoming refreshingly cool this time of year, with, with a light north breeze blowing in off the lake. Before taking his chair, he opened the curtains, letting in the fresh air and sun.

Today his sons Tad and Willie were playing games, including "Free Staters and Confederates" on the lawn. His oldest son Robert was away at West Point, reopened under Free State authority. Mrs. Lincoln shopped the farmers' markets on Saturday mornings, buying meat and produce with her allowance from the Free State government. She had returned a few minutes ago and set the fire in the kitchen stove. He thought about getting up to warm the cold coffee on his table but dozed off instead. The voices of his children playing outside filtered through his sleep and into his dreams.

In his dream, he relived one of the happy days of his early youth in the backwoods of Kentucky, when he had sought refuge in the refreshing dry coolness of a limestone cave near the family's cabin on a humid hot summer day. He was reaching the age where his mind worked backward into the past, as if encapsulating his life into a whole experience recalled in its entirety. Memories he hadn't thought of in decades were becoming vivid again.

When he awoke from these pleasant dreams, he felt melancholy that his life had passed so quickly. The old world he had been born into --- the world of log cabins and forests teeming with bears and wildcats and wild Indians, had transformed, as in a flash, into a world of cities, railroads, telegraphs, and steamships. With the laying of the transatlantic telegraph cable, it would soon be possible to send messages anywhere in the country, and even to Europe in an instant.

Progress was bound to be even more rapid after the war. The new century was only 38 years away, closer in time than the world he'd entered 54 years ago. He would not live that long, but perhaps his children would. What wonders would they live to see? Would they live to see voices and pictures transmitted over the telegraph wires, and gigantic balloons moving across the skies as easily as ships navigated the seas? Would they live in a world of sparkling white cities, with beautiful parks and streams flowing in between magnificent buildings? Would steam power perform the labor of human and animal muscles? Would they live in a world where people lived long and healthful lives, instead of leaving the world so early as his first son Eddie had? He could see this new world in his mind so vividly he almost sensed he was living it now.

We will create this new world driven by invention and progress, but only if we are able to break our bonds with the Confederate Union and get out from under its backward-looking belief that wealth consists only of land, slaves, and cotton!

His secretary John Hay arrived an hour before noon with the latest edition of the **New York Tribune**. Lincoln trusted this paper, published by Horace Greeley, a man of Free State loyalties operating freely from inside the Confederate Union. It was considered the only reliably honest paper on either side of the military frontier.

He perused the paper, then called out to Mrs. Lincoln, "Mother, please come here for a minute."

"What is it, Father?"

"There is copious news today. There's an obituary for Jefferson Davis's son Joseph. It says he passed away while Mr. Davis was in Kentucky."

"Poor Mr. Davis!" exclaimed Mrs. Lincoln as she saw the headline. "It's why I was always afraid of living in Washington. It broke my heart to lose our sweet boy there." Her eyes teared as she remembered three-year-old Edward Baker Lincoln, who had succumbed to fever in 1850. "I would have lost my sanity if any more of our children had died there."

"I couldn't have borne it either," confessed Mr. Lincoln. "My defeat in 1860 seemed so unfortunate at the time, but perhaps it saved the lives of one or both of our boys by bringing us here. Perhaps it ultimately saved the lives of many people by allowing us to establish our house of freedom." He put down the paper and thought for a moment. "I was wondering if perhaps I should send Mr. Davis our condolences. I don't know if that would be appropriate at a time when he leads the government doing its best to conquer us."

"Send him condolences if you feel you should, Father," advised Mary. "Mr. Davis will understand and appreciate it. It may even help us make peace with him when the time comes."

He nodded. "Thank you, Mother, I will do it. There is other news of significance as well. Mr. Davis has announced that as soon as he recovers the Free States, the expansion of the Confederate Union will end. He says there will be no conquest of Mexico and no badgering the British to sell the Canadas. He has also announced the creation of what he calls the new State of Jefferson. It is to be a whites-only Confederate free state stretching across southern Illinois, Indiana, and Ohio, up to latitude 40."

"How far away is that?"

"It's just north of Columbus and Indianapolis. And well north of Springfield."

"I don't like that," said Mrs. Lincoln. "We will lose our home."

"They'll have to conquer us first, Mother. Governor Yates and General Barrie will fight to the last man before giving up Springfield. If Sherman and I have anything to say about it, we'll fight our way into Springfield with our main army, then complete the work driving the Confederates back to their side of the Ohio River."

"I know you will do it Father, now that Sherman is helping you."

"Thank you, Mother." Mr. Lincoln smiled and took her hand. "You are helping too. As First Lady, you are doing our new country proud."

"Oh, Father," she said, and kissed his cheek.

He put down the paper and dozed again until Mrs. Lincoln called him for lunch. The Free State government had finally got around to providing the Lincolns a housekeeper, but Mrs. Lincoln did the cooking, as she insisted that only she could cook the coarse but hearty food he had grown fond of on the Illinois frontier.

He called in the boys, bantering with them as they ate the beef and green bean casserole Mrs. Lincoln had prepared. He had just returned to reading the paper when the doorbell rang. It was Edward Dickinson Baker, Mr. Lincoln's dearest lifelong friend from Illinois, the namesake for Mr. Lincoln's deceased son, and now a Senator-in-exile from Confederate-occupied Oregon.

Baker had travelled from Oregon via a British steamer from Vancouver Island to the Isthmus of Panama; and after crossing Panama, by steamer to Montreal where he'd telegraphed his estimated day of arrival. Mr. Lincoln remembered it as being October 16, six days from now. Had he misremembered the date, as he was prone to misremembering many things at this stage of life, or had the telegraphers got it wrong? *I'll be generous with myself by assuming **they** got it wrong*, was his amusing thought.

Mary and the children rushed to greet their old friend with hugs and kisses. Mr. Baker reached into his handbag and presented a beautiful Northwest Indian wood carving to Mr. Lincoln, an Indian-woven shawl for Mrs. Lincoln, and arrowheads for the children.

"We were just talking about you," Mr. Lincoln explained when they were alone together, "but unfortunately not in a happy way." He held up the paper, so Mr. Baker could see the obituary. "Jefferson Davis's boy has passed away in Washington, sadly reminding us of the passing of our Eddie."

Mr. Baker lowered his head in remembrance. "I don't know why the Lord takes so many children before they are old enough to experience life."

"We will never understand the things of this life," surmised Lincoln. "Mary is glad we are here in Cleveland. She had a premonition that had I been elected president of the old United States, that we would have gone off to Washington and lost one or both of our boys to the fevers that plague that city, as has so sorrowfully happened to Mr. Davis's boy."

He called for Mary, who asked whether they wanted coffee or tea, then motioned his friend to sit down.

"Tell me about the Far Country of Oregon. What do they think of our War for Free State Independence?"

"They haven't given it a fair hearing," replied Baker. "Presidents Pierce and Buchanan packed the state offices with Democrats. The only things people hear are what the Confederate Union Democrats want them to hear."

"They did elect you Senator on the Republican ticket in 1860, despite all the campaigning the Democrats did against you," Lincoln recalled. "I presume there's hope of getting them back on our side once we've established our Independence."

"That's what I came to talk to you about. Many of our friends from Springfield who went out there with me in '58 want to fight the Confederates. The Confederates are holding three hundred thousand square miles of the Pacific Coast with a few hundred people in the state and municipal offices, backed by a few hundred Regular Army men. I believe their hold can be pried lose by a few thousand of our people properly armed and led."

Lincoln leaned back in his chair and drank his tea while he thought about Baker's proposal. "I would be reluctant to incite an uprising of irregulars in Oregon that might result in harsh reprisals. I don't want this war to end with any more bitterness than can possibly be avoided."

"We won't have to do it alone," Baker advised. "The British have a naval station at Esquimalt on Vancouver Island. If we can persuade them to use their navy to deliver weapons to our people on the Pacific Coast, and perhaps to show their support by patrolling the coast down to San Francisco, then we have a fighting chance of organizing a successful uprising that would bring Oregon, Washington Territory, and even California over to our side."

"By all accounts, Oregon is a magnificent country," acknowledged Mr. Lincoln. "President Jefferson understood that we could not fulfill our destiny without it. He sent Lewis and Clark out to claim it, at a time when we could barely enforce our claim to this land we are standing on now."

"It *is* a magnificent country," Baker concurred, "of lofty mountains, forests, rivers, and seacoasts. It is rich in timber, farmlands, fish, furs, and perhaps gold and silver. It has a stimulating climate, refreshing in summer and moderate in winter. Most importantly, it presents us with a window on the Pacific Coast that looks to the rising nations of Asia. We must have a Pacific window to trade with them and become a great power in both great oceans. As President Jefferson understood, we cannot fulfill our destiny without possessing it."

Lincoln got up and walked to the window. Through the trees, he saw a mist of golden-hued air rising off the cool waters of Lake Erie. The sight always inspired him. Such a vast expanse of water was still a novelty to a man grown up in the inland hills, forests, and prairies. It excited his yearning to explore new lands beyond the horizon.

"I can understand how possession of Oregon is as necessary as possession of Ohio," he answered. "Without access to the Pacific, our spirit would be constrained. We would wither as a small country, confined by our limited access to a few Atlantic ports. You are right that we must obtain a Pacific window. We are colonizing the distant islands of Hawaii in anticipation of moving westward across the Pacific, as we moved westward across the North American Continent. We should devote as much of the Free States' resources as can be spared to the project of liberating the Far Northwest.

"Thank you, Mr. President!"

"If the British will agree to transport you and some our military officers out there with enough weapons and ammunition to organize a regular uniformed fighting force, then I will back it. We'd best consult with Secretary of State Seward. He has negotiated our commercial and financial treaties with the British. If he will encourage us to believe we may obtain British assistance, then you will shortly be returning to the Far Country, with a fair chance of making it *our* country."

9. The American Shores

Floyd's Knob, Indiana, October 15, 1862

Jefferson Davis had taken to calling it "The Military Capital," the encampment of tents and wooden barracks booming on the Indiana hills above Louisville. Dick Taylor had quietly purchased the land from an absentee landowner, then up a military telegraph line from the exchange in Louisville, so Davis could communicate with his generals on their distant fronts. Here Davis intended to guide the Confederate Union's re-conquest of the Northwest, bringing the Rebellion to a close.

From his perch on the high ground, he observed the military camps and supply yards spreading south from Louisville and up the golden-leafed ridges of hills south of town. He could see clearly on this early autumn day. A cooling breeze from the north had carried off the clinging pall of smoky humidity hanging low over the city. Intermittent clouds moved swiftly overhead, their dark flat bottoms carrying the seeds of the coming winter's rain and snow.

The transition of seasons reminded him, as it reminded all men, that time was ephemeral. He must show measurable progress in conquering the Rebellion, or it would conquer him. The Fire Eaters kept shouting: "Let the Damn Yankees go! They ain't worth keeping!"

If he did not show progress toward suppressing the Free State rebellion, the Fire Eaters would elect enough of their people to Congress to call off the war. Then they would try to foment the secession of the Cotton States. The Confederate Union might be dissolved from both sides.

He had worked late into the nights, breathing in the fresh air of the highlands, watching the moon and stars pass overhead, and planning to defeat the Yankee Rebels. He fell asleep by candlelight in his tent, waking refreshed as first light dawned over the eastern Ohio Valley. The intensity of his work masked his grief over losing his son Little Joe, especially his sorrow at not being at his side during his last days, nor attending his funeral. Rather than exhausting Davis mentally, the work exhilarated him, in an excitement he hadn't felt since his younger days as a hero of the Mexican War.

He unwrapped a Cuban cigar, struck a match on a boulder, lit it eagerly, and inhaled its rich aroma as he scanned the horizon toward Louisville. He contemplated the ancient military dilemma of a general who drives his men deep into the enemy's territory, but spreads his forces thin; whose further advance is balked by attenuated supply lines; while his officers are burdened with governing the enemy's country.

There must be no more dispersions of effort, no more muddled objectives, and no more railroads snarled by engineers who have no idea where to deliver their men and materiel. Like Stoneballs advises, we must thrust a rapier, with all our strength, into the heart of the Rebellion.

But where? The Yankee Rebels appear to have anticipated McClellan's plan to use the prisoner exchange to break their lines around Indianapolis, since they now demand small exchanges of men at many points along the front, spread out over several months. At least, they have agreed to release the infirm immediately, but that will not help us militarily.

He considered reinforcing Robert E. Lee, whose army faced Grant's across a dog-leg front on the Mississippi River along the Illinois / Iowa border, looped around the corner of Iowa at Keokuk, ran on out across the top of Missouri, and then down the Missouri / Kansas line.

Lee's position at the western extremity of the front resulted from his failure to destroy Grant's army during June's offensive. Can anything be gained by reinforcing him now? If Lee could not destroy Grant's army by surprise in June, I do not think he is likely to do so now that Grant is fully alert and fighting in prepared positions.

He next considered reinforcing General Thomas J. "Stoneballs" Jackson's group of six divisions at Blue Island.

Jackson could have taken Chicago if all our forces were concentrated on that objective at the outset. But that horse has left the barn. Chicago is now a fortified city that cannot be taken by direct assault of any force we can field, certainly not at a cost we can afford. Jackson's method is to strike deep into the enemy's rear and destroy him in battles of maneuver. I must find some place other than the static front around Chicago to employ his talents.

To the South, Jackson's line hooked around the chain of swampy lakes south of Chicago where it joined John Logan's corps of Southern Illinois men. The cavalry of Morgan and Forest, attached to Logan's command, screened the Illinois / Indiana line down to Vincennes where it met General William Harney's line across southeastern Indiana to Cincinnati.

I could order Jackson to attack toward Fort Wayne to cut Chicago off from Indianapolis. However, the Rebels have fortified this line as heavily as their line between Springfield and Decatur. Even if our attack should break through, Sherman can employ his reserves to cut it off at its base. The same result could be expected if we attack further north to break Chicago's communications at Michigan City.

There is also the isolated Rebel position in Central Illinois. It is commanded by Governor Yates, a fanatic, who will order his men to fight to the last and die in place, as Nathanial Lyon did in St. Louis. The Yankee Rebels would trumpet their losses as martyrs gladly giving their lives in a noble cause, while our Eaters would scream about our casualties incurred in taking two Rebel towns of minor importance.

Finally, there is Ewell's corps, fighting its way along the Baltimore and Ohio Railroad toward southeastern Ohio. Perhaps we could reinforce him sufficiently to turn north to take Wheeling or even Pittsburgh. We could use those as bases for an advance toward Cleveland in 1863. Taking Cleveland would split the Rebels in two just as surely as taking Chicago. However, once they were certain we were attacking toward Cleveland, they would transfer men back from Chicago and the Connecticut Valley to resist us from both directions, while our men struggled to advance over difficult terrain lacking railroad connections.

It is not easy even to maintain our present positions. Combat casualties have lessened on the static fronts, but disease has multiplied, thereby depleting the ranks faster than bullets. Our men are demanding furloughs. If we grant them, many will not be scrupulous about returning at the designated time. "Why not take in the harvest while I'm home? The

101

war will still be there next spring." If we don't furlough them, they will simply desert "We have done our part; now it is time for others to do theirs."

I cannot put volunteers under the rigorous military discipline of shooting deserters. Nor can I ask Congress to impose conscription without stirring up a hornet's nest of opposition. Unfortunately, our policy of employing our people at generous wages in war work has made many prefer to prosper in safety rather than risk their lives in battle. What can I tell the people to inspire them to enlist, and to remain in the ranks until the war is won?

He clipped off the lit end of his cigar and put the stub back in his tobacco pouch. He stretched out on a bench one of Taylor's men had knocked together from oak trees, clasped his hands under his head, and tried to relax his mind, tired by a long night of strategic planning. The pleasant breeze cooled his head. He dozed.

"Hello, Mr. Rip Van Winkle!" The familiar voice of Dick Taylor awakened him. He got up stiffly, pain from the old Buena Vista wound shooting through his foot. He flinched, then greeted Taylor.

"Have you had enough of railroad business for one day?"

Taylor laughed. "Let's just say I've received more complaints than compliments. What's your business today if I may ask?"

"I'll be dog-gone'd if I know," confessed Davis. He gave a synopsis of his thoughts to Taylor and asked his opinion.

"It seems the war's stalemated where the Rebels have been able to shelter their armies in fortified cities," surmised Taylor. "My top-of-the-head recommendation would be to push where the Yankees are least able to resist. Keep the pressure up in Central Illinois. Look for opportunities to break their line between Springfield and Decatur. Allocate as many men as McClellan can spare to Jubal Early's corps moving into southeastern Ohio.

"Don't neglect the coming of winter on the stationary fronts. Make a start now on getting the men settled into stout winter quarters. Make sure they're well-supplied with warm clothes, food, ammunition, and firewood. That may be all we can expect to accomplish before winter sets in. Maybe things will look more favorable for offensive operations on those fronts next spring."

"Next spring," lamented Davis. "That will be our third year of war. I never expected it to last so long. By the way, I received a communication from Mr. Lincoln this morning. He expressed his condolences for Little Joe. He said there are many things in life he doesn't understand, but one day we will meet again in a perfected world, where we will understand the purpose of these sorrowful losses we experience in our transient earthly life."

"He's a gracious man," concurred Taylor. "A tragedy he's against us. I think the Rebellion would have failed had he withheld his approbation."

"After receiving his note, I'm inclined to agree," Davis confessed. "Why didn't he join with us in preserving the Union, as McClellan, Stanton, and Logan did?" He reached into his tobacco pouch, pulled out his clipped cigar, and handed a fresh one to Taylor. He lit both, then blew a gigantic puff of smoke toward Louisville.

"Yankee arrogance got the better of him, I suppose," surmised Taylor. He pointed his cigar toward the Ohio River. "I remember going across that river as a child. A Yankee captained the ferry. When we neared New Albany he said, 'We are now approaching the *American*

Shore.' My father rebuked him for implying that Kentuckians were not Americans. The captain said he meant no insult, but wasn't it true that Southerners thought of ourselves as citizens of our states first, and Americans second?

"My father sternly reminded him that George Rogers Clark and his Virginia militia wrested this 'American' shore from the British and Indians during the Revolution; that Thomas Jefferson persuaded the Confederation Congress to decree that it must be admitted to the Union as free states; and that George Washington connected the Potomac with the Ohio by canals, allowing us to settle the Northwest, and keep the British from reclaiming it in 1812."

Davis chuckled. "I can just imagine Old Zack laying down the law to that Yankee, the way he did with me when I courted your sister! He was certainly right to do it. We Southerners conquered this land and held it while the British and Indians ran the Yankees back to New England. I garrisoned Chicago when it was just two shacks and a puddle. Then I was sent to Wisconsin where I reported to your father and courted Knoxie. This country belongs to us more than to the Yankee Rebels. And, oh, how they fought us every step of the way when we wanted Florida, Louisiana, Texas, and the Southwest! If they'd had their way, we wouldn't have acquired anything west of New England. They'd still be trading with the British and spending their Sundays hectoring us about our slaves."

Davis took a final puff of his cigar, threw it down, and snuffed it with his foot.

"I have always felt at home among the fair-minded people in the North. I admire the Yankees' mechanical ingenuity. They helped us roll the wheel of progress forward to the end which our Founders intended.

The problem isn't the Northern people. It's that the Republicans nominate so many unreasoned Abolitionists to represent --- or, I should say to *misrepresent* --- them."

Taylor reached down, picked up a stone, and threw it out into the sky toward Louisville. He watched it disappear through the tree canopy five hundred feet below. He blew a smoke ring from his cigar.

"I was educated at Harvard and share your view of the Yankees. The main question is whether it will be possible to separate the Northern people from their Abolitionist agitators, the way you and Douglass separated the Southern Fire Eaters from our people of reasoned judgement. We'll have to deal with that question again from this side of the Ohio if we beat the Yankees back into the Union."

"How do you think we'll solve it?" asked Davis.

"Well...." Taylor paused a second while he carefully considered his reply. "I think we should decide whether we really want to force the Yankees back in with us, before we lose thousands more of our men fighting them in their fortified cities. I wonder if we should consider offering them a peace proposal conceding the independence of some territory they hold."

Davis raised his eyelids. "What territory would you concede them?"

"Let's answer that question by considering the territory essential for us to hold," replied Taylor. "We must retain possession of New York City and New Jersey. We must recover Illinois, Indiana, and Ohio as far north as Latitude 40, so we can establish our new State of Jefferson.

"We must cut the Rebels off from the West, so the western territories between here and the Pacific are brought into the Confederate

Union as loyal states. If our objective is to limit the Rebellion rather than conquer it completely, then we do not need to batter our way into Chicago. We can complete our occupation of northern Illinois west of the Des Plaines River, then move into Wisconsin. It's better to occupy a lightly defended state than fight our way through a fortified city where our enemies have concentrated."

Davis glanced northward toward Chicago as he considered the proposition, then looked back at Taylor. "Avoiding a set-piece battle for Chicago would let us to move more men into Ohio, as well as Wisconsin. We might even send some to help Lee fulfill his heart's desire to clear Grant out of the Trans-Mississippi. If we can accomplish those things, we can conclude the war on terms we can rightfully call victory."

Taylor's glance turned northeastward. "We will confine Rebels to the country between New England and the eastern Great Lakes. They will become a Greater New England that looks to Britain as its mother because it is too small to threaten us. Let them join with the British in ruling the seas, while we fulfill our destiny of ruling the heart of this continent as Americans."

"Ah, yes!" responded Davis. "I'm so glad to hear you say 'American.' The word was going out of style, since we have started calling ourselves Confederates. I will start referring to our country as the 'Confederate Union of **America**,' so we can keep the 'American' appellation for ourselves before the Yankee Rebels steal it." He felt a burden lifting from his shoulders.

*That will get the Yankees **and** the Fire Eaters off my back. I am henceforth fighting to preserve the homeland of the American people, which will no longer include the Yankees --- and if the Fire Eaters don't keep their peace, I'll kick the hell out of them too.*

Davis anticipated the future. "I will propose an armistice with recognition of the Yankee Rebels' independence along the lines you propose. If they refuse an armistice on those terms, the war to suppress the rebellion must become harsher. I will announce an Armed Occupation Proclamation, like we did with the Seminoles in Florida. It will cover the lands formerly owned by Rebels now in our possession or that may fall into our possession in the future. That will bring land-hungry men into our army from here and abroad. We will re-settle those lands with our people and the Yankee Rebels will know they will never get them back. What do you think?"

"A sound policy," confirmed Taylor. "The more we press the Rebels back, the more afraid they'll be of losing everything, and the more willing they'll be to accept peace on our terms. If they are averse to peace, we can fortify our positions and let them beat their brains out attacking us. Even a mule gets tired of being beat. They'll have to make peace eventually."

"After we conclude the war, we must maintain the peace on our terms," vowed Davis. "We must put an end to Yankee arrogance like that captain who told your father that only the north bank of the Ohio River was an 'American' shore. Let the Yankee Rebels call their country whatever they want. They can call it 'Hell' for all I care. We are the heirs of the American destiny Providence ordained and our fathers bequeathed us. Both shores of the Ohio and the Mississippi are American shores ---- Confederate American shores --- from the warm waters of the Gulf of Mexico to the frigid waters of Lake Superior, and west to the Pacific, now and forevermore."

10. "An artifact of Yankee ingenuity"

Washington City, October 20, 1862.

"How are you, sir," asked Secretary of War Edwin Stanton, as tenderly as his nature allowed.

"I've been better," replied Davis. "Thank you for coming to Little Joe's commemoration last night. I know you're asleep on your feet after working long hours in this office. Your presence meant a lot to Varina and me."

"It was the least I could do for a family I love," said Stanton, with a feeling he seldom expressed. "I've had these tragedies in my family. They are especially difficult when the stress of high office also weighs down upon you." He motioned Davis to follow him. "I'm reluctant to heap more cares upon you, but I want to show you something."

Davis followed Stanton to the door of an anteroom in Stanton's War Department office. Stanton pulled out his key chain and opened the locked door. They went inside and to a table of machined components. Stanton picked one up. "I'm sure you know what this is."

"The firing mechanism for a breechloading rifle?"

"A clerk in Ambrose Burnside's manufactory smuggled it across the lines to McClellan's headquarters. It's the breechblock for Christian Spencer's repeating rifle. But that's not the half of it." Stanton pulled out a metallic cartridge. "Here's what makes it effective: a metallic cartridge with the primer inside. Burnside's clerk says they can pre-load seven in the stock, then fire them off at the rate of one per second. It's a war-winning weapon for them, if they can manufacture the rifle and the ammunition in sufficient quantities soon enough to make a difference."

"An artifact of Yankee ingenuity," said Davis, fingering the cartridge. "Those people know how to make things, even if half are crazy. Ambrose Burnside is good man and good engineer to boot. If only he'd stayed loyal to the Union as you and McClellan did."

"This isn't Burnside's design," Stanton corrected him. "He's making it under license from Christopher Spencer, as the Free State Government has decided this will be their standard repeating rifle."

"How do we know this?" asked Davis.

"The clerk who purloined it is working for us," replied Stanton, "She's Burnside's former fiancé. We presume she gleaned the information from him."

"Eeeeeyyyyyyyyooooooowwwwwwww!" exclaimed Davis. "The Lord certainly works in mysterious ways!" He'd heard the gossip about Burnside being rejected at the altar years ago by a woman of tarnished virtue. He never bothered to find out if the story was true. Apparently, it was. "He's a good man, but not a wise one to trust a woman of that character with military secrets. She must be top-shelf at her trade, as a.....spy." Davis was too polite to call any woman, no matter how tarnished, a prostitute.

109

"According to Burnside's floozie, the rifle is accurate and reliable," Stanton continued, "but they're having difficulties manufacturing the cartridges," said Stanton. "She says they won't have enough cartridges to field the rifles until the middle of next year. We'll need a comparable weapon by then if we expect to continue the war."

"What are our choices?"

"Colonel Raines in our Ordnance Bureau thinks we need a three-pronged response:

"First, mass-produce the Sharps rifle. It takes paper cartridges, which are easy to manufacture.   In a pinch, it can take cartridges for our muzzleloaders. One of the variants has a paper primer roll that improves its rate of fire and reliability. Raines figures it's about a four-fold improvement on muzzle loaders, while the Spencers are about ten times more effective."

"Better to have enough of a weapon four times as effective than to have nothing of one that's ten times better," affirmed Davis.

"That's what Colonel Raines said. He thinks we should study the Spencer to see if we can simplify it enough to manufacture at our Ordnance Bureau. If we succeed, we'll have to figure out how to manufacture the metallic cartridges. That's at least a year, maybe two, down the road. Until then, we must concentrate on getting our men the Sharps.

"His third proposal is to develop armored protection for our soldiers, so they'll be able to withstand the rapid fire from Spencers."

"Hmmmmmm," replied Davis. "Some of our soldiers wore armor plate early in the war. Most threw it away during their first march. They said it kills more soldiers by exhaustion and heatstroke than it saves from enemy bullets."

"That calculation would change if they came under repeating rifle fire, wouldn't it?" asked Stanton. "We could find ways to carry armor in wagons and distribute it to men on the firing line when the battle came. Raines says the armor doesn't have to be iron. We might find a way to make it out of pressed cotton, sawdust, or even paper. How many soldiers have claimed they were saved by carrying a Bible over their hearts that stopped a bullet?"

Davis chuckled, for the first time since Little Joe had passed. "Wouldn't Stoneballs like that --- making Bibles a required part of their uniforms! But I understand your point. If we are ingenious enough to invent these weapons, we are ingenious enough to find ways to protect ourselves from them. We need to get working on it."

Davis and Stanton returned to Stanton's large office. Davis sat down on the sofa and stretched out on the thick upholstery. "I've forgotten what comfort felt like. I've been riding eight out of ten days by train. My back is stiff as a board."

"Have a shot of bourbon, with me. That will loosen you up."

"Thank you," said Davis, sipping the drink. He felt his knotted muscles unwind. He did feel better! He stretched out again.

"Until we get control of the Baltimore and Ohio, it's going to be tough traveling between Jefferson and the East. I didn't mind it so much this time because I wanted to make campaign stops in Nashville, Atlanta, Charleston, and Charlotte, on the way. But we have to open a direct link from the Seaboard to the Ohio Valley."

"Then I think we should ask McClellan to reinforce Early's Corps," advised Stanton. "We need to finish cleaning the Insurgents out of the Kanawha Valley, then expedite the arrival of Early's men to Ohio. They could cut in behind Cincinnati and lever the Yankee Rebels out of the north end of town after they secure the B&O."

"It sounds like you don't expect McClellan to do much around Philly," surmised Davis.

"He's moving like a snail. The Insurgents aren't doing much either. They seem to feel, as we do, that the war will be decided at Chicago."

Davis sipped the bourbon.

"Dick Taylor thinks we should forget about Chicago and move on up into Wisconsin. He says we'll break their backs if we install a Confederate government in Madison and cut them off from the West. Dick and I think we should then offer independence for the territory they hold north of Latitude 40, and no further west than Indiana and Michigan."

"Oh?" said Stanton. "Do you really think they'll mind their business if we let them go?"

"They'll have to stick to their knitting if they're confined to New England and the eastern Great Lakes watershed. If they refuse to make peace on those terms, we'll have to beat them into submission. In that event, I'm considering invoking an Armed Occupation Act, like we did during the Seminole Wars. If we can't negotiate a peace, we'll have to conquer it, and soon. We've got to conclude the war before they're able to manufacture those Spencer breechblocks."

"The longer the war goes on, the higher the risk of British intervention," added Stanton. "Expropriating the Insurgents' property might be enough to bring them into it. They may claim we're waging a pirate war that devalues their investments in the Rebel States."

"I've considered that," replied Davis. "I figure it this way: First, the British will find a way to involve themselves in this war anyway if it goes on much longer. Secondly, we won't have to resort to conscription if we reward our volunteers with land. Third, it will curtail enlistments in the Yankee Rebel armies if they think it puts their property at risk. And finally, If the British do jump in, it might work to our advantage by inducing moderate Free State men to join us. Would they really fight with the Limeys against Americans? What do you think?"

"It's hard to say," Stanton equivocated. "But the more I think about it, the more I like this Armed Occupation Act."

Davis could see by the look in Stanton's eyes that he was contemplating the hefty legal fees involved in seizing Yankee Rebel property and selling it to Confederate-loyal people.

Davis sipped the bourbon. "I'm going to stay here a week and tend to my business at home and with the government. "Then I'll be back in Louisville to help Dick and Stoneballs get organized for a move into Wisconsin. I'll leave it to you and Raines to organize the work on improving our rifles and developing armor for our men."

He drained his glass of bourbon and felt relaxed for the first time since the war began. "Yes," he said with certainty. "We'll clear the Yankee Rebels out of Wisconsin and cut them off from the West. Then I will offer them peace with independence. If they refuse, I will announce the Armed Occupation Act and conquer a peace. If we have to deal with the British, we'll defeat them too."

11. "They diddled us again!"

Cleveland Ohio, November 25, 1862

Mrs. Lincoln saw her husband up early, summoned by a knock on the door. He was opening a package of military correspondence delivered by an army courier from Chicago. He called for his secretary John Hay, asking him to summon Secretary of War Andrew Curtin. Mrs. Lincoln could tell by his furrowed brow her husband was gravely worried. "What is it, Father?" she asked.

"They diddled us again, Mother!"

He held up a copy of *The Chicago Times,* delivered with the military correspondence. The *Times* was much thinner for being published in partially evacuated Chicago, but no less sensational. The headlines on yesterday's paper were as hysterical as they'd been back in those grim days of June when the Confederate vanguard of Indian Territory divisions commanded by the great warrior chiefs Stand Watie and Opothle Yahola made their appearance outside the city:

Confederates Advance, Terror Spreads!

Massacre of McClernand's Corps by Confederate Red Savages!

12,000 Captured and Burned Alive!

"My God!" exclaimed Mrs. Lincoln. "This is worse than the massacre of Custer's men at Blue Island."

"We'd best wait until the facts are all in," Mr. Lincoln cautioned. "The newspapers have been known to exaggerate --- like the reported 'massacre' of Custer's men at Blue Island. It was our men's bravery in fighting so hard to save Chicago that cost Custer's command its heavy losses, not anything having to do with Confederate butchery. The Confederates cared for our wounded and paroled them back to our lines. I trust they'll do the same with McClernand's men."

He read a note from General Ormsby Mitchel. "Mitchel reports that McClernand's Corps sortied out from Chicago to attack the Confederates moving northwest around the city. They encountered Jackson's divisions from the Indian Territory. They were worsted in the encounter and are regrouping in good order nearer their base in Chicago...." He rolled his eyes. Mitchel's report probably went the other way in understating the defeat. He skipped past the details of the reported losses, then surmised: "The Confederates appear to be shifting their forces into Wisconsin, maybe hoping our officers would do something rash, and they did it. Why do they keep getting buffaloed by the same old tricks?"

"The Confederates are cowards," hissed Mrs. Lincoln. "They're afraid to fight our men in Chicago, so they're running away to Wisconsin instead. You and Sherman will catch up with them and thrash them like you did in the other battles."

"Thank you for your vote of confidence, Mother! Sherman is in the East. We must bring him here to deal with the Confederates in Illinois and Wisconsin. Then if we can get Sumner, Wade, Chase, Stevens, and the rest of those hotheads settled down, we'll be able to take rational measures to defeat the Confederates and send them back where they came from."

"Leave Sumner to me," said Mrs. Lincoln. "He promised to help me select our winter clothes. I'll call on him right away and keep him busy today, so you'll have time to devise a plan. While I enjoy selecting *your* wardrobe with advice from a man of refinement," she added with mock snootiness.

"I suppose I'm not a man of such refinement?" asked Mr. Lincoln playfully.

"Ha! It took me near twenty years to teach you to eat peas with a fork, instead of with molasses on a knife! If not for me, you'd have been run out of politics before you ever left Springfield."

He laughed boisterously. "Thank you, Mother. I'm gratified that you succeeded in teaching this backwoods Illinois 'Sucker' a paltry learnin' of manners. I'm proud that such a cultured man as Sumner adores you. Who would have thought a rambunctious Kentucky girl from a slave-owning family would be so much admired by a stern Yankee Abolitionist?"

"He's just a lonely old bachelor, that's all. He enjoys my company and sees in me all the women he craved to marry when he was young but were driven away by his stern temperament. I must say I like him. Can't say why, but I do."

"Perhaps because you like the challenge of charming ornery rascals. Judge Douglas and I fit that description. You may be the only woman who's ever been courted by two presidents! I, and the people of the United States of Free America, are grateful you chose me instead of Judge Douglas."

"I was thinking of marrying him," she confessed, "until he took me to the ballroom at the American House. He spit a plug of chewing tobacco right on the shiny new floor while we were dancing! I spent the rest of the evening dancing around it." She wrinkled her nose and frowned. "I could not conceive of going through life avoiding tobacco every time Stephen spit it on the floor!" Then she laughed, tousled her husband's hair, and kissed his cheek. "Compared to him, *you* turned out not to be such a ruffian after all! You've lived longer too. Imagine me being a widow at my age."

"Well, I am grateful you preferred me to him. You know, for all his crudeness, Judge Douglas was the most remarkable man I've ever known. I met him when he was twenty-two, when he'd just arrived from Vermont without a penny in his pocket, and barely more education than me. He was elected Secretary of State and then appointed to the Illinois Supreme Court before he turned twenty-eight! Too bad he squandered his destiny fighting for slave owners to take their slaves willy-nilly wherever they pleased. He lacked a moral conscience about some things."

"He was a man of the earth, who loved the things of this earth," recalled Mrs. Lincoln. "He liked money, and the company of wealthy men. You are a man of the spirit, who keeps company with principled men. I love you for that."

"Thank you, Mother. You grew up in one of the wealthiest households in Kentucky, yet you never minded sticking with me all those years when we had nothing. You have remained steadfastly true to me, even now, when I am leading cause that seems lost."

"You will not lose. I decided to cast my destiny with a man who wins in life. I made no mistake in choosing you."

"Oh, Mother, how you have cheered and warmed my heart! You've made me remember how my father set me on *my* path to destiny by moving us into the Free States. He hated cruelty, whether it was a man beating a horse, or the sorrow of a slave trader selling a family of Negroes in chains to separate owners, so they would never see each other again. He felt the Free States were the new country, where white men could live free from slavery as much as Negroes. He said that in Kentucky the wealthy men with slaves bought the good land and shoved the poor men without slaves off it. Crude and unlettered as my father was, he was a man with **American** principles, who believed that every man ought to be the captain of his destiny."

"I felt that way too," confided Mrs. Lincoln, "that Kentucky was the old country that wouldn't make progress, the way Illinois would. Most of my family stayed in Kentucky. Two sisters moved to Alabama. They invited me to live with them, but I didn't want to live in slave country. It will be the same in a hundred years as it is now. A few slave-owning families owning all the good bottom land, while the poor whites get a few acres of rocky soil in the hills. Their people talk about the glory days of the past when they won the South from the British, Spanish, and Indians. They don't think about the future the way the people in Illinois do. I came to see my older sister in Springfield and never left." Mary looked discomfited. "Father, do you think the Confederates will bring their slaves **here** if they win?"

"They're capable of it," he replied. "Even if they don't, they'll keep us under their thumbs. They're planning to cut New England down to one state. After they carve out the State of Jefferson, there's nothing to keep them from packing what's left of Ohio, Indiana, and Illinois into one state. We wouldn't have many free states left to represent us in the Senate. I expect they'd find reasons to subordinate us to that 'Military Capital' Jefferson Davis is creating around New Albany. It would become an oppressive country."

"Maybe we could move to the Canadas," suggested Mary. "They're only sixty miles away." She nodded across Lake Erie, occluded by grey skies and a rainy, sleeting mist, toward Upper Canada, just beyond the horizon. "I've heard a few people in town talking about going there if our independence fails."

He sighed. "We'd be admitting that our American Revolution has failed, if we're compelled to seek asylum in a country ruled by a Queen. All the blood sacrificed by our fathers; all the words written by Washington, Jefferson, Madison, and Adams rendered worthless. It would be a crying shame, having to admit that the people can't be trusted to govern themselves, and that only government by monarchy can be sustained."

"Don't they elect a Parliament?"

"The Nobles do; the mass of people don't. They have an imperial heritage and maintain a haughty, anti-democratic attitude. If we cannot maintain a separate independence, then I think I'd rather throw back in with the Confederates. At least we have family ties with them and are familiar with their ways. We'd be treated like unwelcome guests in a house we used to own, but eventually we'd get back on our feet."

"Not a pleasant choice either way."

"Let's pray we don't have to make it. The fight isn't over. The Confederates are moving away from Chicago, and not into it. We've got strong and undefeated armies defending our line from New England to Philadelphia to the hills above Cincinnati and on up to Chicago. Then there's Grant's Army of the Mississippi. We've got the same number of men under arms as the Confederates. They've been sneaking around us; not defeating us."

And we've got another trick up our sleeve with the Spencer repeaters, if we can hold out long enough to get them to our men.

"I'm certain that between you and Sherman, Grant, and Secretary of War Curtin, you'll be more than a match for them," Mrs. Lincoln assured him. "Anyway, I'll have Sumner eating out of your hand before this day is done. I'll leave *your* breakfast cooking on the stove."

Mr. Lincoln smiled and took Mary's hand. *Thank you, Lord. With all the tribulations you have handed me, at least you have given me a wife who loves me, and who loves our country. Please guide me, and our commanding officers, on how to accomplish what we must accomplish to fulfil our American destiny as the land where all men are created equal and endowed by You, their Creator, with the rights of life, liberty, and pursuit of happiness.*

There was a knock at the door. In came John Hay and Secretary of War Andrew Curtin. Mr. Lincoln greeted them.

"The Confederates have renewed their attack in Illinois," he informed Curtin. "Let's do what we can to assist our generals in meeting the crisis immediately, while waiting for the return of General Sherman. We must take charge of the situation before the Joint Executive Committee of Congress...."

"...threatens to dismiss you again!" interjected Hay. "I remember you forestalled them last time with your story about the Chess Automaton."

"Oh, yes!" replied Lincoln. He smiled. "That was hunky-dory, if I must say so myself. Too bad I can only tell it once."

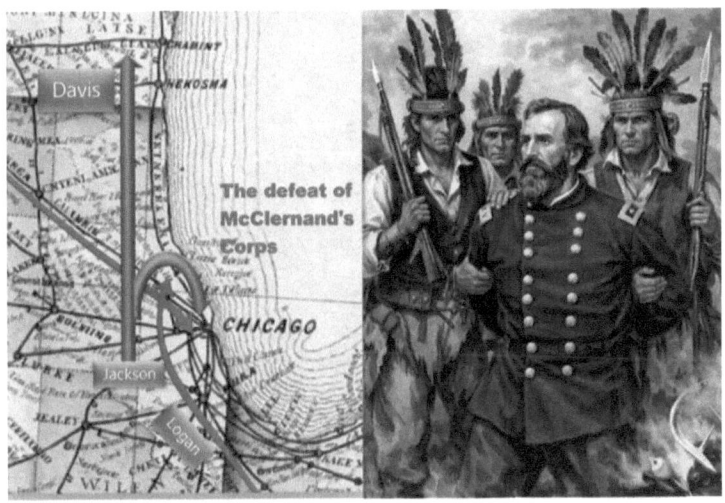

12. "The collision is at hand"

Ilion, New York, November 26, 1862

Blam! Click, click, **Blam!,** click, click **Blam!** Click, click, **Blam!,** click, click **Blam!** Click, click, **Blam!,** click, click **Blam!**

Sherman worked the action on the Spencer Rifle expertly. The first few times he'd fired it, he'd jiggled it while clearing the spent cartridges, slowing his rate of fire. Now he worked the lever action smoothly, ejecting the cartridges cleanly. He kept the rifle on target, firing one aimed shot every three seconds, grouping them closely around the center of the target board at fifty yards. He quickly reloaded seven rounds into the buttstock and half-cocked the rifle to chamber a round.

Blam! Click, click, **Blam!,** click, click **Blam!** Click, click, **Blam!,** click, click **Blam!** Click, click, **Blam!,** click, click **Blam!**

"I never get tired of firing this rifle!" he said to Ambrose Burnside, who looked on approvingly. "Wish I had another day to enjoy it."

He set down the rifle with reverence and took the letter out of his pocket delivered by military courier less than an hour ago. He read it aloud: "Confederates are moving around Chicago and into Wisconsin. McClernand's division defeated outside the city by Jackson's divisions, who occupied Evanston yesterday. Confederate cavalry patrols reported operating inside Chicago. Please return to the Northwest and take charge. - A. Lincoln."

Sherman folded the letter. "Well, dammit, it's time for us to get back to the stern business of war. I'm leaving for Cleveland on the military train tonight. I'll consult with the President, then go on to Chicago, if we still possess it. You'd best get back to New England and keep an eye on the Confederates there. Burns, I'm counting on you to run your department autonomously. I can't be everywhere at once."

Sherman and Burnside stood on the firing range outside the Remington Arms Factory, contracted for final assembly of the Spencer repeating rifles, at Ilion, New York. Heavy wet snow fell from squalls blowing in off Lake Ontario fifty miles away. Occasional sunbeams filtered in between the traveling curtains of snow, reflecting sparkles off the choppy waves in the Erie Canal. The rails of the New York Central next to the canal glistened wet as snowflakes melted on contact. The canal and railroads had brought the Industrial Revolution to the Mohawk Valley. The air rang with the sound of hammers as carpenters nailed roofs over buildings housing new production lines, and over the roofs of barracks housing the machinists and laborers working them.

"Yes, sir!" exclaimed Burnside. He pointed to Sherman's rifle, still spilling copious smoke from its barrel. "With these rifles, we'll kick the Confederates back across the Ohio and out of New England! It's not only the rate of fire, you know, but also the reliability. In battle only about half of muzzle-loaders are ever fired. Men become unnerved and forget to set the percussion caps. They keep ramming loads into the barrel and pulling the trigger. They can't tell they're not firing, in the heat of battle, surrounded by smoke and noise. The Spencers are reliable because the primers are contained inside the cartridges. Just load them and shoot. Confederates might as well be shooting bows and arrows compared to these rifles."

Sherman admired Burnside, an accomplished industrial engineer and designer of his namesake Burnside Rifle. Burnside's position in the army had fostered acceptance of these modern rifles, despite opposition from the old fogies who said they cost too much to procure on tight military budgets and expended too much ammunition. Without Burnside's proof of concept, Spencer's more capable design would have been delayed several years. It was characteristic of Burnside's humility that he championed Spencer's design as if it were his own.

Burnside had entered the Free States' pantheon of heroes for more than just his firearms innovations. He'd insisted on defending Providence despite Sherman's inclination to abandon it for more defensible ground. He said he'd rally his fellow citizens to save their city, and he and they had done it, by cleverly salvaging the port for the raw materials needed to manufacture Burnside rifles and ammunition. These rifles, firing twice as many metallic cartridges as the Confederates' muzzleloaders, and being impervious to damp weather, enabled Providence to hold out during last winter's grim months when Confederates besieged the city. He bought time for Sherman to establish his "Sherman Line" along the Connecticut River Valley, a haven for loyal New Englanders evacuating Confederate-occupied Boston and other ports. Lincoln had taken to calling Providence "The Hero City of Free America."

He was proving his worth yet again in working with Sherman, Christopher Spencer, and the Remington sons to mass produce the Spencer rifles. Spencer had moved his machine tool molds and dies out of Boston just before the Confederates closed their ring around the city. Confederate raiding parties then moved inland to burn the Federal Arsenal at Springfield, Massachusetts and the Colt Factory at Hartford, but were too hurried to wreck the sturdy industrial machinery. Sherman and Burnside supervised the retooling of the machinery at the Colt and Springfield factories with Spencer's dies, then organized the final assembly here at Ilion.

"I wonder if the Confederates have gotten wind of what we're doing with these rifles?" Sherman speculated. "They seem to be in a hell of a hurry to finish this war before we get enough of them to make a difference. We have plenty of spies in our lines, as you well know."

Burnside grimaced. "Oh, please, don't remind me!" At the end of October, he'd caught his old flame, Leticia Moon, trying to smuggle his engineering and production reports across the lines, presumably to McClellan's headquarters in Boston. What else had she smuggled before he caught her?

Sherman chuckled to himself. *Burnside is a nice fellow, but people do take advantage of his good nature.*

"I've learned my lesson," Burnside assured him. "Now we are taking all possible precautions to conceal our Spencer component manufacturing."

Sherman could not resist taking another jibe at his brilliant but naïve friend.

"Just be careful. People are fickle. In a civil war, they'll leave you jilted at the altar when they think the fortunes of war have shifted to the other side." Sherman was referring to Burnside's embarrassment when Miss Moon had jilted him on their presumed wedding day, a few years ago. "No offense, Burns, but let's not presume to trust anybody more than we should."

"No offense taken, sir! She has no shame. She came back to me pleading poverty, so I gave her a clerking job. She was there doing the Confederates' dirty work, and a lot of dirty work on her own account. They say said she was engaged to sixteen men on their side of the line and to thirteen on ours!"

Sherman roared laughing. "If only our men were as promiscuous engaging the enemy as that worthless piece of arse is promiscuous in engaging her body!"

He became serious. "If you catch any more Confederate spies, hang them, women or not. We can't allow anybody to remain within our lines and work against our government, without incurring risk."

"Maybe we won't have to hang too many," Burnside, a compassionate man, said hopefully. "The disloyal people will pipe down when they see what we are doing to the enemy with these rifles. We'll roll the Confederates back like melting snow in May."

Sherman put his arm on Burnside's shoulder. "Burns, please be careful about how you talk about these guns. We've got to attack the Confederates immediately, using the weapons we have. Davis's Armed Occupation Proclamation has spooked a lot of our people. They're scared of losing their property if they don't lay down their arms and swear allegiance to the Confederate government. Our Radicals are liable to impose martial law and began mass executions of those who do. If we don't restore the situation around Chicago at once, they'll be antsy to replace Lincoln with Thad Stevens or Salmon Chase. Then our neutral

Democrats will revolt and we'll have a civil war within a revolution. We can beat the Confederates, but we can't beat ourselves. We'll have to beat the Confederates now with what we have now."

"May I inquire as to where you'll attack them, sir?" asked Burnside.

"I've been thinking to strike the Confederates around Chicago in February, after the blizzards leave them sick, hungry, and shivering. I was counting on employing about sixty thousand of your best winter-hardened men. I don't think McClellan's going to do anything in New England. He's only attacked us at places he thinks we haven't defended. He won't spill his men's blood attacking fortified positions. Therefore, it's a misallocation of forces to have so many of our men idle in New England. I was planning on moving your men to Grand Haven, Michigan, then across the lake to Milwaukee, to come down behind the Confederates' rear. Pin them between the Fox and the Des Plaines, bayonet the guts out of all we catch out in the open, and cut off the rest from reinforcement and resupply. Wait for them to surrender once the cold, hunger, and disease gets the best of them."

"Like Washington's Crossing of the Delaware!" enthused Burnside.

"Yes, but that won't happen now, not with the Confederates occupying the Wisconsin shore and moving into Chicago from the north. We'll have to think of something else." Sherman blew on his hands to warm them. "I'm thinking that you should start moving your best men on multiple routes to Fort Wayne and Columbus. I'll figure out what to do with them when they get there. If you can give me a hundred thousand, I'll take them. You're responsible for the defense of New England, so I'll leave it to your discretion. Give me every man you can responsibly spare, consistent with your duty to defend New England. Send them however they are armed. With standard muzzle-loaders or with your Burnsides. I don't care what they have as long as they have enough ammunition to get through a big fight."

As Sherman expected, Burnside demonstrated hearty cooperation. "I'll leave for Hartford tomorrow morning and get the men moving west as soon as I arrive."

Sherman liked that about Burnside. He executed his orders as enthusiastically as if he had given them himself. Sherman didn't think Burnside had enough self-confidence to command an army in the field. But if he was no lion in battle, he was a past master of defense, as he had proven at Providence. And a loyal subordinate, a rare bird among self-important general officers.

"Thank you, Burns. Please make the best use of the railroads by moving the men on multiple routes, including the Grand Trunk through the Canadas, if you need it. We have credit with the British. We might as well use it."

"Yes, sir. But what about these Spencer rifles? We've got seven hundred field tested in our inventory, and we'll have about twenty-five hundred in a month at the rate we are producing. We could bring a couple of regiments of our best men here and equip them and train them as they arrive."

Sherman twisted his neck until it cracked, as he often did when deciding a question. "My inclination has been not to release them piecemeal, as this would reduce their effect and warn the Confederates to begin producing their own repeaters. There is also the problem of ammunition. These rifles fire ten to twenty rounds per minute. They won't do us much good if we don't have enough rounds to maintain their rate of fire for more than a few minutes. Unfortunately, we devoted more of our efforts to manufacturing the guns than manufacturing the ammunition. It will be another month before we have enough rounds stockpiled even to supply the seven hundred rifles we have now for a prolonged battle."

"Ah, yes," said Burnside. "Ammunition is the bottleneck. I wish we'd thought more about it at the beginning. We should have set up cartridge manufactories near the fronts, so all the men would have to do is pick the guns up here, then receive their cartridges when they got there."

"Well, that's the nature of war," Sherman consoled. "It's never possible to think of every contingency beforehand. I'd like you to work up a plan for copying the ammunition production we have here and duplicating it in Cleveland, Columbus, Indianapolis, Philly, Fort Wayne, Detroit, Grand Rapids, Buffalo, and anywhere else we have enough gunsmiths to know how to make them. The way these things shoot, we can never have enough cartridges."

"My men from the Burnside Rifle Company know how to make them," Burnside advised. "I'll send them out in teams to each town. Once the production line is set up in one town, we'll move on to the next. I'll get you the men you need the stop the Confederates now, and the rifles and ammunition we'll need to drive them out of our country by spring."

"There's one thing more, Burns. Don't overplay these rifles, not even when we have them in enough quantity to be decisive. They'll help us, for sure, but they won't win the war by themselves. Our men must win it the old-fashioned way by fighting the Confederates man-to-man like we did at Gettysburg, the Wabash, and Camden. They'll have to defeat the Confederates with their blood and courage. I don't want our men thinking they won't have to risk their lives, even when they're equipped with these fine rifles. Don't tell them we have better rifles on the way, or they'll shirk until they get them. Let's surprise them and the Confederates when we have enough Spencers to make a difference."

"Yes, sir," said Burnside, but Sherman could tell he was crestfallen.

"Is anything wrong, Burns?"

"I was hoping the Spencers would win the war once the Confederates saw them, and our men wouldn't have to die in large numbers to liberate our country."

"It might have turned out that way if the Confederates had gone into winter quarters for the rest of the season. Since they didn't, we'll have to force the issue now. At least the Confederates won't go around saying, 'The Damn Yankee Rebels couldn't outfight us, so they conjured up their fancy rifle to outshoot us.' If we beat them with our old rifles now, the lesson will stick in their craw."

Burnside, an agreeable man, conceded the point. "It's not like they never tricked us, by trying to sneak into Gettysburg, New England, New Jersey, Wisconsin, and all the other places they thought we hadn't defended. Those people have spent most of this war trying to avoid fighting us man-to-man."

Sherman set his jaw forward. "They can't avoid it any longer. Neither can we. The collision is at hand."

13. The Badger's Nest

Springfield, Illinois, November 28, 1862

Eddie Bates reached the Governor's House exhausted, just after ten o'clock on a late-autumn evening. He'd walked in from the Illinois State Arsenal a mile east of town, created by Governor Richard Yates when Illinois seceded from the Old Union and joined the United States of Free America. The windy night, and the glow of Confederate campfires reflecting off low-lying clouds to the west, recalled the night five months ago when he'd made his first journey to Yates' office. He had arrived unannounced then; this time Governor Yates had summoned him.

Yates was a military amateur whose perspective included a political dimension professional military men usually ignored. Whereas professional officers saw places like Springfield as points to be evacuated when their supply lines were outflanked, Yates understood that the defense of Illinois' capital would loom large in the hearts of other Free Staters. When the Confederates shattered Grant's line with their attack up the Illinois Valley, he resisted orders by McPherson and Schofield to retreat with the eastern half of the broken army into Indiana. He'd rallied fifty thousand soldiers and civilian volunteers to hold this portion of the front. They were stiffened by Phil Sheridan's cavalry division that Yates had jawboned McPherson into leaving behind.

Yates' defense of Springfield and Decatur --- a triangle sixty miles wide at its base and fifty to is apex at McLean --- doglegged the Confederate advance around the two railroads to Chicago, thereby allowing Ormsby Mitchel time to build a defensive line in front of the city. The fifteen hundred square miles Yates controlled was the most productive land in Illinois, with enough corn, hogs, and cattle to keep his men fed until the harvest started coming in at the beginning of September. He cleverly extended his ammunition by ordering his arsenal workers to disassemble the inventory of artillery shells to make two million additional cartridges and percussion caps.

And there was his makeshift manure-and-urine works to make saltpeter --- a subject of occasional ridicule, but general admiration. Yates understood that regardless of whether a single ounce of gunpowder was ever produced by this crude method, the message: "We are here to stay" would ring loud and clear to Free Staters and Confederates alike. His curly-haired visage became a symbol of Free State determination. He was called "The Soldiers' Friend" for his untiring work in feeding and equipping the men at the front, followed by his long hours of comforting the wounded and dying in the hospitals. His defense of Springfield in the West, along with Sherman's and Burnside's defense of the Connecticut Valley and Providence in the East, were the bookends binding the Free States together.

The Confederates loosely cordoned Yates' perimeter with two corps commanded by George H. Thomas and John C. Pemberton. Illinois was a big state, and the Confederates had not the force to occupy all of it, nor to prevent the Free State men in Central Illinois more freedom of movement than siege protocol desired. Yates, Barrie, and Sheridan moved their men rapidly along the railroads inside the encirclement to counter Confederate attacks. Confederates had taken to calling Yates "The Badger" because he could not be defeated by above-ground attack. Somebody was going to have dig him out of his hole.

Jefferson Davis, exercising energetic command of the Northwest, had arrived to do the digging. He had lit a fire under "Slow Trot" Thomas, first reinforcing him with Cheatham's division from Pemberton's Corps, then ordering him to attack with the full force of the divisions commanded by Hood, Helm, and McCullough from the northwest, and Cheatham's from the northeast. Thomas's converging attacks had snipped off the apex of the encirclement and driven the Free Staters back to defensive positions four miles north of the railroad between Springfield and Decatur, looping back around the towns to connect with Grant's original fortifications four miles south of the railroad.

Davis brought in Alexander Porter's siege artillery, concentrating it on the line midway between Springfield and Decatur. Thomas and Porter were trying to cut the Springfield / Decatur railroad, thereby splitting Yates' territory into isolated pockets that could be stormed or starved into submission.

Thomas' fierce attack focused the Free Staters' attention toward the northern front of the encirclement, thereby allowing Davis to pull Pemberton's divisions commanded by Floyd, Pillow, and Polk out of the line to the south and send them up to Chicago. That released Jackson's battle-hardened mobile divisions to advance around the city and into Wisconsin. Davis ordered Dick Taylor to backfill the vacated southern line of encirclement with raw recruits expedited from the training camps around Louisville. Taylor was right about Davis needing to take personal command of the armies. Robert E. Lee, crabbing along the Mississippi, was in no position to exercise the flexible command structure required to unbalance and confuse the Free State armies.

Yates, needing every man to defend what was left of his crumbling positions, had parlayed with General Thomas to exchange some recently captured Confederates for the release of previously captured Free Staters from their paroles. Eddie was the first parolee eligible to return to duty.

"Eddie Bates here to see you, sir," announced Governor Yates' secretary when Eddie arrived, amidst a spattering of rain on the window.

"Come in, Eddie!" Yates started to embrace him, then recoiled at the smell. "What have you been doing at the arsenal?" Yates barely refrained from holding his nose.

"Collecting manure for the gunpowder works," replied Eddie, who in civilian life kept fastidiously clean. "I didn't have time to clean up before coming here."

"What sort of work did you do before the war?"

"My wife and I run a bakery up in Michigan."

"A bakery? Why didn't you say so? I could have put you to better use cooking vittles for our men."

"Sir, white folks don't ask Negroes what they wants. White folks tells us what to do. They don't crack any whips in the Free States, but they order us around just the same."

Yates grimaced. "That's going to stop," he said, as if he'd heard the complaint from other free Negroes. "Our revolution cherishes equality for Blacks. Unfortunately, word hasn't got around to everybody, including me. I should have asked you about your line of work before letting my officers send you to the manure pits. I should have sent a driver over to the arsenal to pick you up. I didn't give you the consideration I would have a white man of your most worthy service."

"It's all right, sir. I know the work is important, or you wouldn't have asked me to do it. I didn't mind working with other Negroes out in the country. At least nobody was shooting at me. I hear the men on the front lines are getting whittled down."

"That's unfortunately true, Eddie. It's why I summoned you. What would you like to do more than anything else?"

"Help win the war, then go home, sir."

"You wouldn't mind getting back in the war as a soldier?"

"I'd be mighty pleased to do that!"

"Your wish is my command," said Yates, holding up papers. "This is your release from parole. We've captured a few Confederates. I offered to exchange them for the release of some of my men. You're first on the list. However, I must advise you that I intend to fight to the last. This parole may very well become your death warrant. You can think it over this evening and accept or decline in the morning."

"I don't need to think, sir. Ever since the slave raiders locked me in that coffin, I've been yearning to fight. Our colonel surrendered our regiment at Bloomington before we fired a shot. Besides, if the Confederates capture me alive, they might send me back into slavery. That Yancey fellow in Alabama has title of ownership to me. They didn't bother me none at Bloomington, but you never know with those people. If I get captured again, it might be by a slaveowner who'll ship me South. I'd rather die than go back to slavery."

"Then fill in your name, rank, and regiment number, date of enlistment, and sign," said Yates, handing him two copies of the release. Eddie completed and signed the copies. Yates handed one ack.

"Keep this with you at all times," Yates warned. "If the Confederates capture you again, this will assure them you're not violating parole. They shoot parole violators, you know. This paper might also keep you out of the slave pen, assuming they don't find out there's a warrant outstanding for your return as a runaway slave. But I don't expect you'll be captured. I intend to hold our positions until we get relief from Schofield's men. We'll hold out 'til it comes, or we'll die fighting."

"I won't be captured," vowed Eddie.

Yates nodded.

"One more thing, if you please," said Eddie. "I've been working with a free Negro named Bellamy. Do you mind if I ask him if he wants to fight with us too?"

"By all means, Sergeant Bates. I'll muster both of you into my headquarters company. We'll fight the Confederates together. If, God forbid, we die together, please remember that I asked you if you were prepared to give your life for the cause."

"I'm mighty glad you did, sir. If more people ask Negroes if we want to fight, more of us *will* fight."

Governor Yates called in his secretary, telling him to procure Eddie a clean uniform from the armory and get him into guest quarters after a hot bath tonight. "Rest well, Eddie," Yates told him. "One serving of your nightmares are over, but there are sure to be others waiting for those who go into battle."

14. "Back in my old stompin' grounds!"

Racine, Wisconsin, November 29, 1862

Back in my old stompin' grounds! thought Jefferson Davis, as he looked out the window from his headquarters in William Hunt's House, owned by one of Racine's few Confederate-loyal Democrats. It was snowing outside, but not heavily. There was perhaps another ten days of campaigning before the heavy winter snows set in. He'd have to stop soon and get his men into winter quarters, making sure the railroads were operating up to the front, the supply roads were corduroyed, and food stockpiled for the weeks of winter.

He reflected upon his first assignments out of West Point, thirty-five years ago. Those were in Wisconsin --- at Fort Crawford and Fort Winnebago, where he was commanded by Zachary Taylor and had fallen in love with Taylor's daughter Knoxie.

Wisconsin's climate had not accommodated weaklings, then or now. During his first month at Fort Winnebago, one of the couriers had left with a message to Fort Crawford on a December morning with temperatures in the 40s. That night a cold wave had blown in, dropping the temperature to 40 below zero. The man had survived by killing his horse, slitting open its belly and crawling inside to be sheltered by the dead animal's lingering body heat. And yet this inhospitable state had gained more white residents in the ten years since 1850 than Davis's home state of Mississippi had gained in its entire existence. Davis thought again of how the lion's share of the nation's future growth would be here in these snowy Northern States, not in the Deep South's steamy lowlands.

This land was part of the Michigan Territory when I first saw it. Not more than a thousand white settlers lived here. Now there are eight thousand in Racine. Another fifty thousand are in Milwaukee, just up the road. Milwaukee would be one of our largest cities if it were in the Slave States. Up here, it is one of many growing Northern cities that will soon become metropolises.

The industry of the people who have come here from many states and foreign nations is there for all to see. The warehouses are full of furs, timber, salted pork, wheat, barley, and hops. The harbor is filled with ships that trade these goods with the growing cities on the Lower Lakes. If we can secure these new states for our Confederate Union, we will nail the board over the Abolitionist Rebels in their rathole.

He sensed he was at the pivot point of the war, whose outcome would be determined by what he did now. He had felt that way once before, at the Battle of Buena Vista, in Mexico, when he had counter-attacked a Mexican force that heavily outnumbered his command, saving his former father-in-law Zachary Taylor's army from defeat. He had known instinctively what to do then, and he sought to discern his correct instinct now.

Should he press on into Wisconsin or turn around and head back to Chicago where an unexpected opportunity was developing? Reports arriving by military courier described a large battle northwest of Chicago. It appeared that McClernand's corps had sortied out of its entrenchments, hoping to ambush the Confederates' northward advance around the city by attacking its flank. Instead, McClernand had poked his snout into Albert Pike's swarming Indian brigades led by the great warrior chiefs Stand Watie and Opothle Yahola, reinforced by John Buford's cavalry division.

McClernand's men were reported to have thrown down their weapons and bolted for Chicago when Watie's and Yahola's painted braves, ravenous to "count coup" after months of indolence, rampaged through their ranks. Buford's cavalry cut off their retreat. A few hundred Yankee Rebels were killed or wounded; the rest captured unharmed. Most were being paroled, but some were adopted into the tribes, either by compulsion, or while consorting under the influence of firewater with the daughters and estranged wives of Indian warriors whose families had accompanied them on the long march north.

At least I won't have to worry about the stinkin' British accusing us of another atrocity and making an excuse to tighten their alliance with the Free State Rebels.

The closest thing to an "atrocity" he had heard about so far was General McClernand, who, it was said, had been captured and betrothed to Stand Watie's daughter "Big Horse" while the great warrior chief covered him with a shotgun.

If the defeat of McClernand's Corps was less sanguinary than expected in Indian battles, it was no less decisive in busting open the back door into Chicago. Jackson's divisions had reached the outskirts of the city in Jefferson and Lakeview townships, while one of Buford's cavalry brigades had reconnoitered into the city center, briefly entering the railroad stations near the river, and sowing panic before rejoining Jackson's main force.

The Free Staters manning the line south of town were rushed north by Ormsby Mitchel to try to halt the Confederates moving into the built-up neighborhoods of the city's northern wards. John Logan, seeing the Free State lines thinning, had pressed home his attack from the Calumet district southwest of Chicago, with a view toward severing the railroads running southeast out of the city along Lake Michigan, then moving his men into the city from the south.

Davis calmed himself, lest the euphoria of unexpected victory unbalance his judgement.

What now? Should I reinforce the attack into Chicago, now that the enemy is breaking; or should I complete the conquest of Wisconsin?

He had reached Racine with Hardee's and Van Dorn's divisions. He could not complete the conquest of Wisconsin without the other divisions of Jackson's command. Should he order Logan to make a close envelopment of the city, but not to fight inside it, while moving Jackson's other divisions northward to join him in Wisconsin? Reinforced by Jackson's divisions, he could take the towns from Milwaukee to Green Bay, and the Fox River Valley towns to the west, completing the campaign's objectives before the onset of deep winter.

He must decide alone. Generals Van Dorn and Hardee were no help. Van Dorn, an amorous character of Don Juan proportions, was off with a woman, rumored to be somebody's wife in "unchaperoned sleigh rides."

He is going to get himself killed by some jealous husband before this war is over.

William Hardee was out surveying the picket line he had set up three miles north of town. Hardee talked military tactics all the time but always made himself scarce when a critical decision had to be made.

Davis opened the door and went outside. This far north, the sun's parabola shortened noticeably every afternoon as it sunk toward the winter's solstice.

The men have been told that Chicago is the objective of this campaign. They are hankering to get into the city and spend the winter in warm, comfortable quarters. They can see the snow in the air. Soon, the nights will be far below freezing. If I continue our advance into Wisconsin, they will blame me for not billeting them in Chicago. Our communications will become extended and vulnerable to disruption Rebel partisans.

Taking Chicago will break the enemy's will more than occupying Wisconsin. We must take advantage of unexpected opportunities. I will order my men to seize Chicago!

15. *"Yet the contest proceeds."*

Cleveland, December 1, 1862

Mr. Lincoln looked ten years older than when Sherman had last seen him, barely more than a month ago. He spoke in a soft tired voice.

"Sometimes you just can't win for losing. If Chicago is lost, Congress will blame me. They will say: 'Lincoln appointed Pope, who nearly lost us the Battle of the Wabash. Then old Lincoln trusted his friend Grant with command of the whole Northwest, and he allowed the Confederates to advance to the gates of Chicago. And now comes Lincoln's friend McClernand who has opened the gates to Chicago, before running off with a Confederate Indian princess.'" Lincoln shook his head. "You know they are liable to wring my neck, Sherman!"

"What nonsense!" replied Sherman. "Everybody knows Governor Yates appointed Pope, Grant, and McClernand to divisional commands. Every officer in Illinois has his position because of Yates, not you."

"True," concurred Lincoln. "But Yates is a hero, who has maintained our foothold in Central Illinois. I'm just an old goat who fouls everybody's barnyard then tells stories that only I think are funny."

Sherman laughed uproariously. "You do look like an old Billy goat who's lost his nanny! But don't forget that you also appointed me to be the General-in-Chief, and I don't think anyone can fault my work in New England and New Jersey, or on the Wabash. You were shrewd in putting Fremont where he helped us the most, and that is no easy place to find for him! He is still writing angry letters accusing me of crossing his front without his permission when I hit McClellan's flank at Camden. But he respects your authority. I don't think anybody else could handle him. Or me. You're doing the job nobody else could do."

"Thank you, Sherman. Just be aware that the Joint Congressional Committee may ask you to replace me as President. I'm skating on thin ice."

Sherman laughed again. "Imagine me doing your job! I've been slandering politicians my entire life. The last thing I'd ever want to do is become one!"

Lincoln smiled. "I sensed that about you. You are not vain and conceited, even though your accomplishments give you every right to be. Since joining us, you have put the success of our cause above all personal ambitions. Grant is like that too. So are Mitchel and Burnside. Even Fremont rode to the sound of the guns, instead of throwing a conniption fit and going home to curse us. So long as our cause is blessed by men such as you, I know we will yet prevail."

"You've been doing your part," Sherman assured him. "Your words after Fremont's victory at Gettysburg have stirred the hearts of liberty-loving men around the world: 'Four score and several years ago,

143

our fathers brought forth, upon this continent, a new nation conceived in Liberty and dedicated to the proposition that all men are created equal.' Those words will live forever. They cannot be conquered by any enemy, and certainly not by the slave-mongering Confederates."

"Well, I suppose making speeches is my small mite of contribution. Perhaps also appointing yourself, Grant, and Fremont to high command. You are right that this is not an easy task, nor is it easy to keep the factions of the Free States from starting a civil war among ourselves."

Lincoln looked out the window. He saw low clouds over Lake Erie in the dim backlit mist of a winter's afternoon. Occasional rays of sunlight appeared momentarily through breaks in the clouds, lighting the falling snow in slanting columns of brilliant white. *There is always a bit of light in every dark situation if you look for it.*

He turned back to face Sherman. "Seward has just returned from meeting with the British in Lower Canada. He is advising me to throw ourselves on their doorstep the way an impecunious mother might abandon her child on the doorstep of a stranger. He thinks we should petition to join the Canadas as a North American Dominion of the British Empire." He shook his head again. "Wouldn't *that* make a fool of me for saying that government of the people, by the people, and for the people will not perish from the face of the earth?"

"You won't have to don the ermine of an earl in the King's government, not just yet" Sherman promised. "I've ordered Burnside to get sixty thousand of his best men moving by rail to Toledo, Fort Wayne, and Columbus. Some will begin passing through here in three or four days. I don't expect McClellan will pull anything in New England. If he does, we've got enough militia troops in the line to hold him. I'll decide how to deploy Burnside's men after I assess the situation in Chicago. I'll use them to relieve the siege if the Confederates haven't taken the city by then."

"I remember we discussed this contingency a few months ago," Lincoln recalled. "I assumed we'd wait until Burnside's men could be armed with Spencers. With the delays in production of the weapon and its ammunition, I figured that would be sometime next spring. I remember you saying you didn't want to send the men in piecemeal. Now it seems the Confederate advance into Wisconsin has forestalled your plan to bring them across the lake and take the Confederates by surprise from the north."

"The Confederates won't be in Wisconsin much longer, will they?" asked Sherman. "Chicago is sucking them in like that whirlpool below Niagara Falls. Let's see if we can whirl them round and around in Chicago until they get dizzy. Then with Burnside's men reinforcing us, we'll scythe them down like Cyrus McCormick scythes wheat! That's what I'm hoping to do, at any rate, if Chicago holds out."

"You're bringing Burnside's men in now, without arming them with Spencers?"

"If we wait until spring to bring them in with Spencers, it will be too late. We'll have to fight now with what we have."

Lincoln looked off into the distance as if discovering a great insight. "You are so right, Sherman. Why didn't I see that? We could have moved the men out here months ago, couldn't we, if we hadn't been so durn set on waiting on them to be armed with those Spencers."

"We became prisoners of our planning," Sherman confessed. "But so were the Confederates. They sat on their tails until Jeff Davis came out here to stir them up. No offense to you, sir, but that's an advantage the Confederates have over us. Their President is also a general."

Lincoln smiled. "You know, there's a rumor making the rounds that Davis and I fought together during Black Hawk's War. The story is that Davis commanded me. A good story, but no truth in it. We've never crossed paths. However, I do remember that Black Hawk's Indians were called 'The British Band.' I suppose that was because of their alliance with the British going back to the 1812 War. We drove the Indians across the Mississippi, and the British back into the Canadas. Now Seward wants me to ask the British to save us from the Confederates. If you live long enough, you see life come back at you like a circle."

"We'll save ourselves," insisted Sherman. "I don't trust the British any more than you do. We've fought two wars to get out from under them, and I don't want to go crawling back to them now. With your permission, I'll leave for Chicago tonight. I'll go to Grand Haven and then by steamer across the lake. Even after the loss of McClernand's corps, we have about fifteen thousand trained soldiers in the city under Hurlbut's and Mitchel's commands, and about that many militiamen who can fight effectively from fortifications. I'll hold the city if I possibly can until Burnside's men arrive."

"Would you mind explaining this to the Joint Congressional Committee?"

"Mr. President, I think it best not to talk too much about what we want to do in Chicago. They'll want me to promise to hold Chicago, come what may. If I fail to give this guarantee they are liable to throw both of us out. If I give the promise and fail to keep it, they will throw us out when we are most needed. Let's make no promises, and we will have freedom of action to do whatever circumstances dictate is necessary. If that includes defending Chicago, we will do it. If we must choose between saving the army and losing Chicago, then we must abandon the city. It is better not to let Congress know anything about this until after the decision is taken."

"I will talk to them by myself, then," agreed Lincoln. "After all, I am the politician! Go now and do what you must to win this war."

Sherman left. Outside, thickening snow squalls blew in off the lake, with wetter, heavier snow covering the city in a solid sheet of white. Lincoln could see steam rising from the warm waters of the lake to the frigid sky where it would shortly freeze and return to the land as snow. Cleveland's knee-deep snows did not melt until April. It snowed even more east of town.

As a young man, he had worked a flatboat down the Mississippi to New Orleans. He thought of the sunshine brightening the Gulf Coast even in the depths of winter. How wonderful the old United States had been as a united country spanning twenty degrees of latitude!

*If the Free States vindicate our independence, we will be confined to the northern latitudes, covered in snow at this season. But at least no inch of our soil will be polluted with slavery. We will fulfill our destiny as the land where all men are free, as our Founders decreed. Providence favored our fathers' cause in the Revolution. Why does Providence seem so reluctant to favor our cause to **preserve** their Revolution?*

He contemplated those thoughts, alone in the house after Sherman left. Mrs. Lincoln and her helpers had gone off shopping for Christmas bunting to decorate the house. His son Robert was at West Point. Tad and Willy were out playing in the snow, probably hiding on one of the flat roofs of the stores and warehouses and pelting passersby with snowballs. John Hay was out with his visiting family. The quietude unnerved him. He decided to write out his thoughts as a ***Meditation on the Divine Will:***

> *The will of God prevails. In great contests each party claims to act in accordance with the will of God. Both may be, and one must be, wrong. God cannot be for and against the same thing at the same time. In the present war between the United Free States of America and the so-called Confederate Union, it is quite possible that God's purpose is something different from the purpose of either party -- and yet the human instrumentalities, working just as they do, are of the best adaptation to effect His purpose. I am almost ready to say that this is probably true -- that God wills this contest, and wills that it shall not end yet. By his mere great power, on the minds of the now contestants, He could have either saved or destroyed the United States of Free America without a human contest. Yet the contest began. And, having begun He could give the final victory to either side any day. Yet the contest proceeds.*

16. "I can't let the Confederates have this city."

Chicago, December 3, 1862

Chicago was going to fall. Sherman could see that as soon as he debarked at the Kinzie Street Pier. Hundreds of panic-stricken shirkers were desperately hoping to board steamers returning to Michigan. They spread exorbitant tales of "massacres" by Confederate Indians as Stoneballs Jackson's vanguard entered the city.

"Twelve companies wiped out, and only one man survived!" shouted a terrified wretch. "They'll scalp you, then burn you alive! It's every man for himself."

Sherman thought about ordering a baker's dozen of these malingerers shot but decided it wasn't worth his time. He had to get to the battle line and restore order, without a second to waste.

Those merchants who had stayed in town to profiteer by selling scarce goods at inflated prices, in violation of the law, were even more pathetic, now having to fear the loss of their lives as well as their money belts. "The Confederates are savages; they'll rape the women and castrate the men!" shouted a balding old man hawking some "medicinal" concoction Sherman surmised consisted primarily of alcohol.

Boats from Michigan, Indiana, and Wisconsin were dropping anchor close to shore to pick up panicked soldiers and townspeople. They were only taking paying passengers. People splashed waist-deep into the chilling waters, waving their money purses over their heads. Sherman saw a burly captain gaff a man like a fish when he tried to climb aboard without paying.

These people are beaten. Let them evacuate across the lake if they can find anyone who will take them. We are better off without them staying here and spreading panic.

Sherman and his guard walked inland to the imposing courthouse a couple blocks south of the river where the Defense Council of Chicago had established its headquarters. The Defense Council was minus a member, since General McClernand had switched sides. Mayor Francis Sherman, a distant cousin, was still on the job, while generals Ormsby Mitchel and Stephen Hurlbut were fighting the Confederate advance through the northern and western wards. A long queue waited to see the mayor. Sherman moved quickly to the head of the line, his bodyguards shoving the queue aside with bayonets.

Mayor Sherman, drenched in cold sweat, rose to greet his distant relative. "Thank God you're here! McClernand got hoodwinked by the Confederates, while Mitchel was away in Michigan, and now we've got a calamity on our hands..."

"I know all about it," said Sherman curtly. Then he mellowed his tone as he realized Chicago might not have been defended at all back in June if not for Mayor Sherman. The mayor was a dyed-in-the-wool

Democrat who nevertheless stood foursquare with the Republican-led Free State Rebels. Because of him, the city's Democrats had mostly stayed loyal to the Free States, denying the Confederates help from inside the city. "Let's see what we can do to salvage it. Where are the police? Aren't they supposed to be maintaining order at the piers? It's a riot down there."

Mayor Sherman shook his head. "A few are still guarding the warehouses and public buildings. Some volunteered to go to the front and fight with the soldiers. The rest deserted when the Confederates reached the city. I guess they figured they'd better save their families. Word is getting around that the Confederates are going to rape, pillage, and burn when they get here. The well-to-do are fleeing by boat. Many others are evacuating to the south. They don't know the Confederates have reached the lake from that direction."

"When responsible men panic, the lesser ones will too," observed Sherman. "What are you doing to maintain order?"

"Mostly trying to calm those 'responsible' people lined up outside before they join the panic. It will be easier with you here."

"I hope so," replied General Sherman. "But I think you need to get out of this office. Walk down to the piers and railway stations. Show confidence. Let people know they should return to their workplaces and keep regular hours until the crisis eases. They will pass the word along that order is being restored, and the panic will subside."

"**Yes, sir!**" said the mayor with enough enthusiasm to satisfy the general. Mayor Sherman walked out the door and calmly addressed the cowed queue. "General Sherman has arrived. You can help him by returning to your homes and places of business and assuring your families, neighbors, and employees that all possible is being done to save

Chicago, and that they need to do their part by working diligently and staying calm."

"Three cheers for General Sherman!" shouted someone in the queue.

"Hurrah … Hurrah! … Hurrah!" came the spirited response. The queue dispersed.

"Good work!' General Sherman told the mayor. "Please go out and take that message to the people. But first, brief me on the situation here. Where are Mitchel and Hurlbut?"

The mayor pointed to the wall map. "Mitchel's last reported headquarters is at Clark and Centre. Hurlbut is holding the Englewood rail junctions south of town. We have a telegraph line to both headquarters."

"Excellent," said General Sherman, "I'll let them know I'm here. I'll meet with both, starting with Mitchel. Is it possible to get there by train?"

"I can have one ready to take you to Englewood this afternoon, but the lines to the north are halted by the Confederates occupying the terminal stations. I have a carriage I'm thinking will do you more good than me, since you have rightly advised me to meet the people on foot. I'm putting my carriage at your disposal."

"Thank you! Do you mind if I take that map with me to plan our defense?" General Sherman ripped down the wall map and folded it.

The mayor's carriage took General Sherman north on Clark Street to the fighting. The two miles of streets were jammed by panicked civilians and wounded and battle-crazed soldiers fleeing the fight.

Sherman's guard moved ahead of the carriage, clearing the path with bayonets. The sounds of rifle and cannon fire reverberated down the streets, booming louder as they neared the front.

They found General Mitchel and his staff engaged in a cacophony of battle about a quarter mile inside the city. There, three blocks in front of him were the Confederates, out in full cry in all their glorious, terrible power! It was as if a caged tiger was suddenly turned loose to hunt. These were Stoneballs Jackson's all-arms divisions of infantry, mounted infantry, true cavalry, and artillery --- each division capable of independent combat that would have required a corps in the pre-war army.

The division on Sherman's left was Roberdeau Wheat's Louisiana Tigers, whose street-brawling New Orleans riffraff terrorized even the Confederate Union's towns they transited. On his immediate front was Albert Pike's Division, consisting of rough-hewn Arkansas mountain men brigaded with Confederate Indians led by the great warrior chiefs Stand Watie and Opothle Yahola. Wagons drawn by Negro teamsters were bringing up ammunition close behind the advancing line. The battle flags of many units, in many variants of the Confederate Union Flag, were flying high and proud.

Sherman felt the hairs on the back of his neck rise, as the "Eeeeeeeee-ooooooooooo yaaaaaaaaaaaaaaaaaaaah!" of the Confederate Yell echoed down the blocks, loud enough to be heard over the rifle and cannon fire. He could sense in the battle cry a spirit rising from the mountains and backwoods forests of Arkansas, the wild prairies of the New Indiana Territory, and the back streets of New Orleans. These were men who loved to fight, who didn't stop until they knocked their enemies flat.

A Confederate battery pulled out ahead of the infantry and unlimbered. It arrived preloaded, with triple-canister. In the next instant the blast wave arrived, concurrent with hails of canister that scythed the Free Staters down … *like wheat going down before McCormick's threshing machines*, thought Sherman, remembering what he'd told Lincoln he'd do to the Confederates.

Confederate infantry surged forward. A flying rod ricocheted off the building over Sherman's head and zoomed in front of him. *That looked like an arrow!* Confederate Indians scampered across the roof tops like cats, ahead of the infantry, letting arrows fly. Another hit the bricks over Sherman's head so hard the arrowhead caromed off.

Mitchel maintained his composure. "Look at this," he said calmly, while pointing ahead, then handing Sherman his spyglass. Sherman saw it. Two Confederate officers on horseback riding toward the sound of the guns. It looked like Stoneballs Jackson and Jefferson Davis! *That's what lit the fire under the Confederates. Coordinated command from top to bottom, where it matters!*

Sherman knew what an energetic commander like Davis would do next, which was what Sherman would do if he commanded the Confederates. Davis would press the attack. Once he was certain of success, he would order Buford's cavalry to attack down the east bank of the Des Plaines River, rolling up what was left of the Free State line west of the city. Then he would order his reserve divisions around Blue Island to join Buford's cavalry in a converging attack into the city from the Southwest along the Illinois and Michigan Canal, while Logan's divisions attacked up the South Shore from Indiana. Any Free State men remaining in Chicago were going to be bagged tighter than roosters in a jute bag.

As the smoke from the artillery volley cleared, Sherman saw Confederate cannons leapfrog forward a block, unlimber, and fire again. This time percussion shells and solid shot plowed the buildings and caromed down the streets. The leg of a soldier reloading in front and to the left of him disintegrated in a spray of flesh, blood, and bone fragments as a bounding cannonball tore it off. The air overhead fogged with brick dust sprayed by detonating percussion shells blowing out the upper floors of buildings. Several more men went down as delayed shock and blood loss overtook them.

"They're eating us up," he said to Mitchel. "We've got to get our men out of the streets and organized behind a defensible line."

He motioned for Mitchel to follow him back to the carriage two blocks to the rear. Another salvo of solid shot and percussion shells slammed into the streets and buildings they had vacated. He studied the map from the mayor's office.

"Let's rally the men a mile behind us at Division Street and bend the line south at Ashland Avenue." He traced the line with his fingers. "We'll fall back south and east of the Chicago River if we have to, but I want the army moving together as a unit. Retreat when you must, but keep your men organized and firing back at the enemy. I'll round up every man I can find and get them to work preparing the Division and Ashland lines."

He thought about riding out to see Hurlbut at the Englewood crossings on the other side of the city but thought better of it. He could not be everywhere at once. Better to help Mitchel stabilize the line north and west of the city. He would telegraph Hurlbut from the mayor's office this evening and tell him to pull his men back from the Des Plaines River and form them in a horseshoe around Englewood, with the flanks anchored on Lake Michigan.

He didn't think the militiamen who remained to defend the city after the loss of McClernand's corps could hold out for more than a couple of days against these veteran Confederates. He would march them south to join Hurlbut's men, then evacuate them by ship or by breaking through Confederate lines south of the city and marching overland to Indiana and Michigan. Getting the men out of the city would at least deny the Confederates a claim to total victory. Burnside's men would begin arriving in Toledo and Fort Wayne within a week. Could they be organized into a force strong enough to fight their way back into the city if they combined forces with his men leaving it?

Burnside's men won't be able to get the Confederates out of Chicago, even if my men join them. Those are the Confederates' best divisions. Once they occupy the fortifications we built around the city, they'll be impossible to dislodge. They knew better than to attack us in those positions until McClernand left a gap in our lines.

Jubal Early's corps has reopened their communications through the Ohio Valley. They can now bring their men out here from the East as fast as we can. The Confederates will use them to thwart my relief of Chicago. **I can't let the Confederates have this city. I must destroy them here! How can I do that?**

A devilish scheme began to form in his mind.

Perhaps by lighting the biggest bonfire since the British burned Washington!

17. Seeing the Elephant

Sangamon County, Illinois, December 5, 1862

Sergeant Eddie Bates and his platoon of colored volunteers piled out of the wagon. The wagon driver wasted no time making his turn and setting his horses on the road back to Springfield at a trot. Ahead lay a dead horse sliced nearly in half by Confederate solid shot. Its torso and upturned head lay twisted at a right angle to its hindquarters, connected only by the backbone and a thin string of hide. Eddie was sickened at the sight of the cavity torn open with the insides hanging out, but with no blood pool around it. Eddie had heard from hunters that deer shot in the heart did not bleed, since the pumping stopped at once. This horse must have died before it knew what hit it.

Boom! .... Boom! ... Boom! ... Boom!

Solid shot from a Confederate battery firing at a distance Eddie estimated to be three-quarters of a mile, screamed in and impacted about 150 yards ahead of him, just in front of the tracks of the Springfield /

Decatur railroad anchoring the last of the Free Staters' defensive lines. Great clods of frozen earth, mixed with pieces of men and their rifles, soared into the sky. The stupendous noise of the cannons pointed in his direction, and the impact of their shots, shook him like a nearby lightning strike. He could feel the air pressure change as the blast waves passed, while the shaking ground vibrated through his feet.

To his astonishment, he was unafraid. He recalled his nightmare back home in Michigan before he enlisted. In that vivid dream he was too paralyzed with fear to parry a Confederate soldier charging him with a bayonet. He woke up screaming and drenched in sweat just before the bayonet reached his belly. Had the dream been nature's way of acquainting him with the terror of combat, so when the time came to fight, he would not be paralyzed?

Before that, he'd experienced the living terror of being kidnapped and locked in a coffin for four days during the slave raid into Michigan that started this war. He had vowed vengeance upon the Confederates ever since. His capture and parole at Bloomington sidelined him to the backwater of "shoveling shit" for Governor Yates' makeshift gunpowder factory. Now his moment had come. He knew he would stand firm on the battleline until killed or too severely wounded to fight.

His mind narrowed its focus to thinking only of each moment. First the future had faded from his thoughts, then the past. He became a creature of the momentous now. The prospect of death obliterating his future no longer paralyzed him with fear. If it happened, it happened, and there was nothing to be done about it. He would live or die on the battleline, but he would not run.

He surveyed his surroundings on this hazy early winter's day. The smoke from the Confederate cannonade hung in the still air. These guns were fired by Alexander Porter's meticulously trained men. The blast from another volley shook the air. Three seconds later, he heard the ear-cracking booms of fused airbursts, spaced almost on top of each other in front of and above the Free State line where the solid shot impacted. The curiously melodious Whizzzzzzz-ZANG-yaaaaaaaaaaang of flying shrapnel reached his ears, as he saw the effect of shell fragments clipping branches off trees and slinging mud when they hit the ground.

He didn't need to be a general to know the Confederates were concentrating their attack on this point, to sever the railroad between Springfield and Decatur, isolating each town. If they were nimble, they would roll up the entire Free State line and march right into the towns unopposed. The state capital at Springfield, the important town of Decatur, and the breakwater slowing their drive on Chicago would be lost. It might be enough to tip the scales decisively toward Confederate victory. Eddie shuddered at the prospect of losing his country and being returned to slavery, as he had not shuddered at the prospect of merely losing his life.

"Over there, boys," shouted a waving lieutenant who sized up Eddie's platoon. The lieutenant pointed to a copse of trees battered by artillery fire about a hundred yards down the line. Another officer standing next to a flagbearer waved them over.

Here again, Eddy didn't need to be a general to know this was the likely point of attack. He could see the furrows plowed by solid shot, some partially covered by tree limbs severed by airbursts. He saw casualties as he and the men trotted to their assigned positions. One soldier lay dead with his legs blown off above the knee, the blood still oozing. The man looked like he'd been running full stride when struck down. He saw other men down and not moving, out of the corner of his eye, as he kept his focus directly ahead.

BANG! BANG! BANG! BANG! Whizzzzzzzzzzzz-ZEBANG-baaaaaaaaYannng!

Four more airbursts over the position he and his men were nearing! The flag-bearer went down with a spurting hole directly over his heart and never moved another muscle. The lieutenant next to him was covered in a spray of blood. His legs gave out, and he fell to his knees, shocked from the overhead concussion and spraying blood. He quickly recovered, picked up the blood-soaked flag, got back on his feet, and held it aloft with one hand. "Who'll carry this flag?" he shouted at the top of his lungs, loud enough to make himself heard in Eddie's ringing eardrums. Three men rose at once and took it from his grasp. They waved it defiantly toward the Confederates together, until the strongest man looked the other two in the eye, and they let him grasp it gently with both his hands. The other two men put their hands on his shoulders. All three yelled "Hurrraahhh!"

A tremendous "Huuurrrrrrrrraaaaahhhh!" resounded from all the men who heard it.

Tears welled in Eddie's eyes. This was what military men meant by *spirit de corps*. It was what kept scared men fighting and holding their ground or advancing into the enemy's fire when their comrades were dropping around them. He was willing, and perhaps even eager, to die in combat, if it would help his new comrades defeat the Confederates and save his new country.

"Quite a ruckus you joined!" said the blood-soaked lieutenant with a calm composure that comforted Eddie. "As you can see, our men are sound. What's your unit?"

"Sergeant Eddie Bates' platoon, sir! We're unattached. We worked for Governor Yates' armory. Yesterday we volunteered to fight."

"Glad you did!" said the officer. "This is where we need you, reinforcing the Illinois Free State Militia. Have your men 'seen the elephant?' "

"No, sir!"

The officer nodded. "I didn't think so. Don't worry. There's a first time for everybody." He addressed Eddie's men. "Load your weapons, then fix bayonets. Stay calm and wait 'til they come up real close --- so close you can't miss. You may only get to fire one volley, so make every shot count. If they keep advancing, stand firm with your legs wide and your bayonets thrust forward and wait for them." The lieutenant showed them by example. "Remember to stay calm and keep thrusting your bayonet at them. Stand your ground. Do not move backward, not an inch. Yell at the top of your lungs. That'll frighten them because they'll know you're not going to break and run for the rear. They will fear you, and they will break, if you stand firm. Do you understand?"

"Yes, sir!" Eddie and his men shouted in unison.

"Remember what you're fighting for," said the officer, "which for you colored men, is for your freedom, as well as for your country."

"*Yes, sir!*" the men shouted louder. The officer moved back to his position next to the new flagbearer, and ordered him to take a knee, as the officer did, to make themselves smaller targets for flying shrapnel.

"Load your rifles and fix your bayonets," commanded Eddie. "Remember what the lieutenant said. Wait 'til they get so close you can't miss. Then fire one volley on my command right into their bellies. Then jab them if they come close."

Eddie and his corporal Gabriel Bellamy were armed with Enfield military rifles. The ten other Negroes were armed with older smoothbore flintlocks Yates' armory had modified to accept percussion caps. They looked ancient compared to Enfields but were loaded with "buck and ball" to deliver lethal volleys, and bayonets if the fighting became hand-to-hand.

When the men had loaded their rifles, Eddie followed the officer's lead and told his men to sit down. No use making themselves conspicuous targets until the time came. Flecks from a towering spray of mud sent flying by a cannonball impacted Eddie's uniform with a thud. His heart skipped a beat as he realized it was all mud, not shards of hot lead. He showed no fear as he looked at his men. He saw some nervous ones settle down when they observed his calm demeanor.

The Free Staters did not return the Confederate artillery fire. Eddie had seen plenty of cannons at the State Arsenal, but they lacked ammunition, their shells disassembled to provide gunpowder and percussion caps for the infantry's rifles. He suddenly became very thirsty. He noticed his leg had started to tremble and he was sweating. He remembered he must stay calm to keep his men calm.

He got up and pointed toward the Confederates. "Ain't it nice of those Confeds to provide us with such a show! Maybe they'll send us some dancing girls too." His men roared with laughter loud enough to hear over the booming cannon and explosions of air-bursting shells. Their laughter calmed Eddie, as his quip had calmed them. They were ready to fight.

More airbursts boomed overhead. One of Eddie's men, who Eddie had taken a liking too, had stretched out prone on the cold ground, resting his head on top of his arms, as if in a peaceful sleep. The man suddenly convulsed as a heavy piece of shell hit him square in the back flat-on from above. He did not bleed, but his heart and lungs must have been crushed inside his body. His body shook and twitched as his life went out of him. "Holy shit," muttered one of the men. The rest kept their silence as they watched the man expire. Like Eddie, they had never seen a man they knew killed beside them.

The cannons stopped firing. Confederates began advancing in rushes of men spaced about five yards apart toward their lines. Officers on horseback rode in front with raised swords at 100-yard intervals. At about two hundred yards the officers on horseback moved back behind the lines, and the infantry halted and opened fire. Another group rushed fifty yards in front of them and did the same. Then the rank behind, having reloaded, rushed forward.

"Fire at will, when you see a target," yelled the lieutenant. "Aim for their knees!"

Eddie's men stood up and aimed their rifles. Clouds of smoke obscured Eddie's view. He jammed his gun as hard as he could into his shoulder and waited for a break in the smoke. He fired at the legs of a Confederate scurrying through a gap in the fog. The rifle jerked up as he pulled the trigger, sending the shot about level with the man's midsection, as intended. Bellamy fired beside him too. Eddie couldn't tell if they hit anybody, but the act of firing calmed him. He managed to tear a cartridge with his teeth, reload, and get the percussion cap set to fire again. His fingers didn't tremble.

The Confederates appeared through the smoke! At about 50 yards they fired a volley that took down some of Eddie's men in the act of reloading. The next line of Confederates came running forward with bayonets pointed at them, just as Eddie had imagined in his dream. "Wait up," said Eddie to the men who had reloaded. "Let them get real close."

"Fire away!" he shouted when the Confederates came within thirty yards. Eddie held his fire while Bellamy next to him added his blast to the booming of the flintlocks, whose barrels kicked high from the recoil of the heavy load of buck and ball. This time Eddie saw Confederates drop. Those who didn't stopped, aimed carefully as veterans knew to do, and fired. This time half of Eddie's men, including Bellamy beside him, went down.

The Confederates charged with fixed bayonets, one aimed for Eddie's gut! At the same time, Eddie saw a man covered in a black coat and black boots come charging forward on horseback, sword drawn high above his head. *What a brave man! Whoever he is, he's their leader. I've got to shoot him first.* He aimed his rifle at the man's midsection and calmly squeezed the trigger. Eddie saw the man's face contort with pain as he fell from his horse.

Eddie turned to thrust his bayonet toward the Confederate charging him. He widened his stance, lowered his shoulders, and shouted with all his might, prepared to stand or die. The riderless horse cut in front of the charging Confederate, breaking his stride. Eddie prepared to charge forward before the man could recover his footing. He never saw the other Confederate, who had broken through the line from the left, turn around and shoot him in the back.

18. "Are you ready for the inquisition?"

Cleveland, December 5, 1862

The first wave of refugees from Chicago transited across the lake to Grand Haven, New Buffalo, and Michigan City. Those who could afford to go further headed east by rail. It took them 48 hours to reach Cleveland, and considerably less than 48 minutes to get from the Cleveland terminal to the Weddell House where the Free State Provisional Congress met. Within four hours of their arrival, the Joint Executive Committee of the Provisional Congress of the United States of Free America had convened an emergency session requesting Mr. Lincoln's presence in their chambers. They sent Speaker of the House John Sherman and Senator Lyman Trumbull of Illinois to summon the president.

Sherman and Trumbull were Lincoln's friends, while the rest were adversarial, especially when the progress of the war was less than satisfactory, as it had certainly been since the Confederates had reached the vicinity of Chicago. The Executive Committee might have replaced

Lincoln months ago, as they had replaced Fremont before him, had not Mary Lincoln charmed Senator Sumner of Massachusetts, thereby breaking the solid ranks of Radical Republicans skeptical of her husband's administration.

Lincoln's secretary John Hay opened the door when Sherman and Trumbull knocked and entered together. "Are you ready for the inquisition?" quipped Trumbull with a terse smile as he greeted his friend.

"I'm afraid I don't have much to tell them that they haven't already heard," answered Lincoln. "The Battle for Chicago is in progress, and we're getting the worst of it, so far. But Burnside's men are starting to arrive from the East. I am certain Sherman will put them to good use as he did at Camden."

"That's all the committee will want to know," suggested Speaker Sherman. "Give them some hope that Chicago will hold out. Or that at worst, its possession by the Confederates will be precarious and short-lived."

"Should we discuss the British offer to guarantee our independence if we join them as a Dominion?" asked Secretary of State Seward. "If we accept their offer, I have no doubt that we will soon remake them into our image as a republic. With their navy and our land, we will rule the world together, and keep the Confederates, and all other troublesome countries, in their place."

Lincoln hesitated a moment before replying. He did not want to rebuke Seward, who had negotiated all reasonable aid from Britain short of their joining the Free States in war. However, Seward seemed much too enthusiastic about wanting to rejoin the British Empire.

*He is like Stephen Douglas, of all people, in wanting to make us into an empire of vast extent. Douglas had a view towards making us an empire by conquering the American continents. Seward wants us to join the British world Empire It is well that those two never got together. Douglas was bad enough, without getting any encouragement from **our** people!*

"Let's not discuss it now," he advised Seward. "If the Confederates learn that we are even talking about joining the British Empire, it will incite them to fury, while inciting some of our people to question our cause. Let us fight our own battles. If we can't win our independence by our own efforts, we don't deserve having it."

He looked out the window a few seconds to gather his thoughts, then looked to the door and motioned the others to follow. "Well, let's get on with it." He asked his manservant, a free Negro hired by the Free State Government, to summon a carriage to pass them through the blustery weather. They ended up filling two. Mr. Lincoln's tall frame was bent so far forward that the space opposite him was unoccupied. Though uncomfortable, he was grateful for the carriage. The snow was wet and mushy on the streets and boardwalks.

Lincoln and his party entered the Weddell House. These grand hotels brought a touch of melancholy to his mind, for their opulence contrasted with the fading world of his youth. He was born into a wild world of Kentucky forests, hills, and springs, and log cabins of his parents' and uncle's homes. Indians, bears, and mountain lions were recent memories. Spanish coins, which could be subdivided into "bits," were his first earnings. He had matured into a larger world in Illinois where farms spread over the prairies. As a lawyer, he'd ridden on horseback to follow the circuit court judges travelling the little county seat towns. He'd shared beds with other country lawyers in tiny rooms upstairs after regaling them with stories around the fireplaces of the little country inns, to the delight of all. He'd slept deeply, in the fullest joy of a small but meaningful life.

He'd only recently risen to prominence that took him to the great cities rising in the East, the Ohio Valley, and around the Great Lakes. They still overwhelmed him with their enormous populations and wealth. Cleveland, with its 80,000 people, and recently swelled by new arrivals of Free State loyalists fleeing the Confederate-occupied territories, was on its way to joining the growing ranks of Free State metropolises.

This is what the Confederates fear. They see the importance of their land, slaves, and cotton fading in a world of immense cities powered by machinery and steam. The industrial wealth of our free cities far surpasses the wealth of slave states. The Confederates know they won't be able to keep their slaves ignorant and oppressed in a world of communication by telegraph, and travel by train. They were afraid to remain with us in the Union, and they are afraid to let us go, lest our power continue to increase, and our example of freedom be communicated to their slaves.

If only we could have maintained our unity! The Irish immigrants stayed loyal to the Confederate Union in New York City, and the Douglas Democrats stayed loyal to them in the countryside of Illinois, Indiana, and Ohio. New Jersey is indifferent to either side and wants only to establish itself as a separate Republic. We are fighting the Confederates with only half our true strength. If we lose Chicago, more of our people will lose faith in our cause, and confidence in our ability to vindicate it. We will lose the war.

He passed the registration counter, invoking happier memories of when he'd arrived for the first time in November of 1860 as part of the First Free State Convention, called in response to the election of the Confederate Union ticket of Stephen Douglas and Jefferson Davis. He had urged the delegates to give President Douglas a fair hearing, and to faithfully maintain their constitutional obligations, including the odious duty of returning runaway slaves.

However, events had moved quickly toward confrontation. Upon taking office, President Douglas had declared the looming occupation of Mexico by France to be a violation of the Monroe Doctrine, requiring U.S. preemption. It soon became clear that rather than protecting Mexico from the French, Douglas and Davis intended to annex it to the United States as slave states.

What would have happened if fate had allowed Douglas and Davis to carry out that scheme? I do believe they would have enticed some of our best Northern men, like Seward, into going along with them. "Let the Southerners have Mexico, and we'll get you northern men the Canadas!" We would have become a slave empire that put the Romans to shame!

That Douglas scheme was disrupted by the Confederates' own extremists before it could be put into operation. Militant Southern "Fire Eaters" had launched their free-lance raid into Michigan to recover runaway slaves, including Eddie Bates. Free State resistance stopped it. The Partisan War, followed by the War of Northern Secession, was on. The French had gone on into Mexico while Americans fought each other.

Fate works in strange ways, thought Lincoln. *The evil schemes of men have a lot more to do with its absurdities than Divine Providence! A merciful God must spend much of His time shuddering over our wicked provocations against each other.*

They entered the grand ballroom, now the chamber for the Free State Congress when it was in session, and convened in an anteroom. Two soldiers assigned to protect Congress stood watch outside.

Lincoln's party greeted Congressman Thad Stevens of Pennsylvania, Congressman Charles Adams, Sr. of Massachusetts; and Senators Ben Wade of Ohio, Zachariah Chandler of Michigan, and Charles Sumner of Massachusetts. Lincoln was unpleasantly surprised to see Secretary of the Treasury Salmon Chase, one of the few men he cordially despised "as not being happy until he can make everyone around him as thoroughly miserable as he is."

In June, when the Confederates approached Chicago, Chase tried to instigate the Executive Committee into removing Lincoln from office and replacing him with Chase. Lincoln defeated the plot by telling the story of the Chess Automaton, making his point that there "was a man in there," and not a machine, who moved the pieces. He made clear he was the "man" they had chosen to command the war, and he would not share commander-in-chief authority with Chase or anyone else. The Executive Committee was shocked into backing down. Would they do so again?

The men sat down around the conference table. Lincoln asked Secretary of War Curtin to give the committee an account of the battles around Chicago. Curtin spoke tersely: Sherman was pulling his men back south and east of the Chicago River. A fierce battle was in progress around the Chicago & Milwaukee Railroad terminal northwest of the junction of the river's three branches. To the southwest, Confederates were astride the Illinois and Michigan Canal, attacking from Blue Island

172

toward the city in corps strength. To the south, Logan's corps was widening its window on Lake Michigan. Reports smuggled in from Free State citizens in Central Illinois indicated the Confederates had renewed their attack against Yates' and Barrie's men between Springfield and Decatur.

Curtin explained that Sherman was bringing Burnside's men in from New England. The first units should begin passing through Cleveland within the next two days. However, the Confederates were also feeding fresh divisions into Northwest Indiana. Pemberton's corps had arrived in the line. Cavalry battalions from Early's Corps were being expedited through southern Indiana to reinforce them. There would be no Free State relief of besieged Chicago.

"I expect Sherman to hold Chicago as long as possible, then evacuate the army by land or across the lake," Curtin explained. "Then he will combine his army with Burnside's and attempt to repeat his victories at The Wabash and Camden."

"We could have moved Burnsides' men out here months ago," thundered Thad Stevens. "We didn't have to wait for them to be armed with Spencers. They fought well enough in New England with what they had."

"We didn't know McClernand was going to freelance on his own and leave the backdoor to Chicago open," replied Curtin.

"Same thing happened with Pope last year at the Battle of the Wabash," added Trumbull. "He advanced without orders and lost his division. If the weather hadn't stopped the Confederates, we might have lost the war then and there."

Thad Stevens grunted. "War is so damn complicated. Seems there are no surefire rules for winning one, other than to keep fighting, learn from mistakes, and keep improving." He looked at Lincoln. "Maybe we need to make a change at the top. I'm not faulting Mr. Lincoln for doing any less than any of us might have done in his position --- and that includes you, Chase. But sometimes a change at the top changes one's luck all down the line. That's all."

"Let me make it easy for you," said Lincoln. He pulled out a note from his pocket. "I wrote this, this morning." He handed it to Thad Stevens who read it aloud:

> *This morning, as for some days past, it seems exceedingly probable that this administration will not be sustained by the confidence of the Provisional Congress. Then it will be my duty to serve the Free State cause in whatever capacity I may, including fighting in the field as an officer, as Fremont so gallantly chose to do, or bearing arms as a private. I ask the Executive Committee of the Congress of the Republic of Free America to assign me where they think I may make the greatest contributions to our cause, and I will serve with all my heart, mind, and strength, in hopes that my example will inspire others to do likewise.*

He expected Salmon Chase to celebrate, as he was considered the most likely candidate to replace him. He had not spoken much with Chase since he'd defused Chase's plot to remove him last June. So far as he knew, Chase still yearned to govern as a dictator. He talked about conscripting all men within his reach, and exiling those who refused, while confiscating their property to impoverish their families. Lincoln looked at Chase with a "Now you can remove me honorably, without having to put a knife in my back," expression.

Chase took Lincoln's note from Stevens' hand and read it carefully. He looked at Lincoln, then looked back at the note. Then he tore it to pieces and threw them on the floor.

"No, Mr. President, it will not be me who casts the first vote to oust you from your office. Our difficulties at Chicago are no fault of yours. I did not believe the city would hold when the Confederates reached its vicinity in June. I thought the city, and our cause, would be lost. But the city has held for six months. I do not see how it could have held if you did not command the trust of our loyal Free State men and women. Those neutral Democrats who remain inside our lines also trust you. They advance our cause even in neutrality by refraining from stirring up trouble in our rear. I cannot honestly claim that I, or anyone else, could improve upon our people's trust in your administration. Now get back to your executive mansion and command our generals to win this war!"

The other men, including the stern ones like Thad Stevens, pounded the table and cheered.

"Is there anybody who wants Mr. Lincoln removed?" asked Speaker Sherman. There were no takers. He turned to Lincoln. "It looks like you've vindicated our confidence in you once again. Thank you for sharing your intentions to work constructively with us, whether we removed you or not."

"You should be thanking *me* for telling him to return to the Executive Mansion," insisted Chase. "Before he tested our patience with another one of his long-winded stories. I don't think I could have stood another one."

The men laughed uproariously.

"It's too bad you had to go and destroy Mr. Lincoln's note," added Thad Stevens with a hint of genuine regret. "It would have made a hell of a keepsake to cherish after we win this war!"

Chase, whose thoughts never veered far from money, frowned. He decided to stay after the others left, so he could pick up the pieces and carefully piece them back together. If Lincoln led them through a successful war, Chase calculated his note could be sold for at least a thousand dollars.

19. Sherman's Cigars

Chicago, December 6, 1862

They called it "Greek Fire" --- a mixture of pine tar, sulfur, potassium nitrate, and whale oil or mineral petroleum derivative, put in a container or pasted on a stick of wood. Since antiquity it had been used to incinerate enemy ships at sea. Sherman figured it would work just as well against a jumble of wooden buildings densely packed into the burgeoning and crudely constructed new city called Chicago, most of it now flaunting the Confederate Union Flag.

He studied the concoction at West Point, making a batch in his chemistry class. After a few hours' experimentation with different proportions of sulfur, potassium nitrate, and oil, it flared magnificently when he dropped a glowing cigar ash on it. Its effectiveness was improved by the addition of gunpowder, containing premixed portions of sulfur and potassium nitrate.

Sherman saw enough raw material at the naval warehouses lining the Illinois Central piers to make plenty of it. They bulged with pine tar, rope, whale oil and the recently developed petroleum derivative called kerosene, along with sailcloth, lumber, and gunpowder, a pyromaniac's dream. Ormsby Mitchel suggested burning it in place, to keep the Confederates from getting hold of it. Sherman had another idea: spread it around Chicago and set it alight while the Confederates were in town.

The booming noise of cannon and small arms, and the pungent aroma of gunpowder, told him they weren't far away. Pike's and Wheat's divisions were full-up on his Division Street line about a mile north. Rooftop spotters on Ashland Avenue could see the divisions of Hardee, Van Dorn, and Buford's cavalry forming up for an assault from the west. Forest and Logan were attacking into the south end of town between the I&M Canal and the Calumet Lakes. The roar of battle came on the howling wind, carrying swirls of snow stinging Sherman's face no matter which way he turned.

Damn it's cold. And winter's only just getting started.

Sherman had experienced enough northern winters to know the snow would taper off in a few days, and a period of sunny skies and freeze-dried air would follow. The wood in the buildings, a lot of them crudely whitewashed or not painted at all, would puff up in the dry air and flame like tinder when ignited. In peacetime, Chicago's fire watchmen kept a tight lid on fires in the city, but with the battle raging, they were no longer on duty. If a fire or two got started outdoors, and a tad of wind stirred the air, the embers would jump from building to building and burn down the city before you could say "Jack Robinson."

I'm surprised this city hasn't burned down already, the way Charleston did last year. All it takes is one stove left unattended, or a cow kicking over a lantern in a barn. If the city burns while the Confederates are occupying it, they'll get the blame. Who will ever know how it started, when soldiers ignite field stoves and makeshift fires everywhere, then start drinking and cavorting?

He looked around, pleased to see that he and the mayor had restored order, at least for now. He had finally ordered a dozen out-of-control soldiers and civilians shot, intimidating the rest. Civilians were evacuating calmly at Kinzie Street, while he had corralled a half-dozen ships at the Illinois Central piers south of the river to await further orders, the captains commanded at gunpoint to keep their ships tied to piers, rather than loading paying passengers and bolting for the Michigan ports.

He motioned for his guard to follow him back to Mayor Sherman's office in the courthouse six blocks away. Order was restored there as well. A modest queue of people waited patiently to see the mayor. Sherman and his guard entered the building, which seemed overheated after coming in from the wind-chilled cold outside. Sherman opened the buttons on his uniform to dry the sweat soaking his undershirt as he by-passed the queue and trotted up the four flights of stairs to see the mayor, his guard huffing to keep up. The mayor's secretary cleared his office and anteroom to ensure privacy, then ushered Sherman in to talk to his distant cousin.

Mayor Sherman greeted General Sherman. "How goes the battle, sir?"

"As satisfactory as circumstances will permit," answered General Sherman. "We lost a brigade of Hurlbut's men when Buford's cavalry cut them off during their retreat from the Des Plaines line; the rest anchored a new line on the lake. I've decided to concentrate our forces here for evacuation out of the city. Hurlbut's men will be arriving this evening. I'll use them to ease the pressure on our northwest by attacking the Confederates trying to cut off the corner of our line at Division and Ashland. If we can rock them back there, we'll get some breathing space for an orderly evacuation."

Mayor Sherman frowned. "Is that the best we can do? Burnside has kept the Confederates out of Providence for over a year. Yates has kept them out of Springfield since May. We still hold the hills north of Cincinnati. Can't we do at least as well here? The honor of Chicago demands it. I don't care if we leave this city in ruins like St. Louis and Cincinnati, but we must fight."

Sherman took off his cap and wiped his sweaty hair. "Well, I confess I didn't think Burnside could hold Providence. He has held it and kept his rifle factories running. He has supplied my men in the Connecticut Valley with arms and ammunition when we sorely needed it. We didn't think Yates would last more than a few days at Springfield, but he's fought magnificently with scant resources, and tied down two Confederate corps. That saved Chicago from capture in June."

"Then why can't we defend Chicago, at least this part of it?" implored the mayor. "Burnside's men are coming to help us --- the same men who saved Providence. Can't we hold out 'til they get here?"

"Mayor, just holding on to Chicago, the way we're holding onto Providence, Philadelphia, the north end of Cincinnati, and Springfield, won't win us the war. Even if we hold our present positions, the

Confederates will continue moving up into Wisconsin. They'll cut us off from the West, then whittle down Grant's army in Iowa. If we lose the West, our people will lose heart and abandon the war. We might as well surrender and ask to be readmitted to the Confederacy at once."

"I don't want that!' exclaimed Mayor Sherman.

"Nor do I." General Sherman chose his words carefully. He wanted to give the mayor an approximate idea of his plan, without letting him know the part about burning the city. "To win this war, we must annihilate every Confederate who has set foot in this city. Inflict a defeat that will shock them to their marrow and knock some sense into them. I'd planned to do that in February, when their men are most fatigued by cold and illness. I planned to trap them in their Des Plaines River positions by coming down on top of them with Burnside's men from Wisconsin."

General Sherman glanced at a map of Northern Illinois on the Mayor's wall. "Now we'll have to trap them inside the city. I'm going to evacuate my men by ship, then encircle the Confederates from the north and west while Burnside's men attack them from the south. It may even work better this way. They'll be so busy celebrating their capture of Chicago, they won't notice the danger. At least I hope they won't."

"Then let my men be the anvil you hammer them on!" exclaimed the mayor. "Look at this courthouse. It's a fortress. We can put three hundred men in here and hold it for a month. Why not, if half as many Texans held that rickety Alamo for two weeks? We've got the men who know how to bleed the Confederates if we concentrate them in this quarter of the city."

"An astute observation," admitted Sherman. "Concentration of forces. One of the first things we learned at West Point."

The mayor looked pleased with himself. "Our honor demands it. We must defend Chicago here, or die in place, like Custer's men died on Blue Island. Chicago must never be known as the city that surrendered without fighting to the utmost. That would darken this city's reputation for all time to come."

"All right, then," said Sherman. "You've convinced me. I'll do the same deal with you I did with Burnside, and Scofield did with Governor Yates in Springfield. If you're convinced your militia will fight to hold this part of the city, I'll keep my men here and fight beside you. That will keep the Confederates occupied while we wait for Burnside's men to get here. If we hold the city until then, you'll be a hero."

"I don't want to be a hero. I just want to save my city."

Sherman nodded. "Burnside said the same in Providence. He proved as good as his word. Now here is what you must do: Have your militia evacuate every civilian in the northern and western Districts. Every last one of them. Get them into this part of town and we'll get them out of here if it takes every ship on Lake Michigan. I want complete freedom to fight my way back into the rest of this city when the time comes without worrying about who I have to kill. Don't leave a single person in that part of the city. Understand?"

"Some will be stubborn and refuse to go. Not all are entirely loyal to our cause."

"Let them stay if they insist on it. It's their lives. If your men see any children left in this city, remove them by force. If anybody gives you any trouble, shoot them."

"Yes, sir. I just hope the Confederates are careful with their fires when they occupy the vacated parts of the city. I would like to see this city retaken with as little damage as possible when you come back."

Sherman nodded.

The Confederates are going to be the least of your worries. They're amateur firebugs compared to what I'm going to do to your city when the time comes.

20. "Enough courage to last any man a lifetime."

Sangamon County, Illinois, December 8, 1862

Eddie, never a heavy drinker, was delirious from the concoction of whiskey and opium powder the local horse doctor had just poured down his throat. Whiskey made him gag but deadened the pain in his back that flamed as if filled with hot coals. At least he could feel that pain. He was more worried about the pain he ***didn't*** feel in his legs.

"Lucky man," remarked the half-educated "doctor" whose name Eddie never learned. "Ball went plumb through you. Nicked your innards but didn't break your back. You'll probably live, if it don't get infected. This'll kill the infection."

He pulled the cork out of a jug of moonshine whiskey, took a pull himself, then sloshed some into the hole in Eddie's belly where the ball had left his body. He stuffed Eddie's ragged shirttail into the wound. Eddie howled with agony. The doctor poured another slug of whiskey into his throat. Eddie spit most of it out but absorbed enough alcohol through his tongue and gums to calm him.

"Lucky man you are," repeated the doctor. "Last soldier I doctored up had a gut full of shot. They left him for dead. When he woke up, he crawled five miles on his belly to get to my house with his guts hanging out. By the time he got there, his innards was stuffed full of dirt, leaves, bugs, and a couple toady frogs. I took his guts out and washed them in a tub of lye soap, then stuffed 'em back in and sewed him up. Now he's good as new."

Eddie winced at the improbable story. He tried to turn away from the loquacious "doctor," but was unable to raise himself. He lay flat on his back on a pile of hay, along with three other men he didn't know. They were inside a roughhewn building without windows that, judging by the smell, Eddie surmised was a barn. A blanket wrap around him kept him off the straw and away from some of the bugs. Though he felt a frigid draft blowing through the failing mud caulk in the walls, he was comfortably warmed by the blanket and an oil-burning lantern.

"Did you doctor the livestock that lived here?" Eddie asked sarcastically.

"Yeah, and they're in *stable* condition, a-ha, a-ha."

Christ, please get me out of here before that quack kills me or I kill him.

Eddie's prayers must have been answered, for the farmer and his wife and daughter brought in a kettle of steaming soup. Eddie marveled that they still had food to spare after all these months of Confederate encirclement. Farmers were clever people who knew how to be parsimonious with their vittles when they had to.

"I saw Governor Yates in town," the farmer informed him while he gently raised Eddie into a sitting position and the wife ladled the soup into Eddie's mouth. "He says you men fought like veterans. He'll be out to see you this afternoon."

"Thank you!" exclaimed Eddie, after swallowing the soup. "Maybe he'll have news about the rest of my men."

"Hope so," said the farmer.

Eddie craved to know what had happened to Gabriel Bellamy and the other free Negroes Governor Yates appointed him to command. None were here. The other wounded men didn't know anything more about the result of the battle, or what had happened to Eddie's men, than Eddie did.

All Eddie knew for certain was that he was on a farm at the east end of Sangamon County not far from the railroad platform of the tiny settlement with the grandiose name "Illiopolis." He surmised the battle must have gone in the Free States' favor; otherwise, he'd be a Confederate prisoner again, and probably dead by now for lack of attention to his wounds. The quack doctor wasn't much merchandise, but at least he knew enough to stuff Eddie's shirt in his wound to stop the bleeding and keep the straw and the bugs out. And he knew whiskey helped wounds resist infection. Eddie recognized his good fortune to be sheltered by a generous farmer who fed the wounded from his scarce larder and warmed them with precious oil that could not be replaced until the Confederate encirclement was lifted, if it ever was. Things could have been much, much worse.

The quack doctor mercifully left Eddie alone to chat with the farmer and his wife and drink in the soup, which gave him a remarkable surge of strength. His spirits soared to the heavens. He didn't see any sunlight filtering into the gray gloom of the snowy air he could see through the cracks in the walls, but it felt as delightful as a sunny June day.

I'm going to live! I'll get to see Emma and my sweet home in Cass County, Michigan again! I swear I will learn to walk again and go back to work in my bakery. I have twice been saved from death. From now on, I will live every moment in joy, as if it's my last.

He thanked the farmer and his wife for the soup and clean drinking water. The farmer's wife said he should rest. He willed himself into a deep sleep.

"How's my man?"

Eddie woke up at once when he heard the baritone voice of Richard Yates, Governor of the Free State of Illinois. It must be afternoon already! He felt he had slept deeply and regained a lot of strength. It might have been his imagination, but he thought he could just barely feel the first tingle in his left leg.

He grasped the governor's hands. "Can't complain too much. I'm alive, and I'm getting better. I'm going to get back on my feet and walk as soon as I can. Then I'll get back in the fight."

"That's the spirit!" roared Yates.

"Please tell me about the battle, and anything you know about my men."

"It was a hard fight, but we held the line and whipped them," said the governor. "Your men bore the brunt of it. Four were killed, and four, including you, were wounded. The other three are resting in tents near the railroad platform. You were the most seriously wounded and the ranking man in your unit, so they brought you here, where you could be looked after by the Knoblock family."

"Do you know anything about Gabriel Bellamy? I saw him fall just before I got shot."

Yates shook his head. "Sorry, but I must have seen two hundred wounded men in the last twenty-four hours. I don't remember many names other than yours. I'll stop back at the station on my way out this evening and see what I can find out about Mr. Bellamy. If I learn anything about him, I'll send a messenger back here to let you know."

"Thank you, sir! You know, I feared we'd lost the battle when they got behind us."

Yates smiled and put his hand on Eddie's shoulder. "Their attack broke down after we killed their Generals Helm and McCulloch, and severely wounded Hood. Their General Ben McCulloch was shot from his horse right in front of your position. They seized about a quarter mile of the railroad but were not enthusiastic about holding on to it. We cleared the Confederates off it before sunset. The trains are running again between Springfield and Decatur. The Confederates have pulled back to their original line. We learned from some of their prisoners that there's a big fight in progress up around Chicago. Maybe they're having to send some of their men up there."

"Was their general who was killed at my position wearing a black coat?" inquired Eddie.

"You saw him?"

"I shot him."

"Then that is yet another significant thing you've done in this war."

"The first two weren't all that heroic," said Eddie. "They happened because the Confederates captured me. There wasn't anything I could do about those!"

Eddie was talking about being abducted by slave raiders in Michigan in May 1861 and captured again by Confederate soldiers in May 1862 when the Confederates broke through the Illinois Valley west of Springfield.

"Well, this is one where you did. You volunteered to fight against heavy odds when you didn't have to. You showed enough courage to last any man a lifetime."

"I was fighting for my life," replied Eddie. "Didn't have no time to think about being brave. I know I don't like being shot. I didn't like killing that man neither. I like it even less now that I know his name."

"There's nothing pleasant about war," said Yates. "But they started it. They could have left us alone and let us go in peace. They didn't leave us any choice but to kill their men. They've killed plenty of ours. Lord knows, I've watched many a boy die in my arms, a couple more of them today. There's nothing worse than watching a boy die before he's had time to be a man."

"Yes, sir," said Eddie. "War is a tragedy for folks who had nothing to do with starting it. But they started it, and I aim to help us finish it, soon as I can get up out of this bed."

"Eddie," Yates said gently, "your wound might not let you recover in time to fight again in this war. You've proved your bravery under fire. When you go back to speaking, you'll rally thousands to fight for us,

189

because you've done it yourself. That's another way to help us win the war. I'll see that you're recognized for what you've done."

A tear welled in Eddie's eye, in awe of Governor Yates and his kind words. There was a man whose wisdom was worth the efforts of thousands of ordinary men. But wisdom by itself wouldn't win the war. It took the bravery and commitment of men like Eddie to combine with the wisdom of leaders like Yates.

"Fate has brought us together and increased our efforts a thousand-fold, over what each of us could do alone," said Eddie. "Every person who cares about our cause needs to fight as if the war depends entirely on himself, because maybe it does! That's what I'm gonna say when I gets back to speaking."

The governor was thinking the same. He put his hand on Eddie's shoulder again and went to talk to the other wounded men.

21. "Let them repent tomorrow"

Chicago, December 24, 1862

President Davis, General Stoneballs Jackson, General McClernand, and his new bride "Big Horse" strolled the north bank of the Chicago River, about half a mile from the lake. The weather suddenly changed, as it so frequently does in Chicago. Last night's bitter snowy cold was banished by warm arid winds blowing in from the West.

These "snow eaters" entered the continent as high-pressure systems crossing the Pacific Coast. They scraped themselves bone dry crossing the Coast Ranges and the Intermountain West. They were heated by compression as they fell down the eastern slope of the Rockies, were pressed on across the Great Plains, and thence to Chicago. During the day, the Confederates marveled as the accumulated snow steamed from the boardwalks, subliming into frisky winds of fifty degrees under milky-blue skies.

Now, three hours after sunset, the temperatures had fallen to around forty-five but did not seem likely to go any lower in the warm winds. It felt even warmer to those acclimated to the below-freezing weather that had set in during mid-December. Coats and mittens were discarded by soldiers and Chicagoans frolicking in the warm breeze.

Davis's party marveled at the stars shining through the thin high clouds, like a spring night in the Deep South. What an evening of beauty and romance, on the night before Christmas, to those hard-bitten veterans on both sides of the lines who were observing an informal Christmas truce!

Davis had expected the city to fall two weeks ago. But the Rebels' resistance had stiffened as soon as Sherman anchored their lines behind the Chicago River. Had Sherman been ordered by his government to fight for this last corner of the city to the last man? Sherman's men had even driven the Confederates back from a sliver of land on the west bank of the river. It was a small but significant gain, anchored by two sturdy railroad terminals, from which the Rebels could not be dislodged.

The snows began falling heavily on December 10th, causing both sides to seek winter quarters in the city. The battle lines had stabilized since then. As was the custom on static fronts, pickets patrolled within sight of each other, but no shots were exchanged. They bantered and traded with each other. There would be time enough for killing when the next campaigning season started in spring.

Most of Chicago's civil population had left the Confederate-occupied districts as General Sherman ordered, except for merchants and prostitutes who didn't mind canoodling with Confederate occupiers. The city was repopulated by tens of thousands of soldiers cooking meat rations they had saved for this holiday and imbibing strong drink while the officers relaxed discipline. It was a glorious night for Confederates who occupied the bulk of the city. Free State men across the river were joyous as well. Confederates on the north bank joined them in singing Christmas carols.

"Merry Christmas, Billy Reb!"

"Merry Christmas back at you, Johnny Union!"

Campfires in the parks and streets added a smoky hue to the air. Not a single rifle shot disturbed the peace. On the Confederate-held sides of the river, the lilting tones of fiddles played by Arkansas mountain men could be heard, while the Indians kept time with their rattles and drums. Free State men on the other side of the river joined the chorus if they knew the tune.

If one listened carefully, sounds of intoxication and debauchery from the Kinzie Street bordellos might be heard drifting in on the wind. Stoneballs despised those who desecrated the sacred holiday, but Davis asked him to leave the men and their concubines alone.

"These are young men, who have had few pleasures being away from their homes for so long," Davis advised his discipline-minded subordinate. "They fought hard to get here, and many will die assaulting the Rebels when we storm across the river after Christmas. Let them repent tomorrow."

"I would rather save my men's souls *before* they meet their Maker," insisted Stoneballs, who reluctantly honored his president's wishes to let the men alone.

The party of four broke up into two unlikely pairs. Stoneballs and McClernand went inside a makeshift restaurant one of the merchants had somehow kept open in his store. Stoneballs had designated

McClernand military governor of the conquered city that a few days ago he had sortied out to defend.

McClernand seemed none the worse for wear. Perhaps his shotgun marriage to "Big Horse" had turned out to be agreeable. Principal Chief Stand Watie had taken a shine to his new son-in-law, presenting him with a dowry of livestock and baubles the Indians had stolen from the towns and farms on their way up to Chicago. Watie designated McClernand his Subordinate Chief who might aspire to leadership of the tribe when Watie passed on to the Happy Hunting Grounds. McClernand sported the hawk feather of a Cherokee Warrior from the top of his beaver-skin hat Watie bestowed upon him. Big Horse was always at his side, purring with contentment, and giving the evil eye to any woman who tried to approach her new husband.

Big Horse and Davis wandered over to the edge of the river to smoke cigars together, while Stoneballs and McClernand chatted about their experiences in the two years of turmoil since the epic election of 1860 that now seemed a lifetime ago.

Big Horse pointed toward the constellation Orion. "You see them three stars in a row? We call them The Three Sisters."

"We call them The Belt of Orion," Davis told her. "The three little stars hanging down are his sword. The four ones around are his body, and the triangle on top is his head." He pointed out the stars as he spoke.

"I see it," said Big Horse.

"Do you know the constellation we call The Scorpion we see in summer?"

"Of course," acknowledged Big Horse, blowing a gigantic smoke ring through her nostrils.

Davis waved expansively toward the heavens. "Legend has it that the Scorpion chases Orion the Hunter, and that is why they are never seen together!"

Big Horse giggled. "That's a good story."

Davis blew another long banner of smoke. "Did you ever think you'd be here in this big city?"

Big Horse snorted. "I've been to New Orleans. It's bigger than this, and a lot more civilized. You didn't think we spent our entire lives in tipis, did you?"

"No, I suppose not," replied Davis. "But this city does impress me. The first time I saw it, half a lifetime ago, it was only a couple of shacks."

"Country's growed up a lot since then," remarked Big Horse. "Some's been good, some bad, I reckon. Father says the Confederates haven't always treated us right, but that's all in the past. Anyway, I like that we're going to have our own state in New Indiana."

"It will be your state to govern as you wish," Davis assured her. "It is your land to have and hold forever. I am grateful for your father and your people overlooking our errors of the past and fighting with us as true comrades now when we most needed friends."

Big Horse finished her cigar and threw the butt into the river. She reached into her cowhide purse and pulled out a bag of chewing tobacco. "Want some?"

"No thanks," said Davis.

Big Horse chewed her plug of tobacco, spit the juice into the river, and looked at the horizon. "Our men must be lighting a lot of fires over there."

Davis noticed the reddish glow spreading southward and eastward across the horizon. The air seemed to be thicker with smoke than it had an hour ago. The attenuated noise of distant bedlam wafted in on the wind.

"Sounds like our boys are having fun," said Davis. "I only wish they would not have so much of it on the night before the holy day."

The reddish glow lining the horizons grew brighter, then brighter still.

22. Sherman's March

Chicago, December 24, 1862

The winds were blowing briskly at seven o'clock, local time, when General Sherman embarked his division of hand-picked men on their March of Christmas Eve. He hadn't planned to burn the city on Christmas Eve, but the dry winds burning through the snow convinced him this had to be the night.

Mayor Sherman's determination to hold the city greatly simplified the march. Instead of loading thousands of men and tons of flammable contraptions on ships and landing them on the tangled lakefront north of the city at night, as was his original plan, Sherman was able to supply his men with the incendiary devices collected at the Illinois Central warehouses. These were pieces of wood dipped in a slurry of oil, gunpowder, and pine tar, and wrapped in sailcloth. History would know them as "Sherman's Cigars."

To maintain security, Sherman carefully screened the officers he selected for this mission. "To win this war we must destroy the

Confederates who have tread their mangy feet upon the streets of this city. Once we began the march, there will be no turning back. Anyone who does not accept the necessity of this mission may remain here." He feared that if any officer held back, more would decline, but no one did.

An hour before dark, at around four o'clock in the short days around winter's solstice, Sherman's carefully picked men assembled at the Illinois Central warehouse to pick up their "cigars." Sherman and Mitchel began marching them in small groups across the west branch of the Chicago River. By seven o'clock they had accumulated three thousand men in and around the *Chicago & Milwaukee Railroad* terminal. Sherman and Mitchel marched them two miles northwest along the Chicago & Milwaukee Railroad to the point where it crossed near the intersection of Division Street and Ashland Avenue.

There Sherman divided his forces. Nearly a thousand men commanded by Ormsby Mitchel marched east down Division Street toward the lake. Another two thousand commanded by Sherman marched southward down Ashland Avenue, toward the Illinois and Michigan Canal.

Sherman's March of Christmas Eve could not have succeeded had the Confederates been alert. But they were busy celebrating their occupation of the city and the informal Christmas truce. Their campfires were everywhere, smoking up the city, and obscuring the progress of Sherman's men. Some survivors on both sides claimed that the Confederates' fires were already starting to get out of control even without the helping hands of Sherman's merry men. However the fires started, they spread quickly on the dry winds. There was no stopping them. Chicago's professional firemen had been evacuated to the small portion of the city controlled by Free Staters.

The Confederates' dispositions sealed their doom. The converging attacks by seven divisions had drawn them deep into the city, leaving their rear areas in the outskirts guarded only by intoxicated teamsters and quartermasters. The city's geography of rivers and canals had split them into four isolated commands not mutually supporting. The effect was to isolate two of the Confederates' best divisions --- Wheat's and Pike's --- in the Northern District of the city, the most intensively scourged by the firestorm.

On the other side of the Chicago River's north branch, Hardee's and Van Dorn's divisions occupied the northwestern wards. From the southwest, Buford's division had cleared the north bank of the Illinois & Michigan Canal. From the South, John Logan's big division, its inland flank screened by Forest's cavalry, had reached the south side of the Free State lines. These groups were not in contact with each other, and thus unable to communicate information of Sherman's march.

Sherman told his officers not to let their men light their "Sherman Cigars" until they saw a pillar of fire emerging from above the intersection of Ashland and Division where Sherman and Mitchel set up their headquarters. If challenged by alert Confederates, Sherman's men were told to say: "Merry Christmas, Confeds! We're paroled prisoners leaving the city." Since they were not carrying visible weapons, the few Confederates sober enough to challenge them decided to believe them, especially when offered friendly toasts with whiskey.

The heads of the marching columns were nearing Lake Michigan to the east, and the I&M Canal to the South, when they observed Sherman's fiery pillar rising in the sky behind them. A few men refused to obey orders to set the city on fire, but most battered down doors and threw bricks to smash windows, while their comrades tossed in their

Sherman Cigars. Fires erupted nearly simultaneously along miles of buildings lining Division and Ashland. Brisk westerly winds did the rest.

The Confederates had over 32,000 men in the five divisions north of the Illinois and Michigan Canal, completely enveloped by flames. Forrest's and Logan's divisions, consisting of a combined 15,000 men south of the canal, had an open escape route to the south, but nevertheless suffered severe losses among their slower-moving units, especially those furthest north balked by the congestion of units fleeing town to the south of them.

Tornadoes of fire swirled over the city, while showers of glowing embers rained down as if a volcano had erupted in the middle of town. Tens of thousands of Confederates, many wild with intoxication, lost their orientation in the jumble of close-packed streets, stampeding in aimless circles until the smoke and flames engulfed them. Even those who reached Lake Michigan expired in the frigid waters when the scorching flames from the west forced their heads underwater.

Free State men, manning their lines along the lakeward branches of the Chicago River, shouted to the nearest Confederates, "Come over to our side and save yourselves, Johnnies!" They threw ropes across the river to rescue their enemies from a catastrophe transcending humanity.

Davis and Jackson took charge of the movement across the river. Many of Stoneballs' men had made the impromptu Crossing of the Wabash back in October 1861 and knew what to do. Stoneballs asked the tallest to move out into the polluted, chest deep water and hold the ropes so the shorter men whose feet didn't reach bottom could propel themselves across. Hundreds of Confederates lost their footing in the fire-boiled river and drowned. Their sacrifice allowed many of their comrades to reach a hoped-for sanctuary on the Free State bank.

Confederates who reached relative safety south and east of the Chicago River helped their Free State rescuers by passing buckets of water up from cisterns to roofs smoldering from showers of embers falling out of Sherman's fiery rain of terror. Little did they know another calamity was about to engulf them.

The Chicago River had become unspeakably foul as the city had grown in recent years. Thousands of tons of slaughtered livestock offal, dead animals, and human and animal waste had been poured into the river and sunk to the bottom where it congealed as malodorous sludge. The descending shower of fiery embers boiled the river, setting its oil-caked surface alight.

The heat percolated down to the lower depths, decomposing the sludge into methane gas that bubbled to the surface, spreading out into a noxious cloud rising above the fifteen miles of the festering river and its branches. At 10:47 a gust from the west blew fresh oxygen into the mix, and a detonation was sparked over the river a half-mile inland from the lake, expanding within seconds into a fireball two hundred yards in diameter. It was the first of more than two dozen detonations heard up and down the Chicago River and its branches during that terror-stricken night.

The fireball incinerated thousands of Confederates at or near the river, along with hundreds of Free State men on the other side, comforting those severely burned Confederates who'd braved the fiery waters to reach anticipated safety. The deafening explosion blew out almost every window in the city, allowing the fires to spread rapidly. Four minutes later, the detonation was heard in Michigan City, forty-five miles away, as a deep rumble coming from the direction of the fiery horizon. Sleepers were awakened by the trembling foundations of their homes.

The thousands of individual fires now merged into the meteorological event known as "The Chicago Firestorm." An enormous updraft was created like the bellows of a furnace. Hurricane winds began lifting those fleeing the flames up into the air and hurling them into the center of the inferno. Survivors on the Free State side of the river watched in horror as soldiers and fleeing civilians on the Confederate side were sucked screaming into the air, their hair and clothes bursting into flame just before their lives were snuffed out.

Chicago's miles-high funeral pyre was clearly visible in Milwaukee 90 miles to the north. Its spreading glow across the horizon was seen in Green Bay, Grand Haven, Fort Wayne, Springfield, Indianapolis; and by some accounts, nearly as far south as Louisville. Fiery embers were lifted into the upper reaches of the atmosphere by the ferocious updraft and blown eastward, starting fires all the way to Ann Arbor and Toledo. These would have been worse still had not the bone-dry winds roaring across the lake sucked tons of moisture into a mile-high fog bank, the humidity somewhat dampening the spread of the inland fires.

Despite heavy snowfalls that set in on the 26th, it took five days for the fires in the city to burn themselves out, and the streets to cool sufficiently to allow surveys of the burned-over areas among jumbles of collapsed buildings, melted lead pipes, and the charred remains of tens of thousands of human beings. Even the area controlled by the Free State men south and east of the Chicago River branches was more than one-third destroyed by the fiery rain of embers, methane gas detonations, and swirling fire tornadoes sweeping eastward before extinguishing themselves in hissing furies of steam over the lake.

President Davis, Stoneballs Jackson, McClernand, and Big Horse survived, although Jackson was in bad shape. Davis and Jackson had stayed on the north bank, encouraging their men to cross as long as possible, then moved on to the south bank when the water began steaming. When the heat became unbearable, Jackson advised Davis to seek shelter in the courthouse where McClernand and Big Horse were helping Free State General Hurlbut care for the injured of both sides.

Stoneballs waded back into the river as it began to flame, exhorting his fearful men on the other side to cross before it was too late. He apparently passed out from methane gas inhalation. He was being carried away from the river by his men when the explosion overtook them. He was found on the snowy afternoon of the 26th, unconscious beneath a pile of his expired men, who appeared to have interposed their bodies between him and the expanding fireball during the few seconds it took to incinerate them. He looked like a badly cooked lobster --- icy cold on one side and burned to a crisp on the other.

Of the 47,000 Confederates in Chicago on Christmas Eve, only about 11,000 in Logan's and Forrest's divisions escaped incineration or capture. However, the ordeal of Logan's and Forrest's survivors was only just beginning. They retreated the way they had come up into the city, which carried them back down into the Calumet Lakes south of town. This was an excellent defensive position astride the Illinois Central, with lakes and marshes constraining the approaches from the south. They hoped they could hold out until reinforcements and rations arrived from Central Illinois, and perhaps from Lee's army on the Mississippi.

It was a forlorn hope. The wintry weather returned with vengeance on December 26th. The swampy ground surrounded on three sides by lakes and sluggish streams shielded the Confederates from attack by the Free State Army in Indiana, but not from howling blizzards and forty degrees of frost assaulting them from above.

Some of Forrest's men survived by shooting their horses and crawling under the piles of their warm carcasses. A few dozen of the hardiest, including the general, escaped down the Illinois Central and eventually reached the Confederate lines. However, Logan's infantry had hurried from the city with barely more than their seared uniforms on their backs. Fewer than two thousand men of both divisions survived the frigid week of December 26th to January 2nd in the barren Calumet Lakes. Logan surrendered the starving remnants of his once-proud division to McPherson's winter-equipped Free State men probing cautiously through chest-high snowdrifts along the roads south of the burned-over districts during the first week of January. Few of Logan's survivors avoided losing toes, fingers, noses, and ears to frostbite.

The catastrophe was hard on Chicago's un-evacuated civil population. The number of Chicagoans who perished in the Northern and Western Districts across the rivers are unknown but would have doubtless been many times higher without Sherman's evacuation order. It is known to have killed over eighteen hundred men, women, and children, and about the same number of Free State soldiers, in the partially burned areas occupied by the Free Staters.

The most prominent fatality in the Free State-occupied district was General Stephen Hurlbut, who Sherman had placed in command of the soldiers remaining in the city. Hurlbut rushed into a burning house on Market Street to rescue a woman's children, who were screaming out the window of her rented room on the second floor. He brought the two children down the stairs and out the front door and was informed by them that their baby siblings were in a side room.

"Who will help me save the babies?" he shouted. He ran back up the stairs, along with a Free State soldier and a Confederate who spontaneously followed. The ceiling collapsed upon them before they could complete their rescue. Hurlbut and his volunteers were found the next morning, collapsed over the ashes of the babies' crib, having shielded the babies from the roaring flames, until death overtook them all. Having been born and raised in the South, then making his fortune in the North, Hurlbut was destined to become a sainted hero honored equally by both sides, as were the volunteers, whose names were lost to history in the chaos that followed.

Mayor Sherman, assuming command of the Free State men in the partially destroyed section of town south of the river, informed Jefferson Davis that his surviving Confederates who had made it to the Free State quarter of town were prisoners of war. Had better security been maintained, the origins of the fire might have remained obscure, and Davis might have acquiesced to his "capture." After all, the Confederates had also been promiscuous with their poorly tended campfires in the parks and streets that night.

However, too many people had witnessed General Sherman's men loading up their "cigars" at the Illinois Central warehouses, then marching across the river. Word spread rapidly that the city had been put to the torch on his orders. Davis, having heard enough accounts of this story to believe it, was having nothing of Mayor Sherman's "prisoners of war" pitch.

"No! No! No!" Davis shouted. "You didn't capture my men in a fair fight. You burned us out with a criminal act of arson then invited us into your lines, where we helped you save what little is left of your city!"

"Nevertheless, you are our prisoners. If any of your men attempt to leave without parole, we'll have to shoot them."

"The first person you should shoot is your pyromaniac cousin," snarled Davis. "He's the one who burned down your shithole town."

In coming days, it would be learned that Sherman's columns of firebugs had not been immune from the destruction. Ormsby Mitchel's column suffered severely when a fire tornado cut off its western half, killing over five hundred men, including Mitchel, in the process. The rest made it to Evanston the next day and watched in awe as the fiery furnace to their south eclipsed the low-lying sun. Even at fourteen miles, they felt the heat on their faces.

Sherman's men, turning west after starting their fires, fared better. The flames were fanned eastward as they headed out of the city for ten miles, the radiant heat nevertheless scorching them through their uniforms, and the methane detonations battering their eardrums, before reforming their column and marching south.

The head of their column reached the I&M Canal an hour before dawn. Around that time the final chain of methane gas explosions detonated over the south branch of the Chicago River. The blinding flashes were followed by the blast wave channeled down the I&M Canal. It was heard two and a half minutes later by Sherman's men "as if a battery of heavy siege guns were fired in our midst." The full realization of what they had done came upon them. Some wept, some prayed. Those of religious spirit remembered the Biblical story of Lot's Wife who turned back to witness the heavenly wrath unleashed upon Sodom and

Gomorrah by a vengeful God. The more literal-minded turned away from the inferno on the horizon lest the sight might turn them into the proverbial "pillar of salt."

At dawn, the survivors gathered, having lost about two hundred men who dallied in the city to loot and were never heard from again. The survivors marched southwest down the I&M canal, reaching the town of Lockport before sunset on the evening of the 25th, many men remarking that it felt as though they had lived a lifetime in the last 24 hours.

They passed the bitter week of blizzards in relative comfort. The townspeople, joyous to be out from under the Confederate occupation, plied them with food, drink, hot baths, warm beds, and friendly women. A cavalry column from McPherson's command located them on January 5th. Thus ended military operations in and around Chicago.

In the following days and weeks, able-bodied Free State and Confederate men alike cared for their agonized comrades and the civil population who had survived the fiery ordeal with severe burns, and lungs damaged by methane inhalation. Alas, many of the injured succumbed to their burns and lung infections. Stoneballs Jackson passed away on January 15th. His last words were, "Let us cross over the fiery waters and rest under the cool blue skies of dawn."

23. "You, the Fiery Devil, as their defender"

Cleveland, January 12, 1863

The complete destruction of communications out of the city by telegraph and railroad, and the curtailment of travel across the lake by the blizzards that set in on the 26th, obscured the origin of the catastrophe to those outside the smoking ruins of Chicago. The telegraph from Michigan City on Christmas morning was terse: "Large fires seen burning Chicago. Explosions heard."

Intimations of an extraordinary event arrived in Cleveland that afternoon with news of wildfires burning for hundreds of miles downwind of Chicago. The following day, the "Black Fog" of lake-drawn humidity, mixed with ashy particulates, submerged downwind cities into an early winter night that began around 2:30 in the afternoon in Cleveland.

People fled indoors until the blizzards arrived to snow the soot out of the air.

The accidental fire that burned Charleston, South Carolina's downtown at this time last year was still fresh on people's minds. Thus, the Chicago fire was presumed accidental by those who knew no better. It would not be the first time a city had burned when occupying soldiers, defending soldiers, and disorderly civilians were careless with fire during the interregnum between defense and capture, when civil government was disrupted, and police and firemen were absent their stations.

Mayor Sherman's secretary was the first to arrive in Cleveland to make an official report on January 6th. On that day President Lincoln, his Cabinet, and the Executive Committee of Congress learned that Chicago was defunct as a procurement and military center; that the destruction was unleashed by direct order of General-in-Chief Sherman; and that Jefferson Davis, Stoneballs Jackson, and John McClernand were in custody.

"We'd better figure a way to blame the Confederates, or we are ruined," stammered cynical Treasury Secretary Salmon Chase. "If our people get wind that Sherman started it, every goddam Democrat in the Northwest will be howling for us to surrender before Sherman burns down any more of our cities."

"Then let's see you go over there and concoct a story," replied the even more cynical Thad Stevens. "You're the most convincing prevaricator in this government."

They that Chase and Secretary of State Seward, who had befriended Jefferson Davis before the war, would proceed by train to Michigan City, and from there by ship to Chicago. Chase was to seek evidence, or invent it if necessary, purporting to show Confederate culpability in setting the city ablaze. Seward was to inform Davis that, in view of the tragic circumstances, the Confederates captured in and around Chicago would be paroled and sent home. He was to escort Davis back to the Confederate line at Franklin, Indiana. He was to ask Davis for a truce while both sides sorted out the catastrophe, and to suggest that they should not inflame public outrage by speculating on the cause of the blaze. He was to point out that the war had become destructive beyond the imaginations of anyone on either side, and to ask Davis to accept a peace that divided the country along the lines proposed by Horace Greeley in August 1861.

On January 17th General Sherman arrived in Cleveland to make his official report to President Lincoln, Secretary of War Curtin, and the Congressional Executive Committee, chaired by his brother Speaker of the House John Sherman.

"By the time I got to Chicago," he reported, "it was apparent to me that if the Confederates were not immediately removed from the city, we would not prevail in this war on terms we would find tolerable. They had broken into Chicago from the northwest before we could accumulate the Spencers and ammunition we were counting on. We could have sustained cartridge fire for only a few hours of battle. After that, the Spencers would have been useless.

"The Confederates had their strongest divisions in the city. Their morale was perfected by the arrival of Jefferson Davis. We would have had to dig them out of the built-up areas of the city where every building is a fortress, with no advantage in weapons.

"They were soon to be augmented by Jubal Early's corps. They were building up their reserves at Louisville with new recruits enthusiastic to obtain possession of our vacated land by the Armed Occupation Proclamation of Jefferson Davis.

"I concluded that Burnside's men could not evict the Confederates from Chicago.

"Had the battles continued, I believe the Confederates would have stymied our armies and imposed peace on their terms --- either by extinguishing our independence or confining us to such a small territory as to make our existence precarious.

"I therefore decided to destroy the Confederates in Chicago. Circumstances did not permit me to consult with the government here. I believe that by destroying the Confederate Army in Chicago, I have saved our country. Chicago can be rebuilt. Our country, had it been lost, would have been lost forever. I regret the loss of innocent life in the city, but it would have happened in any event if we had tried to retake the city with Burnside's men --- a battle that would have cost us many thousands of soldiers' lives, that I do not believe would have succeeded. My conscience being clear, I am prepared to accept censure."

Mr. Lincoln rubbed his chin, while all waited for his response.

"I would not censure you," said Lincoln, "even if I was certain your actions were excessive. That would be tantamount to censuring this government, which appointed you to your position. It would open your actions to endless controversies, which would be followed by recriminations that would undermine and discredit our cause, perhaps fatally. That would be even more tragic after the sacrifices we have suffered.

"I deem it best to put this event behind us. You will remain in your present position as General-in-Chief. Do not say anything further about the incident. Tell your officers not to discuss it."

"Yes, sir," replied Sherman, with evident relief.

Lincoln looked him in the eye to let him know he still maintained his president's confidence. "What do you think the Confederates will do now?"

"Shorten their lines," answered Sherman, with a quickness indicating he had given the question considerable thought. "If it were me, I'd try to hold the line from Champaign to Peoria, then renew the attack on our men between Springfield and Decatur before we can reinforce them."

"Our spies report, as you've already mentioned, that Richard Taylor is organizing new divisions around Louisville," Secretary of War Curtin informed him. "They're using McClellan's method of quickly building new divisions by pulling regiments out of their veteran divisions and using them to leaven their inexperienced men."

"An effective method," confirmed Sherman. "McClellan and Taylor have shown their ability to mobilize large numbers of troops, equip them, and get them into the field. I expect they'll attack us in as many places as possible, with everything they have, in hopes of overwhelming us before we can bring our Spencer repeaters to bear. I expect Stanton will light a fire under McClellan to renew the attack on Philadelphia, perhaps with an amphibious assault as in Boston."

"Then let's see if we can stop this war now," said Lincoln, "on terms we and the Confederates will find tolerable." He fixed his gaze on General Sherman. "Let us pray that Seward and Davis will call forth the better angels of our nature." *And that no more of our cities will make their acquaintance with you, the Fiery Devil, as their defender.*

24. *"They're wild horses, so let them run"*

Relief for the survivors in Chicago proceeded slowly, the fires and methane gas explosions having leveled the piers and warehouses. The first ships to arrive unloaded their cargoes into boats moving cautiously through acres of burnt debris clogging the shore and river.

It wasn't until January 13th that a road was cleared through to the center of town from the south, allowing deliveries of food, medicine, and blankets. By that time hunger was severe, causing many wounded, sick, young, and old to expire. The Defense Council decreed the evacuation of survivors due to the mortal peril of plagues spreading from tens of thousands of decomposing bodies when the thaws began. The city was to remain uninhabited until a salvage operation followed by planned reconstruction could commence. The fortifications around the city would be re-occupied as a military cordon to prevent the passing of lawless elements bent on looting.

Salmon Chase poked around the ruins without obtaining any definitive information about Confederate culpability in setting the blaze. Although he obtained verbal testimony from survivors alleging the Confederates were negligent with campfires, the extent of the destruction made it impossible to pinpoint origins of fires apart from where Sherman's men were known to have sparked them. In his report, Chase spun out a yarn about how the dry winds of December 24th made the fire inevitable in the closely packed city, implying that Sherman had done everybody a favor by igniting a controlled burn rather than letting the conflagration spread haphazardly on its own.

Davis, McClernand, and Big Horse remained in the city until the passing of Stoneballs on the 15th. They decided to have his body embalmed in Michigan City, then forwarded to his family in Virginia. McClernand's role in the loss of Chicago, and his subsequent allegiance to the Confederates, was controversial. Considering the tragic circumstances, it was decided to let him leave with the Confederates.

Seward accompanied them by ship to Michigan City, then by train to the Confederate lines at Franklin, Indiana, twenty miles south of Indianapolis. A sentimental man, Seward had ministered to Davis when they were senators in the prewar United States. Each evening during early months of 1858, he had read the day's proceedings to bedridden Davis, blind and agonized by infected eyes. He had no affinity for Senator Davis's pro-slavery politics, but nevertheless comforted him during nights when his life and spirits ebbed.

Seward pleaded with Davis to consider the stalemate resulting from the destruction of a Free State city and a Confederate army as an opportunity to negotiate "a lasting peace that all Americans may consider victorious." The war, if not stopped now, would become even bloodier. Could they not end it, along the lines Horace Greeley had proposed, before it consumed an entire generation? But Davis's desire to avenge the deaths of his martyred army didn't abate until the train reached Franklin. There they were to part company --- Seward returning to Cleveland, Davis to Washington, and McClernand and Big Horse to New Indiana. Big Horse, who'd gained a husband while losing her father at Chicago, had been listening to Seward implore Davis to make peace. As they exited at the station, she took Davis aside.

Her eyes were wet with emotion, for she understood how difficult the proposition of peace was for a President who'd witnessed the immolation of his army, including her father. The tears were also sweet, for she anticipated getting home to begin a happy life with her new husband, who, with the passing of her father, was destined to wear the golden eagle feathers of a Principal Chief.

She tugged gently at Davis's arm. "Remember how my people and yours shed rivers of blood fighting each other? And how you sent us out of our homes on the Trail of Tears? Now we're reconciled as a family in our country. I don't reckon we'll ever reconcile with the Yankees. They're wild horses, so let them run. We've got plenty to keep us busy in our house. Won't you smoke the pipe of peace with Mr. Seward?"

Davis closed his eyes, remembering the destruction of Chicago. Amid the terror, he recalled Northern men imploring his soldiers to cross the river to safety. The methane gas explosions killed many who responded to humanity's call to wade into the flaming river to help fire-seared Confederates. The Confederates also did their part, especially the unknown soldier who'd been the first to heed Hurlbut's call to enter the falling-down building to "save the babies."

These Northern men are not going to plot another desolating war against us, even if we let them go off into their country. Their Abolitionists will try to inflame them against slavery, but they will not force the issue by invading us. The bonds of humanity, and of being Americans, even if our capitals are in different cities, will keep us at peace. It is time to let them go.

He looked at Big Horse and nodded.

"You're right. We have much to do in the Confederate Union, enough to last lifetimes. It will get done faster and with much less dissension without Yankee Abolitionists agitating to end slavery as the preeminent issue."

Their eyes met, both having the premonition they would not see each other again. Big Horse threw herself into Davis's arms and felt his hand caress her back. Out of the corner of her eye she saw her husband gossiping with a lady while waiting to collect their baggage. She looked at Davis for the last time, smiled, and went flying over there to break that up.

Davis found Seward by the locomotive, talking to the engineer. He motioned for Seward to follow him outside. Once clear of the crowd, he told Seward he was prepared to accept an armistice on terms befitting separate nations. Seward suggested that since the independence of the Free States had thereby been mutually acknowledged, they should meet again here in Franklin, on or about March 1st to negotiate a treaty to submit to their respective congresses for ratification.

25. "A fraternal American people"

Franklin, Indiana March 30, 1863

"The map still looks strange to my eyes," said Seward as he and Davis read the newspaper reports of the treaty they'd submitted to their respective governments for ratification "It will never look as beautiful as when we were one country." He shook his head. "Oh, too bad, that our people were not big enough to maintain it as one!"

"I also wanted us to remain as we were," Davis pointed out. "You remember the first thing I did after taking my Senate seat in '57 was to persuade Congress to fund the new Capitol building. I wanted it to be large enough to accommodate the new senators and representatives we would require as we fulfilled our Manifest Destiny to expand to the Pacific."

"At least your senators and representatives will now have ample space to bring in comfortable furnishings," replied Seward. "Our Free State Congress is still using folding chairs in a hotel ballroom in Cleveland."

Davis laughed. "But now you are free to build your permanent capital in Cleveland, or anywhere you want. We're stuck with Washington. I was hoping to persuade Congress to build a new capital in the highlands across the river from Louisville. They won't hear of it. They've invested in Washington properties and will never give them up."

"Washington has been a sad place for you, losing your children there, and you nearly losing your life," said Seward with sympathy.

"It killed Stephen Douglas too," added Davis, "although he was pretty far gone from over-imbibing strong drink when elected. Even more than that, I wanted a new capital that reflects our westward expansion. Washington was the capital of the old United States. It was built on the border between the North and South as a compromise. Our dividing the country proves the compromise failed We've lost the North --- that many Southerners never wanted --- and gained our fair portion of the West, as you've lost the South and gained your part of the West. We should have a new capital, for a new nation. It belongs being in the Ohio Valley, the new center of the Confederate Union, at a high enough elevation to be healthy."

"We've had that question come up as well," Seward informed him. "Cleveland is good for us, because the axis of our country runs along the Great Lakes from New York and Boston to Chicago. Cleveland is at the center. However, people are governed by tradition. Tradition demands that our capital be placed in Philadelphia. Tradition will likewise require your capital to remain in Washington. You can improve its health by asking your Congress to fund a sanitary sewage system."

"I suppose that's the best I'll be able to get from them," acknowledged Davis. He raised his finger. "I'll tell you what I *am* going to do, though, and that's get our Congress to build our Confederate Military Academy on the high ground across from Louisville, on the encampment Dick Taylor and I set up. I'll get that appropriation if I have to promise every Senator and Congressman's nephew a patronage office. I'll insist on an appropriation for a Summer White House there, so the President and his family can spend summers safely away from Washington City. And, if, God forbid, we're ever at war again, it can be a haven. I fear the British could burn Washington as easily today as in 1812."

"Hopefully, we've seen the last war on our continent," said Seward. "We'll have to steer clear of alliances with European powers that would entangle us in their wars."

Davis grimaced. The British had done everything for the Free States short of fighting beside them. He decided to keep the conversation pleasant by not bringing that up. "Ah, well, we've done enough thinking for one day." He pulled two Cuban cigars out of his vest pocket and handed one to Seward. "Let's go outside and enjoy these."

They donned their coats and walked out of the administration building of Franklin College. They walked along the graveled path through dormant gardens, crunching patches of late winter snow underfoot. March was a transition month in Central Indiana. When the sun shone through breaks in the clouds, the temperature warmed at once, and summer seemed near. Winter returned when scudding clouds blocked the sun and brought back the cold gray gloom.

Franklin was a convenient border town where the military frontier intersected the railroad from Indianapolis to the Ohio River. Soldiers from both armies ambled about, sometimes chatting and trading with each other. Many nodded politely to Davis and Seward. They hoped they'd be going home soon, if Davis and Seward crafted a sound treaty ratified swiftly by both nations' congresses.

"We live in two houses, now, but we're still on the same street," commented Seward, as Davis lit his cigar. "Our people will continue to move across the border, marry across the border, and do business across the border. I don't see any need for a rigid regulation of trade or immigration between the countries. Most restrictions on travel have heretofore been imposed by Southerners, who wanted to keep our Abolitionists away from their slaves."

"There are few places in the South that don't welcome Northern educators and businesspeople --- so long as they stick to their knitting and don't agitate our slaves," insisted Davis. "Now that we control our borders, we'll feel more secure about slavery. Our people never relaxed their vigilance after John Brown's Raid. That, more than anything, made the war inevitable."

"Yancey's slave raid into Michigan started the shooting."

"He's as a guilty as Brown," confessed Davis. "As Secretary of War Stanton said in his speech the other day: 'The evil hearts of wicked men on both sides of the Ohio overruled the wise councils.' "

"That's why dividing our country was necessary," posited Seward. "Our Abolitionists and your Fire Eaters played both ends against the middle. They cut the ground out from under our people of good faith and plunged us into a war that few people of good will wanted. Now that we're separate nations, we can keep them from stirring up any more trouble."

Davis stopped, flicking the ashes from his cigar while he thought how to reply.

"I felt during the war that we had to bring you 'Rebels' back into the Union," he explained. "Because if we didn't, your Abolitionists would continue to strengthen their position, then attack us when they felt strong enough. I think of it more the way you do now: that dividing the country will keep the Abolitionists and Fire Eaters from combining forces to stir up trouble. They won't be able to frighten our people into making war against each other."

He inhaled deeply and blew a thick cloud southward, as if aimed specifically at Yancey and his fellow Fire Eaters. "Not that they won't stop trying. They're still castigating me for renouncing the acquisition of Mexico, and for asking our Congress to exclude slavery from our new states of Jefferson, and our portions of Kansas and Colorado. They're saying that if they wanted a 'Black Republican' to be their president, they'd have voted for Abe Lincoln in 1860."

Seward blew a long banner of smoke that merged with Davis'. "They provoked a war to get out from under the old Union. Now they're out from under it and complaining louder than ever!"

"Tell me about it," answered Davis. "They've got nothing to complain about, nothing at all. We've got enough land for new slave states between Texas and California to last us until the turn of the next century. By that time, we'll have figured out how to modernize the slave system to bring it into line with the realities of steam powered manufacturing."

"They're angry because they will no longer control your government," inferred Seward. "The seat of the Cotton South is the Seaboard from Virginia to Savannah and then on across the lowlands to New Orleans. The new seat of your country will be the Ohio Valley, along the line of Baltimore and Washington to Cincinnati, Louisville, and St. Louis. The immigration of free peoples into the Valley, and the development of industry, will strengthen the Confederate Union. I expect the development of the Free States of your country will pressure the Slave States to give up the ghost of slavery. Because it will be your own government taking the initiative to restrain slavery, the slaveowners will not feel threatened as they do by our Abolitionists, who can also be unreasoning."

"I'm glad you understand," said Davis. "It was essential for us to have the Ohio Valley. Its cities will attract our share of immigrants who will bring their commercial skills to our country. It will allow us to fulfill our larger destiny, instead of limiting our prospects as a smaller slave-holding country under the thumbs of the Fire Eaters."

He was gratified to have held the Ohio Valley as consolation for the destruction of his army at Chicago. In the final weeks of hostilities, Jubal Early's corps, aided by Confederate-loyal militiamen, had pushed through two tiers of counties on the north bank of the Ohio River, the heart of the prewar Stephen Douglas Democratic Unionist country. "Grease and slide back into the Union!" the people told each other as they saw the Confederate Union flag rising over the courthouses, after two years of Free State military law.

Early reached Cincinnati in time to lever the Free Staters out of the fortifications held so stubbornly in the north wards, forcing them back to their next line of defense around Xenia. The river and the Baltimore & Ohio Railroad through Cincinnati linked the Confederate

Union's East Coast with its new Northwestern State of Jefferson, now augmented with Ohio's river counties. Davis had accepted New York City's destiny as part of the United States of Free America in return for Seward accepting the Ohio Valley's destiny in the Confederate Union. Davis planned to make the evacuation of New York City palatable to his Congress by pointing out that the Confederate Union's bankers should not be unhappy to be out from under the hegemony of New York's financial powers.

The swap of New York City for southern Ohio allowed them to negotiate the border west of Pennsylvania along Latitude 39°30' all the way to the Pacific Coast. Davis liked the geometrically pleasing line. It was an almost exact demarcation between Confederate Union and Free State loyalties, that would discourage the ambition of either nation to incite a future border adjustment war.

Seward was equally pleased with the swap. Possession of New York City made New Jersey's pretensions as a sovereign republic untenable. Seward anticipated a trip to Trenton soon to persuade its governor and legislature to "voluntarily" rejoin the United States.

"Perhaps we always had separate destinies," he ventured expansively. "You are a people of the land. We are a people of the sea. We will open a highway from New York to Oregon. We'll put our ten thousand wheels of manufacture in motion. We will multiply our ships and send them forth to Japan, China, and India. The nation that draws the most materials and provisions from the earth, and fabricates the most, and sells the most of production and fabrics to foreign nations, must be, and will be, the great power of the earth."

"I admire the commercial spirit of the Northern people," replied Davis. "I felt as much at home speaking in New York, and Boston, and

Portland, as in Mississippi. Even as two nations, we will share a common American spirit of liberty to pursue opportunity. I will stand for re-election in 1864. God willing, I will remain in office until March 1869. That will be long enough to forge an enduring peace with the United States of America."

"It appears that fate destines me to be your partner in peace," Seward conjectured. "Mr. Lincoln is very tired and frail. He says he does not desire to remain in office beyond his current term, if peace can be concluded before then. I will succeed him in 1864, if that is what he and the people want."

"In the Senate, we rarely voted the same way," Davis remembered. "Nevertheless, you treated Varina and I as members of your family. She still talks about your 'earnest, tender, interest' when you brought her a nurse during that blizzard. When I was bedridden with neuralgia, the blindness was so depressing, and the pain so terrible, that I thought very darkly. I might have died if you hadn't been at my side every night, reading to me the proceedings of the Senate. I saw in you the human form of an angel. The bond of compassion you and others of good will have created in the North and South will heal the scars of war and make us a fraternal American people, even though our governments will henceforth assemble in different capitals."

26. The Bookends of Death

Cleveland, April 3, 1863

The "bookends of death"
President Lincoln's friends
Elmer Ellsworth and Senator Edward Dickinson Baker

Mr. Lincoln found no objections of substance on his first reading of the treaty. He did not feel well today, so he decided to listen quietly to the opinions of his War Cabinet, which included members of Congress, with him here in his parlor.

His fever and persistent cough came near the end of Cleveland's long winters when the weather alternated between the first signs of tepid warmth and the last snows. Today there were no signs of spring. The windows in the presidential house were shut, and the furnace roaring. Snow squalls blew in off the lake, adding to the four inches on the ground. He was wrapped in a blanket, warmed inside by his fever and outside by the fireplace. John Hay persuaded him to take a wee nip of "medicine" in the form of brandy in his coffee. That delighted Mr. Lincoln, for being such a rare indulgence. And bless it, the "reinforced" coffee did warm his body.

He went into a reverie where he imagined himself floating on the warm waters of Lake Erie, under a gentle sun, during a late-summer holiday. He thought he heard the voices of his children, Tad and Willie, playing on the beach, but perhaps it was their voices from the upstairs hallway. Was someone asking if he wanted lemonade when he came out of the water? As he awakened, he understood it to be Congressman Thad Stevens asking Seward a question about the treaty.

"It is organized as an instrument of secession of the Confederate Union from the United States," Seward explained. "Although the designation of the United States as the continuity nation and the Confederate Union as the secession nation is only a matter of semantics, it nonetheless has important connotations. We will retain the name 'United States of America' and its symbols. Our legal history begins in 1788 with the ratification of the Constitution. The Confederate Union of America is to begin its legal existence upon ratification of this treaty by both nations."

Treasury Secretary Salmon Chase began ruminating on the financial aspects of the treaty:

"The national debt as of January 1, 1861 is to be apportioned by census population between the two countries. Each side to maintain the military and civil property in its possession at the close of hostilities...I don't see anything about embassies. The Secretary of State should talk to Davis about it as an addendum. It would save us significant expense if we can take possession of those embassies without having to acquire new ones. Other than that, the financial aspects of the treaty look reasonable."

"I'm glad the financial clause meets with your approbation," said Ohio Senator Benjamin Wade. "You don't seem terribly upset about our ceding the lower third of Ohio to the Confederates."

"It has to be done," quipped Chase. "How else are we going to rid ourselves of Stanton, Pendleton, Vallandigham, and all those others turncoat Democrats who made their bed with the Confederates?"

"Good riddance to Congressmen Bill English and John Logan and their ilk in Indiana and Illinois, too," added Thad Stevens. "We don't need them or their voters in Free America. They were anchors on the ship of progress."

Senator Sumner remained critical of the treaty. "There will be hell to pay in Massachusetts when they learn we're handing over five-sixths of Kansas to the Confederates. Our Massachusetts emigrant aid societies left their blood in the soil to make Kansas free."

"We get Missouri north of 39°30'," countered Seward. "We can barter land swaps between our people in Kansas and the Confederates in northern Missouri."

"It's better land we'll be getting in Missouri," Lincoln's friend Senator Lyman Trumbull counseled. "Better soil, less prone to drought, and more sheltered from the most brutal cold snaps."

"We need to ratify the 39°30' line while we can get the Confederates to accept it," prodded Seward. "I worked on Davis for weeks to get him to agree to it. He said the Confederates had to have 40° in exchange for giving Boston and New York back to us. Let's ratify the treaty before they have second thoughts."

"It's a fair swap," concurred Lincoln, now fully awake. "We couldn't have accepted 40° as that would have put Columbus,

Indianapolis, and Springfield on their side of the frontier. The war would have continued, maybe for years. Lord only knows how it would have ended, after we soaked the land in blood. You did well to get Davis out of New York and New England, and to talk him down to 39°30' in the Northwest. We'll be secure with that border. Like you said, the best land is north of it."

"Is it too late to swap New Jersey for the rest of Kansas?" asked Senator Charles Sumner, who might or might not have been jesting.

"I'd swap New Jersey for a bottle of twenty-year Port." remarked the ever-cynical Chase. "Transcendentalists *and* Democrats, the worst of everything! We've got enough loons already without taking in those crazy Jersey birds."

"You think they're crazy because you aren't educated in *philosophy*," quipped Stevens. "Thoreau, Emerson, Whitman, Hawthorne, and Melville have made their nests there. You've never read anything that wasn't printed on a banknote."

The rest laughed so hard that even Chase didn't show offense. Thad Stevens enjoyed provoking people. For once, Chase let him have his fun without responding.

Stevens thumbed through to the back pages of the treaty. "International Agreements: The treaty commits both nations to maintaining the prohibition on the African slave trade, and to jointly patrolling the African Coast to cut off its source. That's fine, but there's nothing about the Confederates agreeing to give up their ambition to expand slavery into Mexico and Cuba."

"There isn't," acknowledged Seward. "But Davis says he doesn't covet Mexico. He said the only reason the Fire Eaters wanted it was to carve out more slave states to balance our free states in the Senate. Now that the Confederate Union is independent of us, Davis says they don't need any more slave territory. He said he's rejected offers by Mexican warlords to sell their fiefdoms to the Confederate Union. He doesn't think that bringing Mexicans, or Cubans, into the Confederate Union will improve it."

"I'm inclined to believe they'll leave Mexico and Cuba alone," suggested Lincoln. They'd have to fight the French, Spanish, British and us to expand slavery beyond their borders. Davis knows they don't need another war for slavery. Maybe their presidents who come after him will be sensible about it too, after Davis sets the precedent."

Lincoln blew his nose, then inhaled the steam from his coffee and brandy to clear his sinuses. "I'm most gratified that you obtained possession of Oregon, Washington, and part of California, though I regret San Francisco is beyond our means. Nevertheless, we have 'our window on the Pacific' as you call it, without which our country could not be complete."

"Davis didn't dispute Oregon as vigorously as I'd expected," surmised Seward. "Perhaps Senator Baker has succeeded in undermining his authority out there enough to make him decide it wasn't worth keeping."

They didn't know that Senator Baker had been killed on March 13th, while leading an attack on Confederate-held Fort Steilacoom on Puget Sound. The British Fleet had then commenced a naval bombardment that breached the fort's walls, allowing Baker's surviving "Springfield Men" to capture it. Then they proceeded to liberate the Willamette Valley and Puget Sound. The news was being conveyed by a British naval vessel sailing around Cape Horn and thence to Montreal via the St. Lawrence. Jefferson Davis, having more direct overland communication via California, had learned of it sooner, while negotiating with Seward in Franklin. He recognized he would not be able to retain possession of the Pacific Northwest and had concentrated on securing the new State of Jefferson in the Old Northwest.

Baker, Lincoln's best lifelong friend, became the last significant casualty of the war. Lincoln's young friend Elmer Ellsworth had been the first to die in May 1861. They were the bookends of death in the war that killed over one hundred thousand soldiers on each side, while destroying St. Louis, Cincinnati, and Chicago; and extensively damaging Boston, Providence, Springfield, and many smaller towns in New Jersey and Pennsylvania. He'd been notified of the death of his favorite brother-in-law, Confederate General Benjamin Hardin Helm, in one of the last battles near Springfield.

"I have grown most heartily sick of this war," he said in an impromptu speech from his balcony on the last day of April. "As have the people of both nations. I have lost my two dearest friends --- one at the bright shining dawn of his life and the other in its late afternoon. Mrs. Lincoln's dear brother, in the noon of life, has been killed fighting for the other side. Let the long night of death be ended. I implore our Congress and the Congress of the Confederate Union to ratify this treaty without further delay."

27. Three Times a Hero

Cass County, Michigan. May 5, 1863

"Why don't you use those beautiful crutches Mr. Mears was kind enough to make for you!" exclaimed Emma Brown to her common-law husband Eddie Bates.

The crutches were carved from oak timbers by Fred Mears, the best carpenter in Cass County. They had rests for Eddie's shoulders and meticulously carved "boots" on the bottom of the legs to maintain Eddies' upright stride. They were the most elaborate of a half-dozen carved walking devices Eddie had received from well-wishers as tokens of appreciation for his wartime heroism. All the crutches and walking canes stood unused in the corner.

"I'm not going to let people see me walking on crutches!" vowed Eddie. "How many times do I have to tell you that to beat it into your thick head!" He struggled to get up and stand on his own two feet. The wound in his back flamed. He clenched his teeth and bore it. He would not walk with crutches, nor would he drink whiskey or opiate solutions to deaden the pain.

"Stubborn as a mule," said Emma, shaking her head. "Same as always!"

"By the way, do you know what tomorrow is?" asked Eddie.

"How could I forget? It was two years ago tomorrow, when the slave raiders busted down the door and took you away."

"Don't tell me you wasn't stubborn to escape and go get the sheriff to rescue us."

"I reckon that's the right kind of stubborn," conceded Emma. "Like I've said a hundred times, the calming power of the Lord came over me. I knew what I had to do without even thinking about it."

Eddie grimaced with pain in his back when he reached the door! Oh, how he wanted a slug of whiskey to deaden it, but he knew he'd better not get started on that habit. He opened the door; the same door slave raiders had busted down.

"Two years seems like a long time ago," he said on the way out.

He shut the door and walked slowly and painfully to the outhouse. The grass was just beginning to show its green. The buds on the trees appeared ready to sprout leaves any day. The sight encouraged him to think of a happy future. He was going to recover his confident stride if it took a year. He finally reached the outhouse, which had no door, pulled down his pants, and sat over the hole.

First time I ever felt more comfortable taking a shit than standing up.

He finished his business and went back in the house. "Can you handle the bakery by yourself today? I want to finish the first installment of my story for Mr. William Lloyd Garrison and Mr. Frederick Douglass. They want me to start with the slave raid. I'll write my side of the story now. You can tell me yours this evening."

He was writing his first story to be serialized in *The Liberator*, the anti-slavery newspaper published by Abolitionists Garrison and Douglass. He expected to be a sought-after speaker and writer for the rest of his life. Would there still be Negroes enslaved in the Confederate Union at the end of his life? *Yes, there probably will be. But there will never again be Negroes captured in the United States and returned to slavery.*

"I'd better get going," said Emma. "I'm running late as it is. Heroes or not, we still gots to earn our keep."

Earn our keep, thought Eddie. He'd been doing it for twenty-five years, ever since his father had passed away and he'd started working for his own account. *I've never took nothing from nobody except what I've earned with my own two hands.*

"Those Confederates need to learn that all Negroes can earn our keep," he said to Emma as she looked at herself in the wall mirror. "We're not their children. We can make money for us and them too, if they'd let us. All our money goes into buying things, or to the bank. That prospers the white folks who own those stores and banks. White folks in the Confederate Union could do better if they weren't working their Negroes for nothing."

"Some of them ain't working for nothing no more," Emma reminded him. "The Confederates put them to work in their factories during the war. Now they want to keep them working to make things they want to buy now. They'd rather work their Negroes for a little money than pay Yankees a lot."

"They'd do even better if they paid their Negroes fair. White folks is slow learners when it comes to doin' right by colored people."

"Speaking of slow learners, you put your shirt on backwards." Emma giggled. "I've been trying to learn you how to act educated for near on fifteen years, and that's done precious little good." She slapped the top of the dresser and laughed again.

Eddie rolled his eyes. "Who's writin' the story?"

"You are."

"Thas' right. I'm writing it because I'm the educated person in this house. Don't you never forget that. And when I'm done writing it in installments for their magazine, they're going to publish it all in a book."

"What are Mr. Garrison and Mr. Douglass going to call their book about you?"

"*Three Times a Hero: The Eddie Bates Story*. That's what. The first time was the slave raid. Of course, you was the hero then; you and all the folks in Cass County who came to rescue me. All's I did was stay chained up in a casket. I didn't die though, so maybe that's what makes me a hero. Second time was when I sneaked out of the Confederate camp after they captured me in Bloomington and went down to Springfield and told Governor Yates what the Confederates were up to. Mr. Lincoln says that's what kept the Confederates from getting into Chicago in June and knocking us out of the war. Not only that, but because we held Springfield, we got to claim our border 35 miles south of where the Confederates wanted it. Third thing I done was when I fought 'tween Springfield and Decatur last December and shot that Ben

McCollough fellow off his horse. That stopped the Confederates from breaking us in two. I still don't feel right about killin' that man. But war is war, I reckon."

"If he's a Christian man his spirit is in heaven, and he's forgiven you," Emma assured him. "It's *your* soul I'm worried about." She laughed again.

"At the moment, I'm just happy my soul is alive right here on this Earth," answered Eddie, "even if I am in an awful lot of pain. It makes me mighty proud that you and me did our parts to make sure there'll never be any more slave raiders bustin' in, throwing us in coffins, and taking us away to places where we'll never see home again."

"We got plenty o' time left on this good ol' Earth," agreed Emma. "We might as well make the most of it. President Lincoln says we're going to rebuild Chicago better than it ever was before. Says they'll be homesteading land to folks who want to go there, clean up the ashes, and open new businesses. I know you're still hurtin', but I reckon we can hire some folks to help us set up shop in Chicago once we get there. Let's go. They're going to need a bakery, and like as not folks will want to come in and hear your story. We can sell your book along with the bread."

"Not a bad idea," said Eddie. "Not bad at all."

She closed the door to get out to the barn and hitch the wagon.

28. A Final Request

Montgomery County, Alabama. May 30, 1863

William Lowndes Yancey took off his hat as he approached the roughly cut pine box coffin. "God rest his soul; he has earned his reward for his labors."

"Thank you, Marster Bill," replied Aunt Annie, the widow of his slave Old Josiah who passed away yesterday. Old Josiah had been Yancey's first slave. His son Young Josiah and other of Old Josiah's children were here, as were some of his cousins and grandchildren. They arrived with passes from neighboring plantations all over Montgomery and Lowndes counties.

Old Josiah had worked Yancey's land when he was young, then become Yancey's manservant in middle age. He traveled with Yancey to Atlanta, Charleston, and Richmond, seeing more of the wide world beyond the plantation than any of Yancey's other Negroes. He was a raconteur whose stories about the lives of slaves gave Yancey and his friends many a hearty laugh. He had sired dozens of children and grandchildren who labored in the fields all over South Alabama.

"He was a good worker and a good man," Yancey told Annie. A tear welled in his eyes. *Dammit, I do miss that old Negro.*

Yancey had dedicated his life to making sure Negroes remained in bondage. He had fought to get the Slave States out of the Union and into a separate country so slavery could be expanded into Mexico, the Caribbean, and Central America. He said the South needed to reopen the African slave trade "so we can buy Negroes where they are cheapest." He said Negroes were shiftless thieves who had to be watched every minute to keep them from stealing everything that wasn't nailed down. He said the only way to make them work was to keep them in slavery.

And yet, he fancied himself a kindly slave master. He didn't allow his Negroes to be worked to exhaustion. He allowed them personal time to hunt and fish on his land. He sold recalcitrant slaves to the dreadful swamps of Louisiana but would not allow his overseers to whip any on his land. He called upon the best doctors in Montgomery to tend them in sickness. He fed them well and talked to them better than he'd talk to a lot of "peckerwood" whites. He wrote them passes on Sundays to visit their relatives on other plantations. When his Negroes courted Negroes on other plantations, he arranged swaps with other plantation owners so couples could live together.

Why not treat Negroes as well as the circumstances of slavery allowed? That was good business. Contented slaves were less prone to making trouble and running away. Negro couples raised big families whose children could be worked or sold. It was a happy world for Whites and Negroes, or so Yancey thought. Yet many in the North, and even some in the South, said slavery's days were numbered. The land in the South available for labor-intensive cotton farming was running out. What should be done with the Negroes who continued to multiply? Without more land to work, their value would fall. They would become idle and prone to crime or even insurrection. That Damnfool Davis had even told the world that the South wanted no more land for slavery!

Yancey felt a sharp pain in his side, reminding him that *his* time on earth was growing short. With the coming of peace with the Yankees, he had failed in his life's purpose of making slavery secure within the confines of a separate Southern Republic.

I was so close! I almost had the South out of the Union in 1860. Then Double-crossing Stephen Douglas had to unify the Democrats by putting Damnfool Davis on his ticket. Even that didn't stop me! I instigated the slave raid that got the Damnyankees out of our country. And then Damnfool Davis had to go and start the war to get them back!

He didn't get all of them, but he got the ones in the Ohio Valley, Kansas, Colorado, and California, which he says are going to remain free states. That's going to start the trouble up all over again, this time with our own people inside the Confederate Union. "Keep your niggers and nigger-owners and away from us" --- that's what they'll say. They won't allow us to reopen the slave trade or conquer Mexico and Cuba. "We got enough niggers as it is, so why bring more from Africa? And who needs those goddam greasers from Mexico and Cuba."

Before long, they'll start agitating us to liberate our Negroes. Alexander Stephens is already talking that way, and he's a goober-grabber from next-door Georgia!

He was closing the last act of his life, this time as a Confederate Union Senator. In the brief time he'd been in the Senate, he had voted against the admission to the Confederate Union of the Free States of Jefferson, Kansas, Colorado, and California. Once again, he failed. Not only would there be no slavery expansion into Mexico and Cuba, but the Confederate Union's own northern tier of states were free soil! He no longer had time to bend history to his will. He knew he would not serve out the term, maybe not even live until the opening of the 1864 session next March.

He returned his attention to paying his respects to Josiah's sons and daughters. When an old slave died, the Negroes celebrated his or her life. They were drinking the homemade dandelion wine they usually kept hidden, singing songs, and telling stories about Josiah --- mostly funny stories, but sprinkled with a few ribald ones about his amorous escapades with slave women.

That old Darky lived a full life, that's for sure. He filled half the slave quarters in this county with his progeny. He did his work though. He deserves a ticket to Paradise if there is such a thing. Do Niggers go to heaven when they die? If there are any up there, I hope I can buy some when it's my turn to enter The Pearly Gates.

He felt another sharp pain in his abdomen. His life flashed before him: His childhood on a slave plantation in Georgia. The shock of his father's death and his mother's remarriage, of all people, to a New York Abolitionist. Then moving to Troy, New York, where his beloved half-brother still lived.

He remembered advocating for the supremacy of the Federal Union as a young man in college during South Carolina's Nullification Crisis, then advocating for breaking the Union when he returned to the South as an adult. Now he was finishing his life as a senator in a Confederate Union far from being the Southern Republic he cherished. The Fire Eaters' revolutionary zeal for spreading slavery throughout the hemisphere was stillborn. The Confederate Union would be a conventional nation like any other, run by fat old men who promoted their business interests by maintaining the status quo.

And what do we have now? A Yankee Secretary of State named Seward who is spending more time in Davis's White House than with his own president in Cleveland.

They were working up new treaties requiring commercial standards and banking laws to be uniform between the two countries, and agreeing to open rivers, railroads, and highways to citizens and businesses of both countries on equal terms. They had an agreement to make Wilmington, Delaware a common center for business incorporation.

At least Northern businesspeople have sense enough to want to keep profiteering from the South. They've clamped down on their Abolitionists and told them to stop agitating against slavery in our Confederate Union. That's good, but it hardly compensates us for losing a slave empire south of the Rio Grande. It's the lunatics in our country we've got to be worried about. Crazy Aleck Stephens is hooting about "A new face for slavery." Het means educating slaves, respecting their marriages and families, and letting them work as sharecroppers and share-wagers. If that's not a short step to complete abolition, I don't know what is.

"Marster Bill?" It was Aunt Annie's voice stirring him from his reverie. "There's one last thing Josiah wanted me to ask you about."

"What is it, Annie?"

"Is there any way possible, you would consider selling George and Charlie to the Southern Express Railway, so they can go to work for wages in Atlanta? That's the last request of Old Josiah. He asked me to ask you about it, in case he passed before he could ask you hisself."

George and Charlie were two of Josiah's grandchildren who would soon be old enough to work the fields.

"Are you certain they want that? It's a hard life working a railroad, and there's lot of temptations in the city that can get a young man in trouble."

"I talked to them about it," confirmed Annie. "It's what they want. They'll work hard, and the way things is goin' maybe they'll be free by the time they's forty."

Yancey's wife Sarah looked him in the eye and nodded. Had Annie already talked to her?

Sarah knows I am not long for this world. She wants me to sell our slaves now so our accounts will be settled when I pass.

"All right, then. I will do it for Josiah. I'll take them to the Southern Express office Friday and negotiate a sale. You'd best say your goodbyes. You likely won't be seeing them again, not in this life."

"Thank you, sir," Annie said. She had gotten what she wanted, by talking sweetly and patiently to her master. Slaves were like that. They didn't hurry around everywhere, watching clocks, counting money, and worrying about the material things of the world as Whites did. Negroes seemed eternal in their patience, like the Earth itself.

Perhaps it was because they did not own their bodies. They could not control who bought or sold them, or whether their families would be sold apart. They lived one minute to the next without worrying about the future. They seemed content to pass this life and move on to whatever lay beyond without worrying much about it. Somehow or another, they seemed to know that one day their descendants would be free. Was it because of the story of Moses leading the Hebrews to freedom, that the White preachers taught them? Yancey thought about that.

242

I hope that part of the Bible is wrong. Setting the Hebrews free was bad enough, but Negroes? I hope I don't run into any free niggers when I get to Heaven.

29. *"Don't wait for the revolution"*

Chicago, July 3, 1873

Jefferson Davis, once again a Senator from Mississippi, knocked on the door of the curator's little house at the Peace Memorial Park on Chicago's lakefront. John Sherman, now President of the United States of America, opened it.

"Congratulations on building this stately monument in this beautiful city," said Davis, shaking his hand. "I am very much impressed."

"Thank you, sir!" replied President Sherman. "And thank you for coming. You haven't been here since the city was destroyed, have you?"

Davis shook his head. *Destroyed by your deranged brother.*

"It's a memory I don't care to recall. We lost too many of our best men that night. Stoneballs Jackson, Albert Pike, Stand Watie, Robe Wheat, Bill Hardee, Earl Van Dorn, and John Buford. And over forty-four thousand other officers and men in the ranks. Hardly a family in the Lower Mississippi Valley didn't lose a husband, son, or brother."

"It was hard on us too," emphasized Sherman. "Stephen Hurlbut and Ormsby Mitchel. About two thousand soldiers, and a similar number of identifiable citizens' deaths. We'll never know how many perished in the northern and western districts." He sighed. "But that was ten years ago. We should be memorializing the ten years of peace since then."

"Maintaining a spirit of good will, after a painful War of Separation, is worth celebrating," agreed Davis. "That's what I'll say tomorrow."

"Please sit down, then. Will you share a bottle of wine with me?"

"I wish I could. But at my age it puts me to sleep. I'd rather stay awake and enjoy the sights of this beautiful new city you've built. Coffee would suit me better."

"Emma?" Sherman called out.

A black lady appeared.

"Do we have fresh coffee?"

"Yes, sir, made it just now."

"With honey, if you have it, please," requested Davis.

The lady nodded and returned a minute later to pour the honey-sweetened coffee. A black fellow followed with a tray of sliced beef, lake trout, cheese, and crackers. He refilled the wine in President Sherman's glass. "Thank you, Eddie," said Sherman.

"Did Varina come with you?" Sherman asked Davis.

"Oh, yes. She and our daughters Maggie and Winnie are having a grand time shopping up a storm on Michigan Avenue. I hope I can settle the bills before I leave."

Sherman laughed. "I know *that* story! You and I are too honest to accept considerations from favor-seekers, and our governments pay us too modestly to live the life of luxury. But we have done our jobs well in recovering our countries from war and in establishing an honorable peace." He raised his glass to toast Davis. "Here's to us, our governments, and our fellow Americans in both countries."

Davis took a sip of honeyed coffee and felt renewed energy. "Hear! Hear!" he said as cheerfully as he had while raising a glass at Benny Haven's nearly fifty years ago. He took a piece of smoked lake trout and put it on an oval toasted rye cracker, adding cream cheese and onion dip. He looked out the window as he ate.

He saw one of those magnificent early summer days, with a cool breeze coming in from the northwest, a cloudless azure sky, and moderate white-capped waves on the dark blue lake. The new city of Chicago was visible beyond the park. Its broad boulevards, parks, and stone buildings were rebuilt according to the plan devised by Cyrus McCormick, Gurdon Hubbard, Marshal Field; and the professional urban planners Frederick Law Olmsted and Daniel Burnham. The city's well-ordered beauty awed Davis, who was no stranger to the city planning of Washington.

His gaze was drawn to the Peace Memorial looming in the center of the park. Beneath the 200-foot marble Spire were the statues of Stephen Hurlbut and Ormsby Mitchel, the United States generals who had perished. Hurlbut's statue had one arm resting on the two young children he had rescued from the fire. His other arm pointed upward and away, presumably toward the burning building where he was told two babies were waiting to be rescued.

Statues of two other men --- a Free State soldier and a soldier of the Confederate Union --- were poised to follow him back into the burning building. The flags of both nations stood beside them. Davis had read the commemoration on his way here:

"In honor of General Stephen A. Hurlbut of South Carolina and Illinois, and the Free State and Confederate soldiers who died beside him while rescuing the citizens of Chicago during the night of December 24 / 25, 1862."

Every morning at dawn, flowers were placed at the base of the Spire. They were taken up in the evenings, as the Spire's long shadow stretched across the green park and toward the deep blue waters of Lake Michigan--- a reminder that the great city's peace, and the peace between the two American Republics, must never again be disturbed.

Today, workmen were hammering on the railings of the temporary speakers' platform in front of the Spire. Tomorrow at noon, Davis and President Sherman would commemorate the memorial on behalf of their countries. It would be ten years to the day since the Treaty of Franklin, ending the War of Separation, was signed.

"This memorial will move the hearts of the hardest men," remarked Davis. "It will remind them to think always of peace, before contemplating the awful step toward war. It was gracious of your government to honor those Confederate men who died while helping Hurlbut, and to allow us a portion of the park to place our memorials."

The Confederate Union was in the process of commissioning a monument to its men who had died here. Davis had suggested a statue of Stoneballs Jackson, wading out into the steaming river to beckon his men to safety. Alas, only about a thousand Confederates from the five divisions north of the I&M Canal survived the crossing and the fiery explosions kindled from methane gas rising above the river.

Davis didn't think there would ever be any statues, here, or elsewhere, commemorating General William Tecumseh Sherman's equivocal role in removing the Confederates from Chicago, though certain aphorisms attributed to him had left their indelible marks upon history:

"To save the city, I had to destroy it."

"Chicago was destined to burn sooner or later. I gave it a head start."

"You can't fry an egg without turning on the stove."

"War is war, and not popularity-seeking."

"I wasn't running for Mayor of Chicago. My cousin already had that job."

"Where is your brother?" Davis asked out of curiosity. "I don't suppose he was invited to the commemoration?"

"No, we didn't invite him," confirmed Sherman. "He's at home in Columbus. These days he spends much of his time litigating the city over his water bills and property taxes. He still loves to fight." He poured more wine. "I know he's considered a gangster in the Confederate Union, but he put a necessary end to the war. It would have become unspeakably brutal had it continued. Fortunately, you and Seward drew the necessary conclusions and made peace with honor."

"Seward, may he rest in peace, deserves more credit than I," said Davis, with reverence to the memory of his friend. "Without him at my side, I would have been inclined to continue the war. We were fired with angry resolve to bring to justice those who murdered our army." He specifically meant Cump Sherman.

"You wouldn't have gained anything by continuing the war," countered President Sherman. "We were arming our men with Spencer Repeaters. Had the war continued, we would have driven you across the Ohio and Potomac. You would have lost all the Northwest, plus Delaware, Maryland, Washington City, and western Virginia."

Davis had anticipated that response. "No, we would have conquered you. We were preparing to arm our men with breechloaders of our design. After what your brother did to our army, we had more than enough volunteers to carry them."

Sherman knew Davis was exaggerating the Confederates' capacity to equip their men with breechloaders. He also knew he'd overstated the effectiveness of the Spencers. Their weakness was, and remained, the difficulty in supplying their ammunition. Even now, the United States equipped its soldiers with Sharps single-shot rifles, not Spencer Repeaters. It wasn't possible to manufacture and transport enough ammunition to supply men whose weapons could fire hundreds of cartridges an hour.

He also knew that Davis *wasn't* exaggerating the Confederates' anger over his brother's immolation of their army. The Confederates could have raised another army, or perhaps two or three, without resorting to conscription. Their Armed Occupation Act would have packed their ranks with land-hungry foreigners, thereby negating the Free States' Homestead Act. They might have fortified Illinois and Indiana with an armed civil population behind the military frontier, penning the Free States into a small area along the Great Lakes Watershed.

Perhaps they would have employed the full force of Porter Alexander's telegraphically controlled artillery against Providence and other Free State fortified cities as they had at Cincinnati. How could the British fault the Confederates for bombarding Free State cities when the General-in-Chief of the Free State Army had just destroyed Chicago?

Sherman shuddered as he contemplated those possibilities. Back in 1862 he'd had a nightmare of the Confederates breaking through to Cleveland, forcing Free Staters to flee across Lake Erie to the Canadas. He'd dreamed of living in a truly cold place in summer. Canada's northern forests, with mid-summer frosts and short growing seasons, would have been where the British settled America's Free State refugees. He realized his brother must have made those calculations when he decided to destroy the Confederates in Chicago, along with thousands of his own men and untold numbers of people who'd refused to leave the city. Cump had calculated the risks of continuing the war and found the odds unfavorable. He decided to shock both sides into making peace without delay, based on Free States independence in a new continent-spanning country.

"Let's just say it would have been a bloodbath that would have engulfed both our peoples with hatred for generations," Sherman offered. "It's best it ended when it did."

Davis wanted to change the subject too. "You know, humanity has a way of destroying things, then putting them back together, better than before. Look at this city. Chicago has become the model for modern cities in the next century. I wouldn't have imagined it could be rebuilt so grandly."

He had reason to be impressed. The wretched shacks, stinking slaughter pens, festering cesspools, and cholera-ridden wells of the poor neighborhoods in the old city were gone. The war had not only destroyed Old Chicago, but dispersed it further around Lake Michigan, all the way to Grand Haven in Michigan. Many Free State loyalists who'd lived in the Ohio Valley before the war had relocated here. Even though four times the size of its prewar population, Greater Chicago was nowadays much less cramped and filthy.

The factories and stockyards were relocated to the Calumet area south of town. Davis had ridden the train up through there yesterday. It was by no means a wealthy district. The factory buildings were no more attractive than they had to be. The workers' houses were modest. But they were separate houses for each family, solidly built on brick-paved streets, with space for parks and schools, and sanitary sewers below ground. The stockyards were still malodorous, but their waste was now incinerated, not dumped into the rivers and groundwater. No doubt it was much less disease prone. Perhaps General Sherman had ultimately saved lives after all by destroying the old city and forcing a modern one to be built upon its ashes.

He appreciated this spirit of progress that advanced more rapidly than in the Confederate Union.

We have rebuilt our Confederate Union's industrial cities of St. Louis, Cincinnati, and Baltimore, but they are no better now than before the war. We can produce what we need in their factories, but we haven't improved the lives of our people who labor there. These Yankees can produce what they need while keeping their factory workers reasonably content. I suspect it has a lot to do with the ideas of those Transcendentalists that we (and many conservative-minded Yankees) called 'loony birds' during the war.

He had seen their banner --- with its motto of "Knowledge, Reason, Morality," under a seal showing a farmer in his field and a manufactory behind him --- flying over houses and businesses in the industrial districts south of town. The Confederate invasion of New England had run them out of their Boston nest. Ralph Waldo Emerson, Horace Greeley, and Walt Whitman had alighted in New Jersey, declaring it a "Transcendentalist Republic" before voting to join the United free States in 1866. Greeley had brought Karl Marx, his European reporter, over to editorialize for workers' welfare. With the return of peace, their ideas had spread across the Free States, and were especially focused here on the rebuilding of Chicago.

"Things happen fast in war," observed Sherman. "Changes that might have taken a hundred years to work their way through the slow processes of peace, suddenly burst forth in war."

"War brings people face to face with their mortality," suggested Davis. "They understand they don't have as much time in life as they thought. I've seen more changes than I ever thought possible in one lifetime, especially up here. I want to know how you managed to persuade your factory owners to pay their people enough to live in those new houses on the southside. In the Confederate Union factory owners pinch pennies till they holler."

"We haven't really persuaded them," Sherman admitted. "They don't favor any proposal that diminishes their profits. We couldn't get them to raise their workers' pay, which would be good for their businesses by giving their people more money to spend buying the things their factories produce. But we did persuade our Congress to enact the federal income tax, over their strident opposition. That's what we used to rebuild this city and the workers' homes you saw on your way into town. The houses were built with public money and sold to the workers at a price they could afford. If they live in them for ten years and take care of them, they'll own them free and clear."

"Like a Homestead Act for city workers?"

"That's it. If we're giving away free land on the frontier, we must do something for our city people. We're hoping to eventually obtain mandatory profit-sharing for factory workers and guarantees against their destitution by involuntary unemployment. That's another thing that has Cump riled up. He's opposed to enacting laws to elevate anybody above what their wages will earn them. He needs to understand that there'll soon be more wage earners than self-employed farmers and shop keepers. People who work for wages must provide for their families at all times, not just when businesses are hiring. I keep telling him that we've got to provide those people with economic security now, before they became tinder for riot and revolution when times get tough."

"Hmmmmmm," said Davis, sliding his coffee cup on the table between his hands. "We need to be thinking about that too. Most everything that starts up here filters into the Confederate Union. I think I'll make the acquaintance of some of these Transcendentalists before I return to the Confederate Senate in December."

"We're living in an industrial age," agreed Sherman. "We must study economic issues involving labor and capital. It is well that we are now two countries and can address these issues in our own ways, instead of strangling ourselves with endless arguments about slavery."

Sherman became sentimental as he poured more wine. "That was the way Mr. Lincoln, God rest his blessed soul, saw it. He felt we needed to put the slavery controversy behind us so we could look forward to the new century. He said that by the turn of the new century, the horse and buggy will be superseded by vehicles powered by steam, or even methane gas, which demonstrated its power in a destructive way here. He imagined powered balloons flying across the country! He talked about having a telegraph in every home and business, so we can communicate instantly to whomever we like whenever we like."

Davis perked up. "I remember John Logan making the same comments when we were meeting at Stephen Douglas' home during the campaign of 1860. He said if we had to keep the country united to benefit together from progress. We didn't stay united politically, but we'll continue to make progress together. I hope so, anyway."

"You've had your share of progress," acknowledged Sherman. "You're no longer the backward-looking land of slaves and cotton you were before the war."

"Thank you for recognizing that," said Davis. "I appreciate it, I really do. We are blessed to be at peace with the United States. It allows us to benefit from your ingenuity. President Taylor is a Harvard man, you know. He's brought in his New England friends to develop national standards for our railroads and manufacturing industries. He's required our railroad companies to use the same standards for rail gauge, and to link their terminals. Before the war, we had rickety railroads that derailed our trains, and bridges that washed out with every spring rain. I didn't think I'd ever live to see the day when we'd be able to travel across our country from Wilmington, Delaware to San Diego in five days."

Davis was comforted by that thought. He'd been vehemently criticized by Southern Rights "Fire Eaters" for declining Horace Greeley's peace proposal of 1861 dividing the countries along the Ohio River. The "Fire Eaters" had lambasted him for prolonging the war and thereby "consigning the flower of Southern manhood to moldy graves in polluted Free State soil we did not need and did not want." However, if Davis had failed to reclaim all the Free States, he had at least pushed the Confederacy's frontier far enough north to secure its own independence from aggression by any combination of Free States and European Powers.

Even more than land, the Confederate Union's security depended on the manufacture of engines. Steam and electricity were replacing draft animals and candles. Possession of the industrialized Ohio River valleys between Cincinnati and St. Louis gave the Confederate Union the heft of industrial engineers, mechanics, and entrepreneurs it required to keep pace with the United States and the world. The nation's security depended upon this, for everyone in military circles said the next war would be a war of engines. The nation that could manufacture the most would prevail.

The Confederate Union's frontier northward of the Ohio River brought over a million citizens within its borders and continued to augment their population with a hundred thousand European immigrants each year. That broadened the Confederate Union far beyond what it could have been as a purely slaveholding plantation country. Historians were beginning to render their assessment of Davis as second only to George Washington in securing the Confederate Union's destiny as a great power of the Earth.

Davis drank his coffee, then put the cup down and wrapped his hands around it to warm them. Discussing these issues put his mind on the political battles he'd be fighting in the Confederate Union Senate when it convened in December. He and President Richard Taylor were members of the Confederate Union Party, popular in the Upper South. Their "newfangled ways" were opposed by the tradition-bound Confederate States Party of the Cotton South. Even so, the political

255

differences were far less than when they'd been with Abolitionists in the prewar United States.

"We learned some lessons from you, too," Sherman reciprocated. "We're organizing our army according to Stoneballs Jackson's principles, which are studied at West Point. We're creating a small, but powerful, all-arms expeditionary force, and an ocean-going navy capable of deploying it anywhere in the world."

"Why do you anticipate war across the seas?"

"We require overseas markets for our surplus productions, if we expect to keep our industrial people employed twelve months a year. The aggressive empires --- I am thinking specifically of France, Germany, Japan, and Russia --- are seeking to carve up the world into closed imperial domains, like the French tried in Mexico.

"Oooooooohhhh," said Davis. "That explains why you purchased Alaska from the Russians. Our people thought Seward was crazy for buying that ice box."

Sherman laughed. "A lot of ours did too!"

"You didn't want the ice," Davis surmised. "You wanted bases and coaling stations on the northern route to Asia. You're going to annex Hawaii to cover your southern flank into Asia, aren't you?"

Sherman's eyes widened. "Please keep it under your hat. I also hope we can count on you to cover our southern flank on this continent, if we must go to war overseas."

"Foreign customers come to *our* ports to buy agricultural products," Davis said with an air of superiority. "We don't need to fight for overseas markets for surpluses of our manufactured goods.

Everything we manufacture, we consume at home. We have no interests beyond our borders."

"You may discover that you do," Sherman countered.

"Why so?"

"Because darkness is descending upon the Old World. Populations in Europe are increasing beyond the means of the land to support them. People are flocking to the cities where they earn a pittance that doesn't permit them to feed their families. Radical, anti-human ideas of communism, militarism, and imperial conquests are again spreading among desperate people. They are listening to demagogues like those who orchestrated the Reign of Terror. Nowadays, tyrants can multiply their oppressions by harnessing steam power and telegraphs. They may learn to control the explosive gas Cump unloosed by accident. They might put it in bombs dropped by balloons to destroy entire cities in an instant. If a trans-oceanic war comes, don't think you'll be able to escape it. We and the British are discussing an alliance to forestall the sweep of tyranny across the world. You'll have to decide whether to stand with us or the oppressing powers."

Davis replied cautiously. "You and your British friends told us you'd go to war with us if we ever tried to expand slavery beyond our current borders. Don't expect us to go to war to defend your interests."

"Then at least refrain from joining the oppressing powers. Your slaves know that slavery has no future on our continent. You've seen for yourself how our workmen are prospering. Your slaves will learn about it and want the rewards of free labor. Don't join the oppressing powers by denying your Negroes what they know they can earn from their labor. Embark them on the road to freedom now, while you still have time to do it peacefully."

Davis set down his tea, looking as if he might walk out. Sherman raised his palm, motioning him to stay.

"I won't say anything else about slavery," Sherman assured him. "You will decide what to do about that in your own good time. But, please, for your own sake, act quickly to hasten its demise. Don't wait for the revolution."

Eddie and Emma came out of the kitchen together. "Was everything satisfactory, sirs?" asked Eddie.

"Excellent," answered Davis. "The fish was smoked to perfection, and the coffee robust. Thank you very much for your attention."

Emma smiled. "You are very welcome, sir."

"Allow me to introduce Eddie Bates and Emma Brown," said Sherman. "They own the grocery store across the street. As you can see, they are serving us better in freedom than they possibly could as slaves. As slaves they would only have brought an adequacy of what we asked for. As free men and women, they have put their hearts and souls into their work in bringing us the best that pride in their work compels."

"When we work for our own accounts, we make money to buy things from White folks," explained Eddie. "I buy my clothes from a white tailor. I sure can't make them myself. I don't reckon my tailor could have gotten anything from me if I'd been a slave wearin' burlap. Confederate Negroes would do right well for theirselves and for white folks too if they was free to work for wages, or run their own businesses, like I am."

"I understand," Davis assured him. "Four hundred thousand slaves have been manumitted in the Confederate Union since the end of the war. We have nearly seven hundred thousand free Negroes now.

Aleck Stephens will likely be our next president. He has a good heart for your people. He wants our Congress to implement 'a new slave code for a new century.' It's going to be slow going, though. President Sherman was just talking about how reluctant the capitalists up here are to share their profits with their laborers. You can imagine how our slaveowners feel about paying free Negroes to work. There is only so much we can do for your people at any given time. But what is feasible for us to do, we are doing."

Davis looked at Sherman. "Your people could buy our Negroes, bring them here, and set them free yourselves."

Sherman's eyes bulged out. "Our people aren't ready for **that!** Last thing they want is more free Negroes coming here to compete for their jobs."

Davis sipped his coffee. "You're honest to admit it. Your Abolitionists were sanctimonious in demanding that we must liberate our slaves right now. But they never wanted to tax themselves to pay us for their liberation."

That remark stung Sherman because they both knew it was true.

"You wouldn't have liberated them even if we had paid you," he said in a voice showing his annoyance.

"That's true, too," admitted Davis, who could also be honest. "Slavery is a social as well as economic institution. Our people are reluctant to accept Negroes as their economic, legal, or social equals. At least not all at once. People are stubborn, and set in their ways, you know."

Emma looked at Eddie and laughed. "Isn't that the truth!"

Davis chuckled. "My wife says that about me." Times were changing more than Davis knew. Ten years ago he would never have talked casually with a free Negro he'd never met before.

Eddie rolled his eyes at Emma's remark, then addressed Davis. "I'm grateful you kept your word to crack down on those slave raiders that used to come up here. I was one of the ones what was kidnapped on the raid that started the war."

Davis frowned. "Those Fire Eaters were bound and determined to have their war. It didn't turn out the way they wanted, thank God. If they had gotten control of our government, it would have ruined the Confederate Union for our people and yours. I imagine there would have been another bitter war between us and the United States."

"I fought at the battles around Bloomington and Springfield," Eddie informed him. "I don't ever want to see no more of war. I still ache from taking a musket ball in my back. Wars are only ever going to get more terrible, with them repeater rifles, big artillery guns, and maybe people setting off methane gas on purpose in a city to kill everybody all at once." He sighed. "I think the best way to avoid war is to be fair with everybody, including Negroes. Please see what you can do to set Negroes in the Confederate Union free, when you think the time is right. That'll help keep the peace, and it will make you more prosperous."

Davis found himself tending toward agreement. "Things take a long time to change, Mr. Bates. Then suddenly they seem to change all at once --- usually at the time you least expect. Do you have children?"

"No, sir. That's one thing the good Lord hasn't blessed me with."

"Maybe it's not too late," suggested Davis. "My father was long in the tooth when I was born. Anyway, I was going to say that Negro children born in the Confederate Union today will live to see the continuing moderation of slavery. My thinking about it has changed as I've watched more free Negroes prosper the way you have. Other slaveowners have seen it too. More are manumitting their slaves in their wills. I expect in a few years, the wage-sharing slaves who have been prudent enough to put some money aside, will begin buying their freedom. The time will come when there are too many free Negroes in the Confederate Union to maintain the rest in bondage."

Davis raised his coffee and sipped it to give him time to think how to conclude his remarks. He knew slaves are most likely to revolt when they get their first taste of freedom, so he did not want to over-promise the day of liberation. "I expect it will take a hundred years," he concluded with reasoned caution, "but, as your president just told me, we'd best start preparing for it now."

"Thank you, sir," said Eddie. "That's a long time, but it's going the right direction. That's something."

"It surely is," said Sherman. "One of our first presidents, John Adams, said the American Revolution was fought to liberate the slavish part of Mankind all over the earth. We in the United States of America have done our part. I think we can fairly estimate that Senator Davis and his government will do theirs, even if more slowly than we would like. The War of Separation is a waypoint in the liberation of all men."

Davis thought about that. "It wasn't the Confederate Union Victory that Stephen Douglas or our Fire Eaters wanted. But it turned out the right kind of victory --- for us, for the United States, and I expect ultimately for our Negroes."

Davis recalled that pivotal moment back in April 1860 when Stephen Douglas had asked him to form the Confederate Union Compact.

If I had declined to enter the Compact with Douglas, the Secessionist Fire Eaters would have taken the Deep South out of the Union. Knowing what I do now, I do not believe we would have succeeded in winning their independence. We would have been defeated and made subservient to the North's government. Now we have attained our independence the right way, by letting the Free States break the Union, while waging a successful war to reclaim our Confederate Union loyalists in the Ohio Valley. We have secured the Confederate Union's future as a major power of the Earth. We are strong enough to deter the Abolitionists and European Empires from any future thoughts of aggression. And if the United States shall find itself at war with tyrants, we will help them.

With that optimistic view, Davis spoke sincerely from his heart to President Sherman and Eddie Bates.

"We've done a lot in this generation. We've secured the destiny for people of the Confederate Union, the United States, and your people, Eddie. Let us be confident that our descendants will do their part to further the advancement of our peoples, and therefore of all Mankind."

Sherman looked Davis in the eye. Davis read his thoughts.

You will decide what to do about slavery in your own good time. But, please, for your own sake, act quickly to hasten its demise. Don't wait for the revolution.

Afterword

When I began this series, I had in mind a blitzkrieg war with one side overpowering the other with one campaign. In the real Civil War, both sides expected the war to be decided by one climactic battle. The winners and losers would acknowledge the outcome, salute each other's valor, then go home.

The resolve of both sides to fight for their respective causes would not allow the war to be decided until many "climactic" battles were fought. Each side called up seemingly inexhaustible reserves of strength to carry it through the weeks then the months and finally the years of near-total war.

The depth of each side's commitment to its cause enabled them to fight past setbacks that would have knocked less committed adversaries out of the war. President Lincoln was frequently discouraged. He believed he was doing blessed work in announcing the Emancipation Proclamation in late 1862. The very next battle resulted in the slaughter of the Federal Army at Fredericksburg. "If there is a worse place than hell, then I am in it," he said.

Mr. Lincoln held firm during these reverses until the tide began to turn in 1863. Then in 1864 the war took another turn against the Union. On August 23rd he wrote:

This morning, as for some days past it seems exceedingly probable that this administration will not be reelected. Then it will be my duty to so cooperate with the new President-elect as to save the Union between the election and the inauguration, as he will have secured his election on such ground that he cannot possibly save it afterward.

Less than two weeks later, on September 2, Atlanta fell to General Sherman and the North's spirits soared. The Union won other victories at Mobile and in the Shenandoah Valley, and Mr. Lincoln was re-elected, albeit by a close margin. He won the State of New York by one half of one percent and lost the vote in his own hometown of Springfield as he did in 1860. Even after Mr. Lincoln's re-election, the Confederates managed to carry on the war for another seven months.

The frequent reversal of fortunes during a long war of grinding attrition is the story of the real civil war, and so it became a part of this alternate history story. The reconciliation described in the last chapter is the happiest possible outcome. Slavery remains in the Confederate Union and is only slowly fading. An industrial and economic revolution is about to sweep both nations. John Sherman is trying to head it off, as he did in real life, by evening the scales between Capital and Labor. The Confederate Union must deal with that in its industrial cities of Baltimore, Cincinnati, Louisville, and St. Louis and also with the dark force of slavery. How might the 20th and 21st Centuries evolved if still darker forces of fascism in Germany and Italy, imperial militarism in Japan, and communist expansion in the Soviet Union and China had not been countered by a united and free United States?

Author's note

Because history is made by people, alternate history requires an exploration of how historical characters may have reacted to alternate events. I've been writing about the Civil War since I wrote most of the December 1981 special issue of *Civil War Times Illustrated* magazine in a special issue titled "Dissent: The Fire in the Rear" about political opposition to the war in the North and South:

I had to understand the political leaders of the North and South and their motives, that I have portrayed in what I believe are true-to-life characters developed in alternate history parameters.   Within the Confederate Union, the story is told of why the Confederates, so committed to state sovereignty, would choose to fight a long debilitating war to recover the breakaway Free States. It turns out that the men in the Confederate Union's high command have a dual nature. Although they talk about the theory of states' rights, they are also Democratic Party Nationalists in the tradition of Thomas Jefferson and Andrew Jackson who regard the Union as a sacred inheritance to be handed down to following generations. They do not believe the Confederate Union will ever be secure if the Free States go off into a separate nation and ally themselves with Great Britain and other European powers. The secession of the Free State North brings them back to their traditional pre-Civil War role as Nationalists.

In this scenario George McClellan, a protégé of Secretary of War Jefferson Davis in the 1850s, does not display the strange combination of arrogance, paranoia, and defeatism that crippled his effectiveness as Lincoln's general during the real Civil War. He sets a much more rapid pace than his plodding half-hearted advances in the actual Civil War.

Jefferson Davis has opposition, just as did during the actual Civil War when ardent Southern Rights men resisted what they saw as the centralizing tendencies of the "Davis Government." In this alternate history, the "Fire Eaters" haven't given up their dream of creating a Southern Confederacy and expanding it into a great slaveholding empire in the lands south of the Rio Grande. In their view the Confederate Union is just another name for the "Yankeefied" government of the old United States they were bucking to get out from under.

About the Author

"Understanding history is a key to understanding the present and extrapolating the future."

- Alan Sewell

I've devoted my life to analyzing historical and current events and applying their historical lessons to today's business and economic issues.

Although every day is a new day, the new days are layered on top of repeating cycles of history as old as Mankind. The more we understand the cycles of history, the more completely we will understand the present.

My writing is focused on American History, starting with the Civil War --- the crucible that forged us into a united country under one flag, with a preeminent and indivisible national government.

I have intensively studied the Civil War, especially its politics and political dissent. Having lived in Alabama, Georgia, Florida, Ohio, Kentucky, Illinois, New York, and Michigan, I understand how the conflict is seen from both sides of the Ohio River. I grew up close to the

Civil War because my mother, raised in Georgia in the 1930's, knew aging Civil War veterans who fought for the South. Four of them were her great-grand-fathers. My father's family were Appalachian Unionists from North Alabama. Discussions about the war were lively in our family.

I have written two articles for the December 1981 *Civil War Times Illustrated Special issue: DISSENT: FIRE IN THE REAR.* These articles chronicle the dissent of the Unionist minority in North Alabama against the Confederacy, and dissent by Illinois Copperheads against President Lincoln's government. I have also reviewed books in CWTI on the Pennsylvania Antiwar Movement and the career of General John Logan in Illinois.

Other Books by Alan Sewell:

August 23, 1864: The Day Abraham Lincoln Won the Civil War chronicles the most critical day of the war:

https://www.amazon.com/dp/B07M6HZR48/

"Short and very sweet, this book leaves a most pleasurable aftertaste; it is as though Lincoln conversed with you."

Abraham Lincoln began the morning of August 23, 1864 by despairing of re-election:

"This morning, as for some days past, it seems exceedingly probable that this Administration will not be re-elected. Then it will be my duty to so co-operate with the President elect (George McClellan, running on the Peace Platform), as to save the Union between the election and the inauguration; as he will have secured his election on such ground that he cannot possibly save it afterwards."

The Union was losing as many as 15,000 men killed, crippled, and dead from disease per week. Men up to the age of 45 were being conscripted to fill the gaping holes. Many deserted or surrendered at the first opportunity. Officers who had turned Lee back at Gettysburg last year had been killed or discharged with wounds. Incompetents and drunkards took their places. Grant's army was suffering staggering defeats at battles it would have won in previous years.

Robert E. Lee's Confederate army was not only holding fast in Virginia, but had recently raided the outskirts of Washington, taking Mr. Lincoln under fire. On August 23rd bad news poured in from all fronts. Lincoln's friends warned him he would not be re-elected. George McClellan, a pre-war protege of Jefferson Davis, would be the next president.

During the course of the day, Mr. Lincoln made a series of decisions that swung the balance back in his favor and enabled him to prevail in November's election, thus seeing the war through to Union victory.

This is the story of that day.

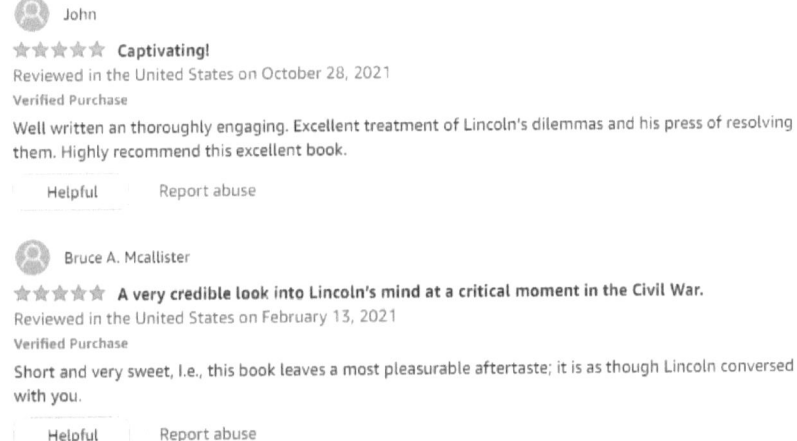

Fire in the Heartland is another novelized true story that tells the hidden stories of the Civil War of political intrigues behind the lines that decided the outcome of the Civil War as much as did its battles.

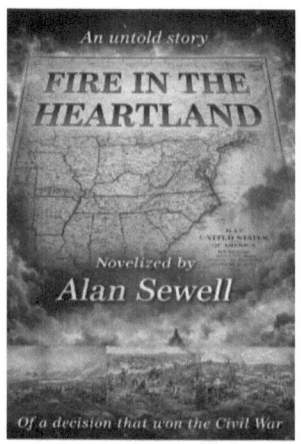

https://www.amazon.com/Fire-Heartland-Civil-story-youve-ebook/dp/B00514WNYG/

I've also been commended for "interpreting the American experience" into critical watersheds when political and economic crises were resolved to advance the country into the next era of its history. These pivot points of American history are analyzed in *The Diary of American Exceptionalism:*

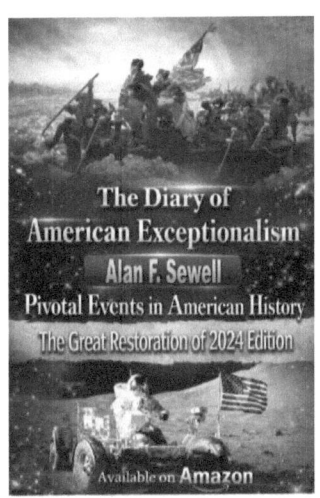

https://www.amazon.com/Diary-American-Exceptionalism-Alan-Sewell-ebook/dp/B01H2HGCNC/